DIRTY POWER

Visit us at www.boldstrokesbooks.com

By the Author

Sex and Skateboards

Dirty Sex

Dirty Money

Dirty Power

DIRTY POWER

by

Ashley Bartlett

2013

DIRTY POWER

© 2013 BY ASHLEY BARTLETT. ALL RIGHTS RESERVED.

ISBN 10: 1-60282-896-2
ISBN 13: 978-1-60282-896-4

THIS TRADE PAPERBACK ORIGINAL IS PUBLISHED BY
BOLD STROKES BOOKS, INC.
P.O. BOX 249
VALLEY FALLS, NY 12185

FIRST EDITION: AUGUST 2013

CREDITS
EDITOR: CINDY CRESAP
PRODUCTION DESIGN: SUSAN RAMUNDO
COVER DESIGN BY SHERI (GRAPHICARTIST2020@HOTMAIL.COM)

Acknowledgments

When I started this story, I had something quite dire planned. The failings of youth can be so entertaining. But then my girl and my bestie didn't like that. At all. So instead, I offer triumph and hope. Partly, because I was told to. But mostly, because they were right. And so I offer hope. Maybe not in the traditional sense. Okay, not in anything remotely resembling tradition. But that's never really been my scene. If these characters can find life and love in the mass of violence and hatred that I have built for them, then maybe we can find it too.

Thanks to everyone who helped me climb out the window when I got stuck in a corner. To my family, my many siblings and all five of my parents. Thanks especially to Babs for being a mom-shaped sounding board. To everyone at Bold Strokes, my other family, for putting up with me. Carsen, for wanting to read the Dirties before everyone else. Also, for coming up with "Dirties." Vixsta, for doing all my research for me. Especially for telling me to make shit up. You're awesome. Jove, for smacking me around. But like in a good way. Cindy, for terrifying me for no reason. I've always liked that about you.

And, of course, thanks to my readers. I hope you realize that you have given me far more than I could ever give you.

All of you, thank you.

Dedication

For Meg, you're the only one I want to get arrested with.

CHAPTER ONE

The knocking on the door was starting to sound impatient. I seriously considered ignoring it. But it wasn't just me anymore. I had the twins to watch out for.

I kissed the top of Reese's head. My head got light. I closed my eyes as I let the smell of her hair assault me. When I opened my eyes again they were blurry. I could stay right there, smelling her hair forever, breathing in the memories, and never move. Forever. The concept didn't seem foreign anymore. It didn't seem so far away either.

The knocking on the door stopped. Shit. I really needed to know who was there. If it was Vito, we were all going to die. Soon.

Slowly, very slowly, I slid up the bed. Ryan burrowed into my ribs. Reese murmured in her sleep. Climbing out of bed without disturbing a sleeping woman was a skill. One that I'd once been very good at. But it was a lot harder with two people. Especially when both of them were on top of me. I shifted my left shoulder up away from Ryan's face. Then I eased Reese's head off my other shoulder and onto the pillow. She must have been exhausted. Usually, she woke up if I was breathing too loud. High standards, that girl.

The knocking started up again. Louder. If that was possible.

I freed my legs from Ryan's, lifted Reese's hand out of my shirt. And then I was good to go. I grabbed the jeans I'd been wearing when we arrived and pulled them on.

I made my way past the still made second bed to the door. The security latch was in place. I left it there and opened the door.

"Hey, Christopher." Damn, I was happy to see him. He smiled. Warmly even. "Just a sec." I closed the door, took off the latch, and opened it back up.

"You've got them with you?" he asked. But then he saw them curled up on the bed. In their sleep the twins had shifted closer until their heads were nearly touching. Reese's hand was over Ryan's.

"Is Breno here?" I asked.

"Downstairs. We didn't know if you had told them yet." Told them that their father was alive and very much wanted to meet them.

"Not yet. And they think I killed you."

"What?"

"Long story. Vito told them."

"Christ." Christopher rubbed his perfectly cultivated beard. Like he was thinking. "I guess you were convincing."

"Very. I think he's gonna jack off to the pictures of your corpse."

"You're disgusting," he said.

I shrugged. I was disgusting. "I'll wake them up. You want to come in?"

"I'd better. Loitering in the hall isn't doing much for my credibility."

I stepped away from the door to let him in. When I closed it behind him, I attached the security latch again.

"Your face still looks like shit," I said.

For real. One eye was black. The other eye was swollen at the outer edge and tinted an angry red. His nose had been broken. Bottom lip was split and puffy. There was a mottled bruise across his cheekbone that extended down into his manicured stubble. The bruise appeared again on his neck where the stubble tapered off. Another long bruise started at the edge of his eyebrow, went across his temple, and disappeared in his hair. A couple butterfly dressings held a jagged split in the center of the bruised skin closed. The left side of his face was battered more than the right side. Because I was right-handed.

"It was worth it. I'm fine," he said.

I nodded. "I know this will sound weird, but can you, like, hide in the bathroom or something? They're going to get enough surprises today."

He didn't even question me. Just went into the bathroom and closed the door partway.

I went back to the bed. I really wanted to wake Reese up by kissing her. But I was pretty sure that, sleeping arrangements aside, she wasn't gonna go for that. So I just shook their shoulders a little.

"Hey, guys, wake up." That didn't work so I had to repeat it a couple times. "Reese. Ryan. Come on. Wake up."

Ryan finally opened an eye. Just one. "Huh?"

"Time to get up. Face the day and all that."

"What for?" He closed his eye again.

"It's hard to explain. Just get up, 'kay?"

"No."

"Reese?"

"Uh-uh," was her brilliant response.

"If I order coffee will you guys get up?" No response. "Okay, but now I have to take your covers." And I did. They tried to hold on to them. Reese even managed to keep the sheet for a second. But I won.

"Damn it." Reese turned onto her back and glared at me. It turned me on a little. "What do you want?"

"To slowly and carefully break it to you that Christopher is here, but you guys are making it hard." That came out wrong.

"What?" Now Ryan was awake. "But he's dead. You killed him."

"Christopher," I called. "Get out here."

The bathroom door opened.

"Hey, kids." He smiled a little. The smile died when he saw their faces.

"Go the fuck away," Ryan said.

"Ryan," I said.

"Yeah, leave." Reese.

"You guys." I couldn't believe them.

"That's good, I guess." Reese turned back onto her side and closed her eyes. "You don't need any more blood on your hands." It was directed at me. And it hurt like a fucking bitch. I didn't need to be reminded of that shit.

"Fuck you," I said.

"Hey, whoa. Let's take this back a notch, all right?" Christopher decided to be the adult. We weren't acting like it. And it was his role after all.

"Blow me." Ryan flipped onto his stomach and buried his head in his pillow.

"Enough. He's an asshole, but he raised you. And there's some shit you need to know. So get the fuck up and play nice."

"Sleep," Ryan said. Reese mumbled something that sounded like agreement.

Fine. They could feign sleep.

"Do you mind waiting downstairs?" I asked Christopher. "We need to talk."

"That's probably for the best."

"Thanks."

He nodded and let himself out.

"Is he gone?" Ryan sat up and rubbed his face. "Cool. We can sneak out the back and he'll never find us."

"So smart." Reese rolled over too. "Why the hell would you let him know where we are?" she asked me.

I ignored her question. "We need to talk. About your parents."

"They're dead. Why damage the memory?" Reese.

"Can you please just indulge me? Maybe get out of bed?"

"No," Ryan said.

"Okay." This wasn't going to be easy. Probably best to just spit it out. "Your dad is alive. He's waiting downstairs to meet you."

"That's not funny," Ryan said.

"Yeah, screw you," Reese said.

"I'm serious. I know this sounds insane. But he's alive and he's here and he really wants to meet you. I spent Christmas day with him and Christopher. And we kind of killed a dude together. We bonded."

"Neat." Reese. So callous.

"They love you. And there's a lot you guys need to talk about."

"Are you fucking with us?" Ryan wanted to know.

"Dead serious."

"Okay. I'm getting in the shower." Ryan got out of bed. Finally.

"Yeah. Wouldn't want to meet Daddy without looking our best." The way Reese said Daddy she may as well have put air quotes around it. Did they think I was making this shit up?

"Dude." Ryan laughed as he disappeared into the bathroom.

Yep, they thought Breno was fictional.

"You really think I would make something like this up?" I asked Reese. She shrugged. "I thought you trusted me."

"Trust is an interesting concept, Cooper." Reese slipped out of bed. She was wearing a pair of Ryan's boxers and one of my ribbed tank tops. And she managed to make it look like couture. She grabbed a bottle of water, sipped some, and placed it carefully on the table. Then she sat down and crossed her legs at the ankles. She stared at me for a long moment like she was collecting herself.

Great. I was in for a lecture.

"You said in Chicago that you trusted me," I said.

"I do. I trust you to keep me alive. I trust you to keep me out of physical danger." She paused. Probably for the drama. "That's as far as I trust you."

"What the hell does that mean?"

"I think you know."

I did not want to have this conversation. Then again, I kind of did. I needed to have this conversation. It was probably too soon. I probably should have waited. Reminded her of the reasons we had been together before we talked. But I wasn't that smart.

"You're the one who broke my trust, buttercup."

"No, I didn't."

"You should have told me about working for your family. You should have told me what they do," I said.

"There was nothing to tell you."

Seriously? She was going to go with it wasn't my business?

"You didn't think it was necessary to mention that your family was organized crime? And, oh yeah, you worked for them." I was laying the sarcasm on extra thick. It didn't help.

"It didn't concern you." She was getting mad.

"It damn well did and you know it. That's a breech of trust, darlin'."

"I'm not the one who fucked some other woman." Reese didn't look away from me when she said it.

I wanted to break our eye contact, but I couldn't. I just couldn't. It didn't matter that it wasn't true. It didn't matter that all I'd done was kiss another chick. It mattered that I had wanted to. I had wanted to fuck someone else just to see if I could.

"So this is it?" I felt my voice break as I said it. The inevitability of four months. Six months. Fourteen years of waiting. The time didn't matter. I'd known somewhere deep inside that she would never be mine, not really. Maybe that was why I'd spent so long hating her. Maybe that was why I'd given her reasons not to trust me. So there would be something to blame instead of just me.

"Don't be dramatic. We had a good run." She waved a hand through the air. "You were right. I lied. You're good in bed. At least you have that going for you."

The way she looked at me as she said it made my insides turn cold. Bile rose in my throat, a thick, heady knot that wouldn't go away. She wasn't looking at me with detachment. Her disinterest was familiar. I could have survived it.

She was looking at me with pity.

I wanted to go find a dark corner and cry. I wanted to run away. I wanted to believe that she still needed me like I needed her. But I'd been doing all of that since she had left me in Mexico. It hadn't brought her back and it hadn't made her love me. So I turned away.

When Ryan emerged from the bathroom, a towel around his waist, whistling to himself, I was digging through my duffle bag pretending that choosing jeans for the day was my only concern.

Reese silently disappeared into the steamy room and shut the door behind her.

"I'm wearing a gray shirt and a red sweatshirt so pick out something else," Ryan said. "I hate when we're twinsies."

"Sure." I dug around in the bag some more, but I couldn't see anything inside it. I turned it upside down and shook it until it was empty. Blue shirt. Gray sweatshirt. Good enough. I was standing there staring at the mess I'd made when I realized that Ryan was watching me. He'd pulled on jeans. His damp towel was trailing out of one hand onto the floor.

"Coop?"

"What?" I said it harsher than I'd meant to.

"Oh, God." Ryan dropped the towel and pulled me into his arms. That was when I realized I'd been crying. "I'm so sorry," he whispered into my hair. "I shouldn't have left you guys alone."

"No," I tried to protest. "I'm fine. Nothing happened." I attempted to push him off.

"Yeah, of course." He locked his arms around me so I couldn't get away.

Then he just held me as I cried into his bare shoulder.

"Some reunion, huh?" Ryan asked when I finally stopped.

"Yeah. Everything I hoped for."

"Here." Ryan picked up his damp towel and offered it to me.

"Thanks." I rubbed it against my face as if that would erase the tears.

"Oh, no, dude. I used that side on my dick. Use the other side."

"Ewww." I threw the towel back at him and laughed. He was disgusting. But he'd made me smile.

"Gotcha."

"Tool," I said.

"It just had to be her, didn't it?" Ryan got serious again all of a sudden.

"What do you mean?"

"All those girls. And it's got to be my sister who makes you cry."

I thought about blowing him off. But this was Ryan. If I couldn't talk to him, then who the hell else was I going to talk to?

"I guess someone had to," I said.

"Yeah, you made enough chicks lose their shit. Someone had to break your heart, I guess."

I shrugged. That was enough analysis for one day.

"So you want me to put some of that antibacterial shit on that cut?" Ryan pointed at my split lip. Smooth subject change.

"After my shower."

"Okay."

"I'm going to need you to change my dressings anyway."

"Dressings?"

"Oh, yeah. I forgot to tell you." I hadn't shown them the full extent of my injuries. It hadn't seemed expedient when we were on the run from Vito. And right then, explaining seemed like a lot of work. So I just stripped off the henley I was wearing.

"What the fuck?" Ryan traced a fingertip over the bandage on my bicep. It was stiff in the center from dried blood. Then he trailed down to my elbow. That one only had a Band-Aid. "Where else are you hurt?" Without waiting for an answer, he grabbed my tank top and pulled it over my head so I was shirtless. I'd never seen Ryan look so mad.

"It's not that bad," I said.

"What the fuck did they do to you?" Ryan lifted my arm to look at the still healing scar on my ribcage.

"It's a bullet wound."

"I can see that. What happened?"

"Shit," I said.

"And what's this one?" He peeled the tape back to look at my arm.

"Knife."

"And this?" He pointed to the lame-in-comparison Band-Aid.

"That one was my idea. We needed blood."

"What?"

"To fake Christopher's death. It's a long story," I said.

"Is he the one who stabbed you?"

"No. The guy who did that is dead."

"Who shot you?"

"He's dead too."

"Jesus. Fuck. I'm sorry." He looked at me with the most anguished eyes ever. Which was weird. Ryan didn't do anguished. He did goofy and stoned. "We never should have left you." He looked away, but not before I saw the tears gathering. It kinda pissed me off.

"You've got to kidding."

"What?" He kept his face turned away. As if I'd never seen him cry like a bitch.

"You don't get to cry for me."

"Huh?"

"You left me. I mean, I get it. She's your sister and all that, but you left me. It was fucking shitty. And I still dragged my ass through hell to fucking find you. So, no, you don't get to cry."

"But, Coop." He shook his head like that would make thinking easier. "That's why I'm sad. 'Cause we shouldn't have left you."

"Fine. But don't expect comfort from me." I was disgusted with him, but I didn't know why.

"I don't." He was lying. I could tell. "Fuck, Coop. Look what they did to you." And then he started sobbing.

"Shit." I'd made my best friend cry. I was an asshole. "I'm sorry. I didn't mean that." He didn't say anything. "Really. I didn't mean it." I kinda did. But I didn't want to see Ryan cry.

"Ryan." He wouldn't face me. "Ryan." I grabbed his long hair to force him to look at me. "I'm fine. We found each other again. It was worth getting shot and stabbed and beaten and hit with that baseball bat and whatever the hell else. If I got you, I'm good." It was only half a lie. He was only half of what I wanted. But that was okay. Maybe the rest would just go away. Maybe I could forget what I'd seen. Maybe I'd forget that I loved Reese and she didn't love me.

"You know all those platitudes and shit?" Ryan asked.

"Huh?"

"If I could go back. If we could trade places. If whatever. I don't know." Ryan swiped at his damp cheeks with the back of his hand. "If I could make you whole again, I would. That's all."

"I know."

"I'll try to—"

We both turned our heads as the water shut off. I grabbed my tank top out of his hand and pulled it on.

"Don't tell her, 'kay?"

"Why?"

"Please, just don't."

"Fine." He looked not happy.

When Reese emerged from the bathroom, we very carefully didn't make eye contact, or any kind of contact. I went in and shut the door behind me, relieved to be alone for a moment. I'd never before felt the need to get away from them. Except for running from Reese my whole life, but I hadn't really meant that. Ironic, considering how hard I'd worked to find them, that once we were together I wanted to get away.

I'd already taken one shower since the twins and I had fled the DiGiovannis. It was cursory. Intended to remove the blood from my hair. But my hair was still stained. It was the kind of filth that couldn't simply be washed out. Not alone at least. I'd either need to wash it about twenty times—and considering the open wound on the back of my head, I wouldn't be doing that—or I'd need one of the twins to do it for me.

As it was, I only got half a shower. I hadn't seen a real doctor for any of my wounds, but I was pretty sure that I wasn't supposed to get them wet. Or soapy. I needed to ask Breno. He would know.

Too soon, I was finished with my shower and just standing there knowing I didn't want to go back out into that room. They would be there waiting for me. Or worse, maybe they wouldn't. They'd left me before. Why not round it out to a nice even four abandonments?

Ennui didn't look cute on me.

Chapter Two

"Just to be clear," Reese stopped laughing long enough to say. "You went with some guy named Esau to torture and kill Christopher, but stopped when you realized our biological father was there."

"Yes." I was studying the elevator lights as if that would make the damn thing come to our floor faster.

"This Breno." Again, I imagined her doing air quotes. "Looks identical to Ryan so you had some inherent knowledge when you saw him. Which made you decide to kill Esau and fake Christopher's death."

The elevator finally arrived. Reese kept talking as we got in.

"And you had a long, bonding type forty-eight hours where you discovered that our esteemed stepfather, Christopher, is gay." Ryan started laughing. "And he, twenty years ago, faked Breno's death. Oh, because they were best friends. Am I getting all this right?" Reese joined Ryan in his laughter.

Ryan cut in. "And they convinced you that they both deeply love me and Reese. Even though they abandoned us to varying degrees." He stopped to catch his breath. "Better yet, they abandoned us because they loved us and each other and our mom so fuckin' much."

I really didn't get why all this was so damn funny.

"Do the part where Coop beats Christopher and they fake his death." Reese smacked Ryan's stomach with the back of her hand. They both escalated to howling.

Thankfully, I didn't hear that part of the story I'd just told them in the hotel room repeated back to me because the elevator stopped and the doors slid open. I walked out, assuming they would follow. They did. I could hear them giggling behind me.

The laughter followed me through the lobby, past the front desk, and into the small restaurant that looked out onto the snow covered Denver streets. They managed to stop laughing out loud, but I imagined they were grinning behind me, waiting for a punch line that would never come. I rounded one of the large pillars and spotted Christopher and Breno sitting by one of the wide windows. The twins stopped when I did, one standing on either side of me.

Reese saw them first. She gasped. One hand lifted as if to touch the surreal scene of her two fathers sitting twenty feet away.

On my other side, I heard Ryan swallow, cough. I turned to look at him and saw that he had gone pale, or as pale as Ryan ever went.

"Fuck that." Ryan spun to walk away, but I grabbed him by the arm and held him in place.

Christopher and Breno hadn't noticed us yet so I pulled Reese and Ryan behind the pillar. They needed a moment before Breno saw them.

"No, this isn't happening," Reese said. Except it was happening.

"I know they have a lot to answer for. And they know they have a lot of explaining to do."

"No fucking shit." Reese glared at me.

"This can't be explained away. Why did you bring us here?" Ryan asked.

I thought about that. Because he was right. It was a little fucked up to spring it on them like this. Okay, I had tried to warn them, but still. I could only think of one reason that wasn't a bullshit platitude.

"Because I thought you would want to know your father."

"Shit just got real." Only Ryan.

"You in?" I asked.

"If you are." He directed it at Reese.

"Damn it." Reese stared Ryan down, but then she nodded.

I could have celebrated my minor victory or gloated or pointed out that I hadn't been lying. But I didn't. I just walked over and sat next to Breno. He spared me a glance. Fear and kindness and relief all in a split second.

And then he saw them. Really saw them for the first time. I wondered what he was feeling, but I didn't know. All I could see were his trembling hands and the tears in his eyes. Ryan and Reese were easier to read.

Reese was pissed. I watched as the anger was forced down, controlled, until nothing showed on her flawless face. That detachment told me more than the anger had. This would be a battle. Reese would win. Or she thought she would.

Ryan's reaction was more amusing than anything. Like the time he had gotten an ant farm as a kid. I thought it was boring as fuck and decided to dismember Reese's Barbies. But Ryan sat there for weeks just watching. He was like that now. Staring at the inevitable and freakish result of nature. Fascinated. I knew in that drug-addled brain of his he was tracing the contours of Breno's features, trying to find the differences, strangely drawn in.

I'd done the same thing. Watched until I knew how they differed. Ryan's mouth was wider, more sensual, than either of his parents'. His eyes, like Reese's, went gray when he was scared or high or excited or angry or aroused. Well, I wasn't sure about Ryan when he was turned on. But Reese's went gray. So his probably did too. Ryan's skin was a shade lighter than his father's. It was smoother too. Though that might have been his surprisingly in-depth exfoliation routine.

"This is Breno," I told the twins. It was kind of obvious that this was Breno, but someone had to say something.

"Hello," Breno said. His smile was weak.

"For real," was all Ryan said. Reese said nothing. It was going to be hard to mediate this conversation.

"We ordered coffee," Christopher said. Good. Someone was going to help with this silence.

They turned to look at him.

"Fuck, man. What happened to your face?" Ryan asked even though he knew what had happened to Christopher's face.

"My God. Coop did that to you?" Reese looked back and forth between Christopher and me with her mouth open.

"Yes," Christopher said.

"So everything you said was true?" Ryan asked me.

"Yeah. Why would I make it up?"

They didn't have an answer for that.

"What exactly are we doing here?" Reese asked.

"For the moment, we are going to figure out a way to get the gold back," Breno said. It was sort of the truth. He wanted to know his kids. But we all knew that was going to be a slow process. Probably best to hide behind the things that needed to be done.

"And how will we manage that?" Reese's tone suggested that she thought it was an impossible task. It was. But that didn't deter Breno and Christopher.

They launched into what they'd found out. And what their plan was. It still sounded insane to me. But I didn't care anymore. I was just along for the ride.

❖

"Have I told you recently that my ass is numb?" Ryan asked. He used his highbrow, imitating-Reese voice.

"Indeed, Ryan, you have," I said with the same intonation.

"Oh, good. I wouldn't want you to think that I was enjoying this."

"Now, now. Look at all of this scenery." I sounded like my father.

"Yes, the Rockies are so exciting."

"You gotta get more into nature, bro," I said.

"If you let me get stoned, I'll totally get into nature."

"You really want to meet up with Breno and Christopher reeking of pot?"

"How long is this drive again?"

It was a non-sequitur. But he'd made his point.

"Fine. Smoke away. But roll the window down. I'm driving and that doesn't mix with weed."

"Love you," he said.

Ryan didn't talk much when he lit his first joint of the day. He'd always told me it was a profound experience not to be muddied by speech. Just like that. Or sometimes it was a profound experience not to be diluted with the changing and fallible conception of reality. Once, he even looked at me and said *ceci n'est pas une pipe*. I never quite figured out what he meant by that.

Besides, I always thought he just lost the power to speak for the first minute or so.

He took his time that morning. First, smelling the unlit jay. Then, turning it, inspecting it for a flaw. When he found none, he lit it. I cranked up the heater when he cracked the window. He inhaled deeply. His closed eyes seemed to smile, but it didn't reach his mouth. Like his muscles were taking orders from different brains.

I ignored him and looked back to the road. It was beginning to snow. I'd volunteered to drive first, but now I was regretting that. Whatever. I was probably better than Reese. Girl drove at like half the speed limit. Add snow, and we would never get to Vegas. And the only other option was Ryan. Who currently had his nose and one hand pressed to the window. His breath fogged the glass.

"It's crazy isn't it?" Ryan whispered.

"For real." I didn't know what I was agreeing to. But I also didn't know the potency of the weed I'd given him. For all I knew it was laced with acid. That would suck.

"I mean, look at it. I saw a picture once, but I never really realized, you know?"

"You've only seen a picture of the Rockies once?"

"No, man. Of his face. It's like mine. Or mine is like his. Crazy, right?"

Oh, now it made sense. He was looking at his reflection. "Yeah, it's weird."

Ryan turned from the window. "Did you freak when you saw him?"

"Totally. Dropped my gun. Almost shot myself in the foot."

"Dude. Guns aren't toys. You gotta be careful."

No shit.

"He really loves you guys," I said.

"Yeah, you've said that like a bajillion times. But he doesn't know us. So it's like he loves us in theory, you know?"

"I guess. Christopher has kept him pretty updated on what you guys are doing and who you are and shit."

"So?"

"So he knows you as well as he can," I said. Ryan stared at me blankly. "Plus he almost kicked my ass."

"Why?" he asked.

"'Cause he found out Reese and I had been..." There it was again. The relationship that had no word. "Dating or whatever. He said I'd corrupted Reese or something."

"Hmmm," was all Ryan said.

"And there was that thing with that chick and Breno tried to strangle me."

"Oh, that," Ryan said.

I didn't have anything else to say about that so I didn't.

"Why'd you do it?" he finally asked.

I glanced in my rearview mirror. Reese was still asleep.

"I don't know. I was mad at her." We both knew that was how I rolled.

"But you fucked some other chick. You cheated on my sister, man." Ryan wasn't mad anymore. Not like he'd been at first. He just seemed sad.

"I didn't fuck her."

"Dude, I saw the picture." Good point. That picture had been pretty damning.

"That was as far as it went. I was kissing her and I just couldn't get Reese outta my head. The chick smelled different. Felt different. She wasn't Reese so I bailed."

"Why haven't you told Reese that you didn't sleep with her?"

"Why would I?" I shrugged.

"Serious?"

"Yeah."

"Because you didn't cheat on her," Ryan said like I was stupid.

"I didn't fuck someone else. But I still made out with someone else. That's cheating."

"Ehhh." He shrugged. "Less cheaty."

"Less cheaty?"

"Less cheaty."

Lessons in morality from a stoner.

"She'll hate me either way. Why fixate on what I can't change?" I asked.

"You love her."

"Are you asking?"

"No. I know you love her."

"Yeah, so?"

"I was answering your question. Don't lay down and take it like a bitch. Fight. Tool."

He wasn't wrong. Not that he was right. But he wasn't entirely wrong, either.

After that, we really didn't have anything to say. So we listened to music until we switched drivers at Grand Junction.

❖

When I woke up, it was dark. I'd been spread across the backseat when I fell asleep, but now I was half falling off it. Because Ryan was shoving me off in his sleep. And his feet were on my stomach. It was a less than comfortable position. I wriggled out from under him and climbed up front.

"I thought Ryan was going to keep you company."

"I got coffee, so I told him he could sleep," Reese said.

"Oh. Got it."

"It's still warm, if you want some." She waved her hand at the coffee cup sitting between us.

"Thanks." I took a sip. Coffee ruled. Also, Reese being relatively nice was good.

"Where are we?"

"Almost to Vegas. We crossed the state line about forty-five minutes ago."

"And then another hour to the gold?"

"Yeah, about that."

"Cool." I reached for the iPod. Reese was listening to Death Cab. Good for lazy summer days. Bad for staying awake on dark, cold nights. And it was fuckin' cold out there.

"I didn't want to wake you guys." She answered the question I hadn't asked.

"Ryan will sleep through anything." I tried not to think about the last road trip we had been on and how Reese had taken advantage of Ryan's deep sleep.

"Play something loud and obnoxious."

"Ke$ha?"

"Sure." She sounded dubious. She should have. I had ulterior motives.

It's impossible to listen to Ke$ha and not be happy. Halfway through the first song, Reese was drumming her fingers on the steering wheel. By the end, she was singing. During the second song, she started rapping about a bottle of Jack, and I was laughing. There was even a little dancing involved.

We almost had fun driving through Vegas. At one point, I looked over at her and smiled and I couldn't feel anything else. Just happy. Sometimes the simple pleasure of driving and listening to loud music with a pretty girl is enough.

Animal and *Cannibal* got us to the familiar stretch of highway where we were meeting Christopher and Breno. Reese dutifully followed my directions off the road until I told her to stop. Their fathers hadn't arrived yet. No surprise. We'd lost time with Reese driving, but Ryan and I thought speed limits were for wimps. So we still beat the old dudes there.

"This is it?" Reese asked.

"Theoretically."

"Wait. You're not sure?"

"Ryan and I both remembered the same GPS coordinates." I shrugged. Proof enough.

"I guess we'll find out." Reese went to open the door.

"Hey, wait." It was an impulse. I probably should have stopped myself. But impulses are like that.

"What?" She looked back at me.

"Are we, you know, cool?"

She stared at me so long I didn't think she was going to say anything.

"Meaning what?" she asked.

"I get that we're...over." Damn, it was hard to say that part. "But do you still hate me?" Because I didn't think I could stand it anymore if she hated me.

"I don't hate you. I don't think I ever could hate you."

"Why? You have every right to. Every reason to."

"I thought I did. But I guess there aren't as many reasons to hate you as I thought."

"Why not?" I asked.

"Because you and Ryan never lie to each other."

"Huh?"

She grabbed the door handle, popped it open.

"I'm not a heavy sleeper like Ryan is," she said. Then she got out of the car.

Fuck me. She'd heard our entire conversation.

Chapter Three

H ave I told you how intelligent this idea was?" Christopher asked.

"Fuck you," I said.

"Blow me," was Ryan's response.

"Actually, our half of the gold is still here." Reese pointed to the hole where the gold was just beginning to show through. "What happened to the half you tried to take care of?"

Christopher opened his mouth to respond, but I spoke before he could.

"If you even think about blaming me for that, I'll punch you in the face again."

He closed his mouth.

"Let's not blame," Breno said. "We have this gold. We will get the other half back."

"Dude," Ryan said.

"We have too many people in here," I said. "Breno, get out. Ryan and I got this."

Breno hesitated, but then he got out of the hole. I watched Ryan's face. He wanted to tell me to stop digging. Misguided protectiveness. But he couldn't do it without telling everyone I'd been shot.

"I'm fine," I whispered to him.

He grumbled something that sounded like, "Yeah, right."

I ignored him and kept digging. After a while, we were just scraping our shovels over the top of the gold.

"That is probably enough. You can hand us the bars now," Breno told us.

"I think we know what we're doing," I said. Me, irritated? No.

"Really?" Breno said. Reese looked at him with the oddest expression when he questioned me.

"Yeah, we got this."

"Have you noticed that you are bleeding?" Breno asked me all superior and shit.

"Fuck." I looked at my arm. I'd stripped off my coat to dig. My shirt was slowly turning crimson over my bicep and on the inside of my elbow.

"Get out of there, Cooper," Breno said.

I was going to tell him to shove it, but Christopher and Reese looked like they were gonna back him up, so I just climbed out.

"Happy?" I asked. I wasn't.

"Ecstatic. Come on." Breno cupped my other arm and led me to the open truck bed. "Sit here. I have a first aid kit in the cab."

"Fine." I watched the twins and Christopher and waited for him to come back. Ryan was tossing bars out of the hole for Reese and Christopher to pick up. Reese and Christopher didn't look happy. Probably because they hadn't done any work yet. We'd given up on trying to make them do physical labor. Their clothes were too pretty.

Breno came back and set a white plastic box next to me.

"Take off your shirt."

"We can do this later," I said.

"Or we can do it now." He opened the box and waited. Not a fight I was going to win. I took off my shirt and sat there shivering in a sweaty T-shirt.

"It's fucking cold."

"I know. I'm sorry. The truck isn't any warmer. Do you think your car will be?"

"No."

"All right. Then I will try to be quick."

I let him tease the tape off my upper arm until the gash underneath was exposed. He frowned.

"It will heal soon enough."

"You tore out a couple of your stitches." He mopped up the leaking blood with a piece of gauze.

"That explains why it feels shitty."

"I'm so sorry." And he sounded sorry.

"It's okay."

"No, I meant that I am sorry this happened to you," Breno said. He was studying my arm like it was the most important thing in the world.

"I'm fine. Really. And it was my fault anyway."

"But if we had contacted you sooner, then I could have protected you." Angrily, he tossed the bloody gauze down. Then he grabbed an alcohol pad and resumed his cleaning.

"Hey." I grabbed his forearm so he would stop cleaning. "Not your fault. You did the best you could."

Breno looked up at me. His eyes were glittering like Reese's. I heard a noise behind Breno. I leaned to look behind him and met Reese's gaze. She was standing there with an armload of wrapped gold bars staring at the strangely intimate scene of her father taking care of me.

"Are you okay?" she asked.

"Yeah." I nodded.

"Is she actually?" she asked Breno.

"Yes. She pulled a few stitches. Once we stop, I can give her new ones if she needs them."

"Good." Reese moved around Breno and dropped the bars onto the truck bed. She seemed pained by something, but I wasn't sure what it was.

"Will they ever forgive me?" Breno asked as Reese walked away. "I'm sorry. Never mind. It isn't fair to ask you that."

"They will. It will take time, but…" I shrugged.

"Thank you." Breno returned to his task.

When he'd cleaned both wounds and put fresh bandages on each, he handed me my shirt. I pulled it on.

"Thanks."

"I'll grab your coat." He closed up the first aid kit.

"No, it's okay. I can't work with it on."

"You're done working."

"No, I'm not. We need to get on the road," I said.

"The four of us are capable of filling in a hole," Breno pointed out far too reasonably.

"Whatever."

I let him retrieve my jacket from my car. With a promise to only observe, Breno let me stand at the edge of the hole.

"How many more are in there?" I asked Ryan.

"Some." He shrugged.

"Wait, you're not counting them?" Reese asked him.

"Nope."

"Why not?" Reese asked.

"Can't count. Too stupid," Ryan said.

"It's fine. We can count them in the truck," I told her.

Reese rolled her eyes and grabbed a couple more bars. Loading was a bitch. Each bar was almost thirty pounds. They added up fast. Not that it mattered to me. My new job was looking pretty.

When Ryan had tossed out all the gold, he and Breno started to shovel the dirt back in. Probably because Christopher was carrying more bars each trip than anyone else. And he was moving faster. Breno needed butch points to make up for it.

"I'm hungry," I announced to the group. As if they cared.

"Bro," Ryan said.

"Yeah, hurry up," Reese told Ryan and Breno.

"There are snacks in the truck," Christopher said.

"Serious?" I ditched them to find food. I was pretty sure I'd only eaten Cheetos and Zebra Cakes since breakfast. In the cab of Breno and Christopher's rented truck, I found a cooler. Bottled water and baby carrots. I kept searching, but that was it. I went back to the hole.

"Did you find the food?" Christopher asked.

"Fucking carrots," I said.

"Yes. And water," he said.

"What's wrong with you?" Ryan stopped working to glare at Christopher.

"What?" Christopher asked.

"Carrots aren't food," I told him.

"I agree," Reese said.

"I want something fried. And covered in melted cheese. Real food."

Christopher grimaced.

"We can stop and get burgers after this," Breno said.

Ryan and I looked at him like he was crazy. He was crazy.

"They don't eat beef," Reese told Breno.

"I don't understand." Breno stopped shoveling.

"Ryan and Coop. They don't eat beef or pork," she explained.

"You kids are vegetarians?" he asked all confused.

"No," Reese answered for us. "They just don't eat beef or pork. Chicken, turkey, and fish are okay."

"Why not?" Breno wanted to know.

"Tastes gross," I said.

"Totally." Ryan.

"What about you?" Breno asked Reese.

"I'm a carnivore," she said.

Breno just shook his head and shot Christopher a look.

"What?" Christopher asked.

"My son's a vegetarian. It is your fault."

"What's wrong with that?" Christopher asked.

"He's a pansy," Breno said.

"Hey." Reese sounded pissed. Ryan and I said nothing.

"He isn't a pansy," Christopher said.

They all looked to Ryan to see if he would say anything. He just shrugged and kept shoveling.

"Shouldn't you be defending yourself?" Breno finally asked.

"I'm comfortable with myself. Don't need to defend anything," Ryan said. No one responded so he continued, "I've worn women's underwear, dressed in drag, and rocked heels. I like pink. Sometimes I paint my nails. I once flirted with a guy just to get a video game. I wear skintight jeans because they make my ass look awesome. If you didn't notice, my hair is long. I think it makes me look pretty. For two years in high school, I wore eye makeup. I stopped because it looked like hell in the morning. I spend more on hair and skin products than Reese does. And if you have a problem with any of that, then keep it to yourself."

I was stunned. That was the longest speech I'd heard from Ryan since freshman year of college when he actually had to give a speech in class. Reese was just as thrown. Christopher, oddly, looked proud.

"No. No problem," Breno lied.

This was going to be a long couple of weeks.

Christopher and I had discussed switching cars for the drive to New Orleans. Like he and I could drive together and let Breno and the twins drive together so they would have time to talk. But after the stop in Vegas that seemed like a terrible idea.

I could have used our day and a half of driving to tell the twins about Chicago and what I'd done there. I could have told them about watching Esau torture people. Maybe told them about the human trafficking operation their cousin had tried to get me to participate in. Or about the way Vito treated me like his kid. With equal parts pride and disappointment. I probably should have told them. Those moments in life may not be good anecdotes, but it's bad to let them fester in silence.

But I didn't say anything.

Instead, we talked about nothing. In the usual strain of familiar nothingness. Ryan mooned a couple cars. We got high and giggled in the backseat while Reese drove. Reese and Ryan played show tunes and sang them really, really loud.

Ryan tried to convince us to go to the Grand Canyon. We said no. He offered to drive. We let him and lost two hours when he decided to go to the Grand Canyon anyway. Turned out it was just a big canyon.

We stopped for a little while in Albuquerque. It was less than riveting. But it was better than being trapped in the car.

In Texas, we made jokes about backward people and horror movies. Until we stopped in Dallas and it wasn't lame. And then we kinda felt like jerks.

Reese was at the wheel when we finally got to New Orleans. Unfamiliar cities are a bitch. She got us lost despite the GPS.

"Where are we going?" Ryan wanted to know.

"I don't know, but figure it out. 'Cause I'm driving in circles," Reese said.

"Should we find a hotel?" I asked.

"Totally. And food. I'm hungry." Ryan.

Reese gasped. "Oh my God. Oyster po-boy."

"Good call. Oyster po-boy," I said.

"I know, right?" Reese.

"You're a genius."

"Obviously." Reese.

"Huh? What just happened?" Ryan asked.

"That's what we want to eat," I told him.

"But you hate oysters. And do you even know what a po-boy is?" Ryan asked.

"Not really. No. Pretty sure it's a sandwich," I said.

"I'm so confused."

"I don't hate oysters," Reese said.

"But you don't like them either."

"It doesn't matter. We want oyster po-boys," I said.

"Why?" he asked again.

"Because we're in New Orleans," Reese said.

We found a hotel, checked in, searched out oyster po-boys, and took them back to our room. I took one bite and immediately spit it back out.

"I told you that you hated oysters," Ryan said.

"Fuck you."

"Want something you can swallow?" Reese offered.

"Please."

Reese reached into the bag on the table and produced another paper-wrapped sandwich. Always prepared, that girl.

"You're the best."

"I know."

"If only someone would get me another beer." I frowned at my empty bottle. Then I pouted out my bottom lip and gave Ryan my saddest eyes.

"So fuckin' needy." He shook his head. But then he got up and grabbed two beers out of the small fridge. He twisted the top off mine before handing it to me. I couldn't do that. Open a beer with my bare hand. But Ryan could, and he knew I found it super impressive.

"So manly."

"Blow me."

Reese glared at us. Then she stole Ryan's fresh beer. He got up and got himself another one with a long-suffering sigh. So put upon.

"So what are we going to do?" Reese asked.

"I'm gonna need you to narrow that question down," I said.

"I meant in the broad sense. Take the money and ditch them? Stick it out? Disappear? Thoughts? Feelings?"

"I vote we give it some time. But it's your call." I shrugged. Not my decision.

"If staying with them blows then we can always take off," Ryan said.

"True. I just didn't like how he talked to you," Reese said.

"Question," Ryan said. We waited, but he didn't ask his question. Or say anything.

"Ryan?" I asked.

"Oh, yeah. Question. What do we call him?"

"Call him?" I asked.

"For real." Reese nodded like Ryan was a genius. "Do we call him Breno? Dad? Breno seems accurate, but weird. And Dad just doesn't make sense. He isn't our dad, not really."

"Totally." Ryan.

"Are you asking me?" I wanted to know.

"Yes." Reese.

"Why would I know? It's your convoluted relationship. Not mine."

"We want your opinion," Ryan said.

"I don't know. What feels right? When you think about him, what do you call him in your head?"

"That dude." Ryan.

"Breno." Reese.

"Then call him Breno. Or..." I grinned. "Just don't directly address him."

"So helpful." Reese.

"Bro." Ryan.

My disposable cell phone rang. The readout said it was Christopher. I handed it to Ryan because I was chewing. He answered, listened for a minute, shrugged, and hung up.

"They just passed Shreveport. Won't be here for like five hours."

Reese and I shrugged. That didn't really affect us much.

"Fruit loop?" I asked.

"Yep," Reese answered.

"Are you talking in code on purpose today?" Ryan asked.

"Gay town," I said.

"Is that some mythical queer talent or something? The ability to find any gay bar within fifty miles."

"Yes," Reese lied for me.

"Like gaydar. It's queer magic." I threw in some spirit fingers for good measure. He didn't need to know I had looked it up online.

"Okay, but I wanna get laid too," Ryan said.

"Not something you need to share with me," Reese said.

He shrugged.

"I'm sure you can find a straight girl," I told him.

Ryan stared at me, all offended and shit. "She has to be hot too. Not just straight."

"I thought that went without saying," I said.

"You guys can keep arguing. I'm taking a shower," Reese informed us.

We let her. I figured I didn't need to tell them I was going to be picturing her in that shower.

Chapter Four

R eese looked fucking hot. Like too damn hot. Normally, that would be a good thing. But considering the number of women who had bought, or tried, to buy her a drink in the last hour, it was definitely a bad thing. She was wearing jeans that were quite possibly made for her ass. And the top was…Well, it wasn't appropriate for the weather.

Damn. When had I become a prude?

"You're gonna break something if you don't relax." Ryan posted up on the wall next to me. He handed me a beer. Then he handed me his beer. With both hands free, he grabbed my jaw and attempted to unclench it.

"I'm relaxed. Get off me." I jerked my chin out of his hands.

"Sure." He took his beer back.

"That chick needs to ease up. Reese isn't into her." I started to push off the wall. I was going to separate Reese from the woman who was standing far too close to her. Ryan grabbed my arm and pulled me back until my shoulders slammed into the wall.

"Leave it. It'll only piss her off."

"She needs help." She didn't.

"Reese can handle herself."

"Shit. I know. I just can't handle it." And I hated myself for not being able to watch Reese. She wasn't doing anything wrong. Hell, she had turned away nearly every woman who had approached her. They all left looking happy just to have managed a minute of conversation. Reese could be nice when she wanted to. She just wasn't being nice enough to me.

"It's okay." He pulled me into a one-armed hug that I seriously needed. "You guys will figure it out."

"Thanks."

"But don't be so damn needy. Makes you look pathetic. She hates that." Apparently, my nice BFF had left the building. Now Ryan was just keeping it real and shit.

"You're so helpful."

"I know."

"Shit. She's coming over here." And she was. Reese was maneuvering toward us. She was somehow sipping a radioactive drink as she weaved around people. That took mad skill. Or maybe not. It was only her second drink. Ryan and I were on four. Maybe five. I wasn't sure. "Serious. She's coming right over here."

"Damn, Coop. What is this? Your first high school dance? Be cool."

"Sorry. Shit. Fuck. What's wrong with me?"

"You're a tool," he answered.

"Thanks."

"You guys about ready to get out of here?" Reese asked once she was close enough to us. "Maybe finish our drinks and go?"

"Sure." I tried to be nonchalant. I think it worked.

"Wait," Ryan said.

We both looked at him, but he didn't say anything else. His gaze was locked on something across the room. I followed his line of sight and found the only sexy straight girl in the bar. Ryan had a talent for that shit.

He still didn't say anything. Just handed me his beer and walked away.

"Damn. Now we need to get another room," Reese said.

"Yep."

Ryan got halfway to the girl before she realized someone was watching her. He didn't say or do anything. But I knew he was looking at her with those sleepy, stoned, bedroom eyes of his. They were impossible to resist. I'd seen women try and fail. The boy knew how sexy he was.

Their encounter took two minutes. Less than, maybe. And then they were gone and stumbling back to our hotel.

"If we hurry, we can get him another room before he takes over ours," Reese said.

"Let's go." I ditched the two bottles I was holding and grabbed her hand. Because the bar was crowded and so were the streets. I didn't want to lose her. Swear. It had nothing to do with simply wanting to hold her hand.

A block later, Reese pointed out Ryan and his temporary girlfriend.

"They're definitely heading to our hotel," I said.

"Yeah, but they're moving slow." If moving slow was a euphemism for making out on a street corner, then yes, they were moving slow. "Cross the street and pass him."

"Yes, sir," I said.

Reese glared.

We got to the hotel and reserved a room on the same floor as ours. The kid working the counter handed me the keycard about two seconds before Ryan and mystery girl stumbled into the lobby. I made sure the room number was scrawled on the envelope he had handed me, then followed Reese to the elevator.

Ryan was too busy doing a thorough tonsil inspection, as all refined boys do, to notice us standing next to him. I stuck the card into his back pocket. That he noticed. He grinned and went back to making out. The elevator came. Which was good because they were kind of gross and noticeable in the lobby of this far too tasteful hotel.

Reese and I waited for another elevator.

"That was fun." Reese glared at the door as it closed on Ryan.

"Yeah, your brother is super classy," I said as if I had never behaved the same way.

"Tonight, he is so not my brother."

"So, uhh, what do we do now?"

Reese shot a non-subtle glance at me. She'd just realized that we were on our own for the evening.

The elevator opened for us. We didn't get into it.

"Let's go back out. I feel like dancing," Reese said.

I did not feel like dancing. Not with any girl who wasn't Reese. And definitely not with Reese.

"Yeah, sure. That sounds fun." I hated myself.

"Come on." Reese turned and headed back to the street. Like an idiot, I followed her.

❖

Dancing wasn't the problem so much. Not like I thought it was going to be. It was hard to be anything except turned on and high when Reese was all pressed up against me and grinding. Not that Reese was the type to bump and grind. But that's what it felt like.

The problem was everyone else in the room.

They were looking at me like I was a lucky bastard. Which I was. Like they wanted to have the girl I had. That was the issue. She wasn't mine. They all thought I'd be going home with her. That tonight I'd know the way her skin tasted. That I'd know what it felt like to get lost in her. Just her. That I'd fall asleep with the scent of her surrounding me.

It was a lie. Made stark by their collective jealousy. They had a better chance than I ever did. Even if it was a slim one.

I was jealous of them.

Not that Reese noticed. Or gave a fuck. Girl wanted to dance and she was going to dance. The only thing she would have noticed was if the music stopped. Maybe not even that. She definitely didn't have the inclination to pay attention to whatever the hell was going on with me.

At first, she kept her distance. Like she had a vague awareness that I might not appreciate her way too sexy body pressed up against mine. But that wore off quickly. I should have known what she was going to do. She'd done it before. But I didn't see it coming. Soon she was just dancing. Arms draped lazily around my neck. Eyes closed. Hips following a beat I couldn't fathom.

And I was more turned on than I'd ever been. Ever.

But I kept it together. Really. I just vaguely moved with her and let her do her thing. The pain building low in my belly would fade. The pulse of want would too. It was worth it for one night.

I didn't lose it until one of her hands dropped. Slowly. Slim fingers traced the side of my neck, a stray thumb caressed my jaw, fingernails scratched oh so lightly across my collarbone. And I was okay with that. I was even okay with her stepping in closer to me while she did it. But when a stray pinkie innocently grazed my nipple, I was so not okay with that.

The bitch was fucking with me.

So I tried to kiss her. It seemed logical. She wanted to turn me on. It was fair play.

Reese dropped back a step, stopped dancing, and looked at me hard. The brief moment of anger was eclipsed by sadness. And that made me lose my shit.

I left.

❖

The arousal faded quickly when I started walking. That surprised me. But my skin still tingled, my hands shook, every muscle seemed to vibrate. I'd felt like that for hours, days. Like currents were running through me. Since the moment I'd seen Ryan strapped to a chair in a warehouse in Chicago. No, before that. Since I'd found Breno and Christopher back in El Dorado Hills. From the moment Breno had hugged me.

After that, it was a thousand small moments. Christopher's hand on my arm. Breno's soft, caring looks. Ryan's constant need to make me real via contact. Reese reaching out to me in her sleep. All human connection. Not the way Alexis touched me. With her, I knew she wanted something. Same with Vito. It wasn't about me. It was about them. But when Christopher or Breno or Ryan, hell, even Reese, touched me, I knew it was out of love.

That simple need to be touched by someone else had been denied to me for half a year. I hadn't known I'd missed it.

Reese knew. And she exploited it. I didn't know why.

So I walked. And kept walking. It didn't make it hurt any less. And my hands didn't stop shaking. I thought walking might make me tired. Weary enough that I could go back and crawl in bed and not hear Reese breathing softly beside me. But I knew I would hear her. Even now, I could feel the whisper of her chest and thrum of her heart. And I ached so bad just to let my heart beat with hers.

So I kept walking.

It was somewhere between midnight and dawn when my phone rang. There was a brief rush when I thought it was her. It wasn't.

"Yeah?"

"Cooper. Where are you?" Christopher.

"The French Quarter." I was fairly certain that was true. I'd been circling the same blocks for hours.

"Are the twins with you?"

"Nope."

"We've been trying to reach you guys for thirty minutes." He sounded worried. And frantic. And tired.

"Ryan found a girl. I don't know where Reese is. What's up?" I asked.

"We're here. Near the hotel."

"Cool. Get a room. We can meet for breakfast in the morning." Why did I sound so normal? I didn't feel normal.

"We can't."

"Why? Oh, shit." They couldn't exactly park the truck and leave it unattended. "I'm on my way. I'll drive for a while so you guys can sleep."

"Great. Thank you."

"Sure." I hung up.

Maybe driving would accomplish what walking couldn't.

I found Breno and Christopher idling with their hazards on a block from the hotel.

"You guys look like shit," I said.

They exchanged an exhausted glance and didn't bother replying.

"You don't mind driving?" Christopher asked.

"It's fine. Get some sleep. I'll call if I need someone to take over."

"Thank you," Breno said.

I shrugged and climbed behind the wheel. I probably should have paid attention to where I was going. Because other than the po-boys, I hadn't picked up much from Micky Knight. Just place names. Not where they were or where they went. The streets I recognized I turned on. The signs pointing to places I'd read about I turned toward. Not a great navigational tool. Which was how I ended up on the Pontchartrain Causeway. Dawn teased me for the first few miles. After that, the sun broke. The water got lighter. Lake Pontchartrain was not a sexy body of water. Kinda blue. And watery. Like Tahoe, except I was driving over it, not around. And it didn't look nearly as deep.

After that, I just followed the highway. The car ahead of me seemed to know where it was going so I stuck with them. I realized I was tired when I nearly fell asleep at the wheel. My head started to fall forward and my whole body twitched. Then my heart started going triple time. Not good. After that, I couldn't not notice how dead I was. The signs blurred into green blobs with smudges of white. The cars ahead of me coalesced into a stream of silver and black and gold above a gray-black strip.

I was fucking dangerous.

The dash lit up with an obnoxious squeal that made me jump. Great, I was also out of gas. I pulled off at the next exit praying for somewhere to stop. The god I didn't believe in was looking out for me. Capitalism, that is, not any of the others.

I pumped gas. And managed to stay upright while doing it. I was a champ.

The convenience store was kind enough to be made entirely out of glass. Safe enough. I ignored visions of having fifteen million snatched out of the truck and pushed into the store. A high school kid behind the counter continued to play on her phone, not at all distracted by my presence. She was a champ too.

I grabbed a coffee guaranteed to make me have to pee long before I was back in New Orleans. Also two Red Bulls and three Mountain Dews because they didn't have AMP. What the fuck backwoods town didn't have AMP?

The girl glanced up from her phone after I'd stood in front of her for a full two minutes.

"Yeah?"

I nudged the drinks in response. Words were hard.

She threw a number at me. I threw some money at her. We had an understanding. It was nice.

"Where's New Orleans?" I asked. Then amended, "Like how far? And do I just follow this road?" I couldn't remember if I'd made any major turns.

"Two hours. Maybe more. That way." She pointed. No more information. I waited. She broke first. "Stay on the freeway. After the state line, you might want to ask someone else."

"State line?"

"Yeah."

"Where the fuck am I?"

"Mississippi."

"Fuck me."

She didn't have a response to that.

I was crossing the parking lot, juggling my coffee and soda and energy drinks—she hadn't offered a bag and I hadn't asked—when someone behind me called out.

"Hey, hey, bud."

I figured he wasn't talking to me.

"Hey, you."

A quick and subtle glance at the pumps suggested he was talking to me. There were only two cars. Trucks, that is. Mine and something big enough to survive a zombie apocalypse. It was older and muddy and dented all over. I kept walking. Slowly. Didn't want to show fear. But all I could think of right then were rapid-fire words like Mississippi and song lyrics and, strangely, the image of a map. I was in that middle section where it was all red.

How the fuck did I end up in Mississippi? Gay slurs had been funny back home. Would they be as laughable here? All those books and movies and songs and shows I'd grown up with. Hick towns and backwoods bars and rednecks. Did I not pay any fucking attention?

"Hey, buddy. Stop, would ya?" And then there was a hand grabbing my shoulder.

I turned to look. Right then, he was my worst fucking nightmare. He hadn't shaved in about two days. His lip bulged with dip. He had a weathered face upward of fifty with tired, dark eyes. He smelled faintly of whisky like it had spilled on his worn shirt and he hadn't bothered to wash it. Coffee and sour tobacco on his breath.

"Oh, hey, what's up?" I tried to be nonchalant.

"You ain't from 'round here." For real, he said 'round here.

"Uh, no."

"Might wanna look out." He lifted a hand. He was gonna hit me. I knew it. I took a step back.

"Whoa there, bud. You dropped this. That's all."

I looked at his hand. It was holding my wallet.

"Shit. Thanks." I tried to take it. My hands were too full.

He glanced at my hands. Then back at my face.

"You're a girl."

I debated lying. Was it better to be a dyke or an effeminate guy?

"Uh, yeah."

"Sorry, you just looked a bit like a fella." And he actually looked sorry.

"No worries. Happens a lot."

"Oh, well. Shoulda been payin' attention." He shook his head like it was his fault.

"It's okay."

"Oh, uh, right then. That your truck?"

"Yeah."

"I'll walk ya. Looks like your hands are full." He still had my wallet.

"Thanks."

"Where you headed?" He started walking with me.

"Uh, New Orleans."

"Vacation?" he asked.

"Yeah."

"Alone?"

"Got friends there," I answered.

We reached the truck. There was an awkward moment where we realized I couldn't get my keys.

"Here." He took the coffee out of my hand.

"Thanks." I opened the door, dumped the bottles and cans on the seat, and turned back for the coffee.

"You okay there? You seem a little jumpy."

"Fine."

"You sure? I'm not tryin' to make you nervous." He handed me the coffee and my wallet.

I decided to be honest. Probably the lack of sleep.

"You hear horror stories. Gay kids in Middle America and all that."

He smiled. Kinda slow. Like it took him a second to get what I was saying and even longer to figure out that a smile was a good response. "Don't gotta worry 'bout that. I ain't gonna hurt you."

"Yeah, I figured that out."

"I'm Gus." Of course his name was Gus.

"Cooper." We shook hands.

"Good to meet you, Cooper."

"Yeah, you too."

"Now you be careful drivin'."

"Thanks. And thanks for grabbin' my wallet. I would have been screwed."

He just smiled, nodded his head once, then I was back on the road.

❖

The girl in Mississippi was wrong. It took me three hours to get back to New Orleans. And, not surprisingly, the insane amounts of caffeine I'd consumed had me jumpy, sleepy, and kinda nauseated.

I called Christopher and Breno, but they didn't pick up. Neither did Ryan. I really didn't want to call Reese. But it was either that or hurl and pass out in the truck. And that was only worth it if I'd consumed my weight in alcohol. Not even then, really. So I called Reese. She didn't answer either.

Fuck.

I decided to do the mature thing. I sent Christopher and Breno a bunch of annoying text messages. And I called both their phones repeatedly. After the sixth call, a sleepy Breno answered.

"Hey. I'm dyin', man. I need someone to take over."

"All right. I will be down in a few minutes." His voice was all scratchy. And he sounded kinda dead. Which made me feel bad.

"Thanks. I'm two blocks south of the hotel. Ish."

"I will find you," he promised.

And he did. Twenty minutes after we'd hung up, he strode to the passenger side and climbed in. He had the same stubble Ryan sometimes boasted. More of a pubescent joke than facial hair. Heavier on the jawline and upper lip. Smooth cheeks. His eyes were bloodshot. Hair unwashed and sticking up a bit in the back.

He looked young, despite the gray in his hair and the slight lines around his mouth. Younger than I'd ever seen him look. It was weird.

"Sorry. I thought I'd last longer," I said.

"Don't worry. I appreciate you driving as long as you did."

"No worries. I left the city. Drove to Mississippi, apparently," I told him.

"Mississippi?" he asked.

"Yeah. So I don't think you'll stand out if you stick close."

"Why did you drive to Mississippi?"

"Wasn't intentional." I shrugged. "Just drove. Ended up there."

"You should head back. You look tired." Breno seemed concerned.

"I am." I opened the door. "Keep me updated."

"I will."

I started walking. My head was swimming. And my feet didn't want to go in a straight line. They felt more curvy than that. At least if anyone noticed me they would just think I was drunk. Stupid kid after a long night in the Quarter.

I stumbled into the hotel and fell into the elevator. Two women got in after me. I leaned against the wall out of necessity. Standing was hard. And I tended to sway. The women shot me a couple glances, but neither seemed particularly curious.

When I got to the room, the security bolt was thrown.

"Reese. Let me in," I called into the small space. Nothing. "Reese, come on. I'm fuckin' tired." I was louder that time.

"I'm sleeping. Fuck off."

"Well, I haven't slept yet. So let me in. Please."

"Ryan's room is for one-night stands. Go sleep there." She sounded pissed.

"Huh?" Confused. That was me. "What?"

"Did you at least get her name?" Her voice was still muffled. Probably buried in a pillow. So it made her hard to understand.

"I don't get it. I'm sleepy. Let me in. You can berate me then."

I heard movement. Then an angry sigh. Then footsteps. Reese slammed the door shut, threw off the bolt, and opened it.

"I said, did you at least get her name? Or a shower? 'Cause I'm not letting you in here until you're fuckin' clean. But I doubt that's a state you'll ever achieve." The glare plastered on her face was record breaking.

"Seriously. What the fuck are you talking about? Let me in." I tried to push her back, but she planted a hand on my chest and shoved. I nearly fell. Balance was tough.

"I'm talking about whoever you've been screwing all night. I don't want the room to smell like your dirty ass one-night stand. So go beg at Ryan's door. He's never cared about your sins."

"I...what? I haven't been screwing," I said.

"Right."

"There's no girl..." Like you. But I didn't say that. "I didn't—"

"What? Get her name?"

I'd done a lot of stupid shit. And I'd slept with a lot of stupid girls. But I at least admitted it when I did. And I'd never lied about it. So her disbelief pissed me off. A lot. It also woke me up. Temporarily.

"Gus."

"You slept with a girl named Gus?" Now she looked confused.

"No. But the only person I've spoken to since I last saw you was named Gus. Also Christopher and Breno. There was a girl in a gas station, but she was straight and underage, and no, I didn't catch her name."

"You slept with a minor?"

"No. I drove the fucking truck to Mississippi so Christopher and Breno could sleep. I stopped for gas. Bought coffee and soda in the store. Dropped my wallet. A guy named Gus picked it up and gave it back to me. Now, I've had a long-ass night and an even longer fuckin' morning. So back the fuck off and let me get some sleep." I shoved her aside. This time she didn't stop me.

I didn't even bother with a shower. Just kicked off my shoes and jeans. Stripped off my shirt. Crawled in bed. I was asleep before Reese even closed the door.

CHAPTER FIVE

Reese woke me. She was perched on the other bed glaring at me, and she looked a little confused and a lot mad. So pretty much typical Reese.

"Ryan called. He wants breakfast."

"Okay." I rubbed my face and stared at the clock. Blurry. I gave my eyes another rub. Less blurry. "What time is it?"

"One."

"Where are we getting breakfast?"

"Some place he heard was good. He said he'll meet us in the lobby."

"Cool." I rolled to the edge of the bed and managed to sit up. "I got to shower."

"Whatever. I'm going downstairs."

"Fine." I didn't have the patience or inclination to argue with her.

Twenty minutes later, I stumbled out of the elevator into the lobby. Ryan jumped up and bounded over to me. He looked happy. At least someone was.

"Morning," I grumbled.

"Hi." He threw an arm around my shoulders and dragged me toward Reese. "You guys ready for breakfast?"

"Sure," I said.

"Whatever." Oh, good. Reese was still in her little mood.

We took off down the street. Ryan seemed to know where he was going. Plus, I didn't have much choice. He still had his arm around my shoulders. And he was bouncing with every step. It was jarring.

"Have either of you heard from Breno or Christopher?" I asked.

"No. Are they back yet? Have you talked to them?" Just-got-laid Ryan was the most annoying person ever. All smiles and excitement and sunshine.

"They got in early this morning," I told him. I was going to elaborate, but that seemed difficult.

"Christopher took over for Breno an hour ago," Reese said.

"Oh, good." I left it at that.

"Should we call them? Do they need us to drive?" Now Ryan was sort of skipping.

"They'll be fine," I said.

"Cool. Okay, great."

"I'll call after we eat," Reese said. I was pretty sure she just wanted to get away from me.

"Here." Ryan spotted the restaurant he was looking for and dragged us inside. It smelled like fish. But not in an old way. In a good way. I was starving.

Ryan kept conversation afloat for a good fifteen minutes. Somehow, he managed to communicate about thirty unrelated subjects all with three-word sentences. It took him that long to realize Reese and I weren't participating in his monologue.

"What's with you guys?"

I shrugged. Reese lied.

"Nothing."

"'Cause you're quiet."

"Tired," I said.

"Yep." Reese.

"Okay." Ryan. That was all it took. He was easily distracted.

Reese was saved from calling Christopher when he called us instead. She nodded and said non-committal things for a few minutes, then hung up.

"He finally reached his friend. But the guy can't meet us until tomorrow morning."

"Shit," was my contribution.

"Oh, well. Whatcha wanna do?" Ryan asked.

"Don't care," I said.

"Nope," Reese said.

"Wanna walk?"

We shrugged and agreed and somehow found ourselves wandering the Quarter again. Ryan stuck to coffee, from three different cafés, until it started getting dark. Then he found a daiquiri. Not sure where it came from.

"Dude, they're seriously into partying here." Ryan was so smart.

"It's New Orleans, dumbass. That's like what they do." I scoffed and looked to Reese for confirmation.

"You're both dumb," she said. Guess she didn't appreciate my attempt at camaraderie.

"Just sayin'. Overkill." Ryan chugged his icy booze.

"Yeah, for real." If Reese didn't want my help, I'd just back Ryan up.

Reese rolled her eyes.

"Dude. Daiquiris." Ryan handed me the almost empty cup he was holding and took off across the street.

"Is he high again?" Reese asked. Interesting. Starting conversation with me all on her own.

"Isn't he always?"

"True."

"So I take it you're not pissed at me anymore?" I asked it all nonchalant. But I was curious as hell.

"Sorry." She hesitated, then pushed on. She should have kept her damn mouth shut. "I thought you were lying about driving. But Christopher said you drove for a while."

"Seriously? That's why you were pissed? You thought I was lying?"

"Yeah. Why else?" Reese asked.

"I had no fuckin' clue. So you didn't believe me, but when Christopher said I drove all morning, you believed him."

"Why are you getting pissed?" She seemed angry at my anger.

"You don't believe a damn thing I tell you." Bitch.

"That surprises you?"

I didn't have an answer for that. So I went after Ryan and his pursuit of booze.

❖

I woke up next to Ryan. His feet were by my head. But that might have been because I was upside down. I dragged myself up the bed until my head was on my pillow. Ryan reeked of rum and citrus, kinda orangy. I couldn't figure out the oranges part. I tried to shove him away from me. He rolled right back to where he'd started. After my second attempt, I realized his pockets were stuffed with oranges. That explained the smell, but it didn't help with reclaiming half the bed. I dug four oranges out of his sweatshirt pockets. Then I checked his pants. Two tangerines. And each of his back pockets had a fistful of kumquats. Miraculously, they were all intact.

My search inspired a lot of questions and very few answers. I rolled over and went back to sleep.

The next time I woke up, Ryan was leaning over me eating an orange.

"Want?" He held out a section to me.

"No. Go away."

"Can't. Gotta meet Christopher. We're going to that artist guy's place. Get up."

"Where did all that fruit come from?" I asked.

"I was gonna ask you. It was on your side of the bed." Ryan pointed. The table on my side did have a large pile.

"I pulled them out of your pockets."

"Huh." Ryan shrugged, leaned over me, and snagged some kumquats. "Tastes good."

"Where's Reese?"

"Shower." He nodded at the bathroom.

"I'll take an orange." It seemed like a good idea. He handed me one. I stared at it for a minute. Opening it was going to be tough.

"Here." Ryan took the orange back and started peeling it.

"Thanks."

When Reese came out of the bathroom, she found us sitting on the bed. We had the ice bucket between us half-filled with orange and tangerine peels. We both had juice to our elbows and Ryan's chin was sticky. It's tough to be angry when you're naked, but somehow Reese managed to glare while wearing only a towel.

"What?" I asked.

"I guess I should just be happy it isn't crawfish," she said.

"That wouldn't be breakfasty," Ryan told her.

"Did you get coffee?" Reese asked.

"Shit."

"I asked you to do two things, Ryan," Reese said.

"I woke up Coop."

"That was the first thing." She said it real slow.

"But I forgot the coffee," he said.

"I figured that part out."

"I want coffee," I said.

Ryan sighed. "Fine. I'll go get coffee."

"Can't we just get room service?" I asked.

"Princess wants a cappuccino," Ryan said. "And it just has to be from that place down the street. Where we went yesterday." Well, that narrowed it down.

"Don't worry about it." Reese sounded all exasperated. "We can get it on the way."

"No, no, darling sister of mine. If you want a cappuccino, I will get you a cappuccino."

"Stop. It's too late," she said.

"Nope." Ryan stood up. "I'm already going." He went into the bathroom to wash his hands.

"You're an idiot."

"An idiot who's getting you coffee," he called over the running water.

"Whatever." Reese rolled her eyes.

"Later. I'll meet you downstairs." Ryan grinned and left.

"He's dumb," Reese said. I just shrugged. Non-committal was the best way to go. Keeping up with Reese's moods was way too hard.

Reese dug around in the dresser until she found a pair of jeans. Somehow, her wardrobe had tripled since leaving Chicago. Ryan and I had given her the dresser since we were still living on the same two pairs of jeans.

I probably should have gotten in the shower. I probably should have pulled on pants and gone with Ryan. I probably should have done anything except sit in bed. I definitely shouldn't have stayed there trying to get a glimpse of the underwear Reese was picking out for the day. And when Reese looked at me, hesitated, and dropped her towel, I really shouldn't have watched.

Fuck me, that girl looked good naked. Like, really fucking good.

I was helpless. All I could do was sit there and watch. Look at the carved plane of her stomach. Stare at the hint of pink in her nipples. Salivate 'cause I knew how her collarbones tasted. My eyes dropped to her cunt. That was when she realized I was watching. She acted like she hadn't noticed, just turned so I was looking at her ass instead. Not that I was going to complain.

My view was seriously interrupted when she pulled on something silky and girly that was supposed to be underwear. No. The view was still good. I wasn't getting the full frontal. Just a side view. The slope and subtle softness of her tits. The roundness of her ass. How did she get such a perfect ass?

"Stop it," Reese said.

"Stop what?" I tossed the remainder of my orange into the bucket. I tried to be cool when I climbed out of bed, but I realized I was soaking wet. There's no cool way to see if your boxers are damp.

"Staring."

"I wasn't staring." My heart was pounding so hard and fast I was going to suffocate. My hands were shaking. I was so turned on, standing was a challenge.

"Whatever."

"I'm going to shower," I said. It was a lie. I was gonna jack off. The only time I'd gotten turned on in the last four months had been when I met Alexis DiGiovanni. And that had only been because she had a striking resemblance to her cousin. Not exactly orgasm worthy. The real thing was so much better. Because right then, after looking at Reese, my body was very much alive. And I needed to come. Bad. But Reese didn't need to know that.

"Fine. I'm going to go meet Ryan," she said.

"Cool."

I dug into my duffle and pulled out a pair of jeans. I didn't even look up at her. I didn't need to. The image of her in all her naked hotness was burned into my flesh. The picture expanded with memories of her above me, beneath me, arched and begging to come. My clit started throbbing. My stomach hollowed. Fuck.

I walked into the bathroom. Tossed my jeans onto the counter. Brushed my teeth. Waited for her to leave.

"I'm going downstairs." Reese tossed her towel into the bathroom.

"'Kay. I'll be there soon," I said around a mouthful of toothpaste. It was less than coherent.

The door to the room opened and closed. She was gone. I spit out the toothpaste. Rinsed my mouth. Then shoved my hand into my boxers. Oh, fuck. I was actually dripping. When I slid a finger between my folds, I groaned and closed my eyes. My hips arched forward.

"What are you doing?"

My eyes flew open. Reese was standing in the bathroom door watching me.

"Fuck."

"Are you jerking off?" she asked.

"Uhh, yeah." It was pretty apparent. Denying it would have been stupid.

"Why?"

"'Cause I want to come." Hard to lie when you've got your hand in your pants. It inspires honesty. Damn, my hand was still in my boxers. I pulled it out. My fingers were wet. I turned and started washing my hands. They were shaking.

"I don't really know what to say."

"Don't say anything. Just leave." I didn't know if I should be mad or embarrassed or both. "This is all I got right now. So let me have it before the picture fades."

"Wait. You're jacking off 'cause you just saw me naked?" Reese asked.

Uh-oh. I thought that part had been obvious.

"Fuck," I said again.

Reese didn't say anything. And I didn't say anything. I looked at my hands. I was still washing them even though they were clean. She looked at me. It was awkward.

Reese pulled out her cell phone. Dialed a number.

"Hey, Coop and I are staying here. You guys okay without us? No, Ryan is downstairs waiting…No. We're fine…Yep. Bye." She ended the call.

"What was that about?" I asked.

"Strip," Reese said.

"Huh?"

"Strip. Get on the bed. Now." She pointed.

I didn't move. So she grabbed my shirt and dragged me out of the bathroom. She yanked the shirt over my head. Pulled my boxers down. Shoved me so I fell onto the bed. I had no idea what was going on. Actually, I had a pretty good idea what was going on. I just didn't know why.

No love was going to be made in this room.

"What are you doing?"

"What do you think?" she asked as she stripped.

"I don't know."

"Don't be an idiot."

Reese climbed onto the bed so she was straddling my head.

"No. Stop."

She froze. "You want me to stop?"

"Okay, no. But—"

"Don't start. Do you want to fuck or not?"

"Yes." I wanted to fuck her so bad. I wanted her to fuck me so bad. I didn't even give a fuck how it was going to happen.

Reese grabbed a fistful of my hair and pressed my face against her cunt. I opened my mouth, took her in. A rush of wetness coated my throat. Made it so I couldn't breathe. I decided right then that the dude who figured out air was necessary was an idiot. Ten seconds later, I figured out that that dude had been a genius. Also, Reese was probably trying to kill me. I tried to pull away to get some air. She held me close. So I kept licking, sucking at the smooth folds of her flesh. Fuck it. If I passed out it would be worth it.

Reese lifted away for a brief moment. "Breathe." I did. She pulled me back against her with a groan. Her hips started to rock. She arched back, grabbed my cunt. Pressed hard against my clit. I was going to fucking come.

Her fingers tightened in my hair. She was close too. She swelled in my mouth. Moisture dripped down my jaw. I flattened my tongue against her clit, but stopped licking. I'd given her too much control. She needed to know that I wasn't going to do everything she wanted. I wasn't going to be everything she wanted.

"Come the fuck on." Reese's hips jerked. A sad attempt to make me keep going. I started again, but slower this time. Building up movement until my tongue was vibrating against her. "God, yeah. Like that." I let her set the rhythm, let her fuck my mouth the way she wanted to. She shivered and came. I didn't. She let my head drop.

"Seriously?" I asked.

Reese didn't move. Just slumped a little. Her fingers were still hard against my clit. But not moving. The bitch wasn't going to let me come.

My arms were over her legs. Held up by her thighs. Just at the wrong angle. But I tried to reach for myself anyway. Reese grabbed my hand and put it between her legs.

"Again."

"But I want to—"

"Fuck me," she said.

We both knew I was going to. So I slid inside her. She was still soaking. As I filled her, she sobbed and gasped and groaned. I pulled her clit between my lips again. Grabbed her ass, squeezed rhythmically. She started calling out to God, then me. She had the order wrong. I was God.

Reese tightened around my fingers. I pushed deeper. Sucked harder. I couldn't understand what she was saying anymore. My head was filled with the rush of her blood and the pounding of my own abused heart. Her thighs pressed closer. I slid out and in, harder this time. Twitched my fingers inside her. Faster. Worked my tongue in time to my hands.

And then she came again. In a sobbing mass of groans. In a collapse of her impeccable control. Came and came again. I didn't stop fucking her. Didn't stop until she weakly pushed my head away and fell onto the bed.

I stayed still for a minute. Carefully, pulled out of her. Let my shaking hands fall to the sheets. Reese was twitching beside me. Damn, the girl was still coming. And she didn't seem to notice or care that I hadn't stopped throbbing.

When I lifted my hand to touch myself, Reese grabbed me.

"No."

"Please. I gotta come."

"Just shut the fuck up for a sec," she said.

I did. For longer than a second. I thought she fell asleep. I wasn't going to try jacking off again. I wasn't stupid.

"Reese?" I whispered.

"Just be quiet."

And then she climbed on top of me. Pushed her thigh between mine. Braced one arm next to my head. Started twisting my nipple with her other hand. Just the sensation of her bare skin pressed to mine would have been enough to make me come. And I did. I arched up against the pressure of her thigh, groaned into the mouth that was suddenly, violently against mine, and came. Reese thrust her leg against me rhythmically. Sucked my tongue in time to her thrusts. I came again. And again. When I collapsed back, spent and shivering, she pulled the blanket over us and held me as I drifted to sleep.

❖

The afternoon light was waning when I woke. Reese's legs and arms were tangled with mine. She was warm and soft and totally naked. I wanted to always wake up like that. And I was terrified I might never do so again.

I decided to just stay there. Not move or say anything. The longer she slept the more I would get. Minutes, hours maybe, passed. The sun went down. Reese slept. It wasn't until there was a gentle rap on the door that she woke up.

"Shit," Reese said.

"Huh?"

"That's probably Ryan."

"Probably." And like that, the dream was over.

"Fuck it. You'll tell him anyway." Reese rolled off me. She found my boxers and pulled them on. Followed by my T-shirt. "You might want to cover up."

I sat up and wrapped the blanket around myself.

"You guys in there?" Ryan called through the door.

"Just a sec." Reese crossed to the door and opened it.

"Hey." Ryan looked at her, looked at me. "Oh, hey." And started grinning so big I thought he might break something. "How's it going? I was gonna ask if you wanted dinner, but no big. It's cool. I'll just come back later. Or not at all. We still have that other room. Yeah, I'll just go there. Okay, bye." He started to turn away, but Reese grabbed his shirt and hauled him into the room.

"Calm down," she told him

"Yeah, sure. I'm calm. Like, whatever. Totally."

"Serious, Ryan. Shut up," I said. I didn't know what was going on, but clearly, Reese wasn't going to make a big deal about it. So neither was I.

"Okay." He sat on the other bed. "So you guys want dinner? I mean, Christopher and Breno went to get food, but we don't have to eat with them. Or I can just go to their room to eat. Whatever."

"I'm showering," Reese said. Then she looked at me. I was hopeful for a second. But then she said, "Make him smoke or something. Otherwise, he'll be really annoying at dinner."

"Okay." What else was I going to do? Ask to shower with her and get denied? Ask if this meant we were back together and get denied? Ask her to marry me and get denied? Bad ideas. Might as well get stoned.

The bathroom door closed. Loudly.

"Dude. Oh my God. Like, dude," Ryan said.

"For real."

He tackled me. "I knew she wanted you."

"Don't get ahead of yourself. I think she just wanted to get laid," I said.

"Dude." He was scolding now. "She's my sister."

"Sorry."

"Let's smoke," he said.

"All right. Hand me some clothes."

He did. We got stoned. Reese got out of the shower and I got in. Showers are awesome when you're high. Then we went to join their dads for dinner.

❖

Dinner was awkward. Ryan was all giddy, but none of us wanted to explain why. I was spaced, but we didn't want to explain that either. And Reese was just quiet. So we all sat in Breno and Christopher's room and ate our takeout and tried to act normal.

"My friend will have the sculptures ready and shipped within a month," Christopher said into the silence.

"Cool." Me.

"Neat." Reese.

"Totally." Ryan.

"So we need to have somewhere to ship them," Breno said.

"Okay," I said. The twins nodded.

"Where would you like to go?" Christopher asked.

They were trying to keep this conversation going. It was sweet.

"I dunno," Ryan said. I shrugged.

"Not the US," Reese said.

"For real," I said.

"All right. Let's narrow it down," Christopher said.

But we didn't have any more contributions.

"Are you kids doing all right?" Breno asked. "You seem... tired." What a nice way of saying it.

"Yep."

"Fine."

"Uh-huh."

"Did something happen?" Christopher wanted to know.

"Nope."

"Uh-uh."

"Just tired."

"Are you sure? Because all of you are acting oddly," Breno said.

"What about Europe?" I asked. Better to talk about locations than feelings.

"Somewhere warm," Ryan said.

"Yeah, Italy. Or Spain," Reese said.

"Somewhere they speak English," I amended.

"Coop is shit at languages," Reese told them.

"You will be fine," Breno assured me.

Reese laughed. Ryan tried not to.

"I'm really bad at not English," I said.

"We will figure it out," Christopher said.

"So do we like need to have a house or something?" Ryan asked.

"That would be best. Some place large enough that a shipment of sculptures won't be odd," Christopher said.

"How do you know this guy will come through?" I realized right then that we had blindly handed fifteen million to some dude we didn't know in the hope that he would do as we nicely asked.

"We are paying him handsomely," Breno said.

"I'm guessing it's still less than fifteen million," I said.

"Yeah, what's with that?" Ryan asked.

"I trust him," Christopher said. Breno laughed.

"What? What didn't you guys tell us?" Reese looked pissed.

"Nothing. He is an old friend. He won't rip us off," Christopher said.

"That is true." Breno was still smiling.

"Spill," I demanded.

"We have evidence of his cocaine smuggling," Breno said.

"Shut the fuck up." Me.

"Seriously?" Reese.

"Not cool." Ryan.

"Don't worry about it," Christopher said.

"You hired a dude who smuggles drugs?" Reese looked livid. "And you're trusting him with all of our money? What if he is arrested in the next month? What if someone kills him? What if someone rips him off? Did you think of any of that?"

"Damn it, Reese. Yes, I did think it through. I'm not an idiot," Christopher yelled.

Ryan laughed. "Sure."

"He's been running his operation for years. Very low level. Other people do his dirty work. So he is unlikely to be arrested or killed in the next thirty days. You're just going to have to trust me on this." Christopher was pleading now. Not a good move. Reese didn't appreciate weakness.

"Oh, good. The fact that it's unlikely makes me feel so much better." She crossed her arms, leaned back, and glared.

"Do you have any ideas about transferring fifteen million in gold bars into a bank account without anyone noticing?"

Reese didn't have an answer for that.

"He is right," Breno said quietly. "This will work. You just need to trust us."

"I don't know you and I don't trust you." Reese stood. "But we don't have much of a choice now, do we? I'll be ready to leave for Florida in an hour." With that, she turned and left.

Ryan and I stood. I may have liked Breno and Christopher, but I wasn't going to risk Reese for them.

"Sorry. She'll chill," Ryan said.

It was the only platitude we could offer.

CHAPTER SIX

I am so fucking bored," Ryan said.
"For real."
"How long do we have left on our shift?" he asked.
"Three hours," I said.
"Three hours? Three hours!" He slumped back against the door of the car, closed his eyes, and stuck his tongue out. "That's it. I'm dead. See? Dead." He stuck out his tongue again, farther this time.
"I told you stakeouts are boring."
"Yeah, but you didn't tell me I couldn't smoke. And it's hot."
"We're in Miami. What did you expect?" I asked.
"It's January."
"It's not even eighty."
"Liar. It's totally hotter than that," he said.
"No, it isn't."
"Yeah huh."
"Nuh-uh."
"I'm hungry."
"You ate an hour ago," I said. "And you're only doing half a shift. I still have seven hours left."
"You should be careful. You might die of starvation."
"Reese will bring me food when she takes over for you."
"You guys will probably just make out for three hours. And I'll still be bored. I'll just be bored in a hotel room."
"You could go be bored on the beach," I said.

"Whatever."

"Dude."

"What?" Ryan asked.

"Dude. There." I nodded at the house we were watching.

"Shit."

We watched the garage door open. There was movement inside, but we couldn't see much. A car backed out onto the street. White-gold Lexus. I let it drive past us. A woman was driving. There was a kid in the backseat.

"She's not even hot," Ryan said.

"Shut up. She's good-looking. Not hot like Reese, but still."

"I can't believe you threw my sister away for a chick who isn't even hot." He sounded disgusted.

"I was in pain. She was nice," I said.

"Asshole."

"Tool."

"Should we follow her?" Ryan asked.

"Yeah." I waited until the car was up the street, then pulled out and started following it. "Call Christopher. Give him a heads up that we might need help with a tail."

"On it."

Ryan got out his phone and dialed Christopher. I gave him street names as we turned through city streets. We didn't go far before the Lexus pulled into a small parking lot. I drove past.

"You see where she's going?" I asked.

"Yeah. Grocery store."

"Tell Christopher."

He did. I pulled over a couple blocks away. Ryan hung up.

"Christopher is outside the store. He says there's only one entrance."

"Where's Breno?"

"Finding somewhere else to watch."

I looked in my mirrors. "I think there's a coffee shop across the street."

"I'll text him."

We waited some more. It was boring.

"Christopher took off." Ryan read his texts. "Breno will tell us when she leaves."

"We tailed her already. Christopher should follow her this time."

"Okay." Ryan started typing.

"I'm heading back to the hotel. We can switch cars and go back to the house."

"Cool."

We had rented three cars, a van, and three bikes for our surveillance. It might have been overkill. But it had taken Breno three months to find this bitch. We weren't letting Joan get away this time.

"Have Reese meet us with the keys."

"Already texted her. She'll be in the parking lot," Ryan said.

Five minutes later, we pulled into our hotel's parking lot. Reese was waiting next to a silver Toyota SUV.

"Hey," Reese greeted us. "She went to the store? Sounds exciting."

"Very James Bond," I said.

"The tail was totally James Bond," Ryan said.

"Yeah. All one mile of it." I rolled my eyes.

"Neat." Reese took the keys to the Jetta. I took the keys to the Highlander. "So I'll see you in a couple hours."

"Yep."

"Don't get caught," she said.

"Never, buttercup."

Twenty minutes later, we were parked in front of the beach house, farther down the street this time. Ten minutes after that, we were bored. Ryan was annoying. Another five and Christopher texted us.

"She's on the move," Ryan said.

"Where is she going?"

"Christopher is following her." More waiting. "Yep. She's coming home."

"Did he get a look at the kid?" I asked.

Ryan typed and waited. "Yeah. Little girl. Practically a baby."

"Shit."

"For real. That's gonna make this hard."

I nodded. But I was already forming a plan.

They weren't going to like my plan very much.

❖

"Turkey burger." Reese handed me a takeout box.

"Fries?"

"Of course there are fries." I was going to ask about a drink, but then Reese pulled out a bottle. "And Mountain Dew."

"You rock."

"I know. How long have you been parked here?" she asked.

"The whole time."

"We should move or something."

"It's almost dark. I doubt anyone can see us."

"Backseat then?"

"Sure." I handed my food back to her and climbed through the seats. She gave me the food back and followed me.

"So what's the bitch doing?"

I shrugged and bit into my burger. It hadn't occurred to me before that this was going to be a bad idea. But having Reese do surveillance of the chick I'd cheated on her with was definitely a bad call.

We sat there while I ate. Some lights went on in the house. Others went off. At one point, Joan walked past a window. Reese went still. Like a predator about to make a kill still. I didn't blame her.

"This blows," I said. We were two hours into our shift. Two hours to go.

"Yep. She's old."

"Totally." I wasn't dumb enough to disagree.

"And ugly." Petty didn't look cute on Reese.

"Yep."

"You're an asshole."

"Yeah."

Great. As if this stakeout wasn't dragging enough, add some awkward tension.

With an hour to go, Reese spoke again. "This is boring."

"You lasted longer than Ryan."

"No shit."

"Wanna make out?" I asked. I didn't think she'd go for it.

"No. Tool." Ten minutes passed. "Yeah, okay."

"What?" I asked.

In response, Reese grabbed my shirt, pulled me close, and kissed me. I wasn't stupid. I kissed her back.

She tasted like strawberry lip gloss and honey. She must have gotten new lip gloss. Weird thought. When she stuck her tongue in my mouth, I stopped thinking. Just pulled until she was on top of me. One of her feet curled around my leg and pulled me closer.

One of us moaned. It might have been me.

"Wait. Wait." Reese pushed against my chest.

"What?"

"This might be a bad idea." Duh. "What if something happens and we miss it?"

"Nothing's gonna happen. She has a kid so she's probably in for the night," I said.

"You're right. She isn't going any—shit."

"What?" I tried to sit up, but Reese was still half on top of me.

"Someone is going up the walkway."

"Shit."

Reese moved so I could sit up. The figure going up to the door was carrying a bag. It looked like a dude. Slender. And judging by the height of his jeans, probably young.

"Did he walk or drive?" Reese asked.

"I don't see a car."

"Bike. By the fence." Reese pointed.

The door opened. Light from inside spilled onto the dim porch. He handed her the bag.

"What's he giving her? What's in the bag?" I asked.

"I don't know, but it looks like she's paying him."

"Sketchy," I said.

"Totally."

The guy took whatever she was giving him and turned away. The door closed. He got on his bike and started to ride.

"He's gonna go right past us," I said.

Reese and I slid down in our seats as he went by.

"Shut the fuck up," Reese said.

"What?" I sat up a little so I could see.

"The bike has a crate on the back."

"So?"

"The crate has a sign," she said.

"What's it say?"

"She ordered takeout. He's the delivery boy."

"Shut up," I said.

"Nope. We are crazy paranoid."

I started to laugh. "For real."

"Your girlfriend really knows how to spend a Saturday night."

"She's not…never mind."

There wasn't much to say after that.

I officially hated street surveillance.

❖

"This feels skeevy," I said.

"You're tellin' me," Christopher said. "Honey," he added as an afterthought.

"Seriously skeevy."

"I'm not asking you to put suntan oil on me. Be happy."

"That's because science has revealed that suntan oil is bad for you," I told him.

"Fine. I'm not asking you to put sunscreen on me. Be happy."

We were stretched out on a big beach towel. Christopher was stretched out on his back looking at the water. We were playing the part of a couple. Gay, not straight. And I was figuring out that drag is hard in summer clothing.

"Why didn't Ryan just play the part of your boyfriend?"

"He's sleeping. You know he was on the night shift," Christopher said.

"Then why can't you play straight for a day? You did it for twenty years."

"Shut up and read your magazine."

"I'm just saying." The Ace bandage across my chest was itchy and hot. And I was wearing a shirt that was just a little too tight. I might have been cranky.

"It was Breno's idea. I think he wanted an excuse to spend time with Reese," Christopher said.

"Whatever." I went back to the magazine I was reading. Or pretending to read. I was lying on my stomach looking up at Joan's house. With sunglasses on, it looked like I was reading. I was trying to get an idea of the layout of the house. It wasn't working.

"Cooper?"

"What?"

"Why aren't your legs shaved?" he asked.

"Fuck you."

"Sorry, I was only curious."

"I'm lazy." I don't know why I decided to answer.

"Oh. It works well for the disguise."

"Yeah, I used my magical ability to look into the future and predict that Breno would suggest that I dress in drag and pretend to be your young, hot lover on the beach."

"You're an ass," he said.

"A great ass."

"Excuse me?"

"I've got a great ass," I said. "That was also part of the disguise. I wanted to literally be a hot piece of ass. So I predicted the need to work my glutes."

"Do you think about the shit that comes out of your mouth, or do you just speak?" Christopher asked.

"I don't even know what we are talking about anymore." It was honest, at least.

"Can you see anything?"

"No. The angle is all wrong so I can only see the upper floors. And there's a couple staring at us."

"What do you mean?"

"Two dudes. Checking us out." I was trying to play it cool, but they had been cruising us for the last five minutes. And now they were walking toward us.

"Damn." Christopher must have caught sight of them.

"Wanna hold hands?" I asked sarcastically.

"As abhorrent as I find the idea, yes. It might keep them from coming to talk to us." He reached a hand over.

"Fuck." I shifted my magazine so I could hold it with one hand. Then I reached over and slid my palm against his. "This is weird."

"You have no idea."

In horror, I watched the two guys saunter closer. They were cruising me. Nope, only one was cruising me. The other was checking Christopher out.

"Here they come. If you flirt I'll fuckin' kill you," I muttered.

"Yes, honey."

"Nope. I don't know what I want to do for dinner," I said loudly.

"There's that Cuban place you wanted to try," Christopher suggested.

"That sounds nice."

"Mmm hmm."

The two guys stopped a few feet from our towel. "Hi there," the taller one said.

Christopher tilted his head back. "Hi." He grinned. That grin was going to be our downfall. Why did he have to be good-looking?

"How you guys doing?" The shorter one this time. He was shirtless and muscley. I wondered if that was Christopher's type. Or maybe if the taller one was. He was more of a pretty boy. The short one was more rugged-looking with cultivated stubble. Christopher had the same kind of facial hair thing going on.

"All right. Enjoying the sun," Christopher said.

"Mmm hmm." I didn't want to speak too much. The voice would probably give me away.

"Vacation?" pretty boy asked.

"Honeymoon," Christopher said.

The rugged one's smile dropped for a second.

Pretty boy covered better. "Oh, congratulations."

"Thanks," I said.

"Yeah, thanks." Another Christopher smile. "Five years and now we're legal. It's pretty exciting."

I smiled at them. I was going for love struck. It didn't work. I leaned over and whispered in Christopher's ear. "Hurry this up."

Christopher laughed. Deep and hearty and far more genuine than I expected. He was good at faking. Not surprising, really. He'd done it for half his life.

"Now if we only knew where to eat tonight. Any recommendations?" Christopher asked.

"Where are you staying?" rugged one asked.

Christopher named a hotel. Not the one we were staying at. They suggested a couple places that were presumably nearby.

"Great, thank you," Christopher said.

I nodded. "Yeah, awesome."

"All right. Congratulations again." They sketched a simultaneous wave and started to stroll away.

"Are they gone?" Christopher asked after a minute.

"Yes." I watched their retreating backs. "That was painful."

"The taller one was gorgeous."

"Keep it in your pants, darlin'." I threw as much disdain into darlin' as I could.

"I'm going to kill Breno."

"Agreed. Epically bad idea. I think we can stop holding hands now." I let go of his hand.

"We are going to have to figure out a better way to watch the back of the house. This isn't working."

"Want to get out of here?" I asked.

"Please."

"Thank God."

❖

"Did you see anything interesting?" Christopher asked.

"No. And I'm bored of surveillance. I can't sit in a damn car anymore. Even sitting on the beach is boring," Ryan said.

"We're all tired of it, Ryan," Reese said.

"My ass hurts from all that sitting," he whined.

"Did you get a decent layout of the house?" I asked.

"I drew you a picture didn't I?" Ryan pointed at the sketch on the table.

We all leaned in to look. Again. It didn't make any more sense this time than when I'd first seen it.

"What is foodage?" Breno pointed at one of the childish squares. There was an arrow pointing at it labeled foodage.

"The kitchen. Obviously," Ryan said.

"And this?" Christopher pointed at another section of the drawing.

"A balcony," Ryan explained.

"What about this section, with all of the arrows and lightning bolts?" Breno asked.

"That's where the alarm panel is," Ryan said.

"Wait. What?" I asked. "You can see the alarm panel? We're in. We just need to watch and get the code."

"No, dude. You can't see the keypad. What kind of shitty security company would install it facing a window?" He had a point. "That's why there are sad faces. See?"

"Oh, yes. It all makes perfect sense now," Reese said in a voice that implied that it did not make sense.

"Fuck you." Ryan pushed away from the table. "I went out there and crawled on top of a fucking lifeguard tower and watched those windows for hours. It was hard. And it was dark. And it took forever. But I made you the damn drawing and I waited until I figured out all the important shit and I totally hit my balls climbing down and it hurt like fucking hell. So just fuck you."

With that, he started pacing. I'd never seen Ryan pace.

Reese and I watched him, stunned. Christopher studied the drawing some more. Breno didn't seem to know what to make of his strange son.

"I see the sad faces now. And this must be the little girl's room." Christopher pointed. "The one that says sleepy time and has a teddy bear." Ryan didn't respond to the indulgence so Christopher went on. "Oh, and these are all windows. The squares with the sunglasses drawn in them. The ladder here." He pointed. "This is a ladder, right?" Ryan glanced over and nodded. "That must be a place where we can climb up."

"Well, yeah. It's not like she just has a ladder chillin' there. That would make it too easy." Ryan stopped his pacing.

"Okay, so how will we get in?" Reese asked.

"Climb through the window," I said.

"But there's an alarm," she pointed out.

"We go in when she doesn't have the alarm set," I said.

"When the hell will that be?" Reese wanted to know.

"She sets it when she leaves," Ryan said. "And once she's inside, she resets it. So I think it's pretty much always on."

"What about when she answers the door?" I asked.

"I don't know." Ryan shrugged. "I don't think she did that when I was there."

I thought about that. I definitely had a plan. It was a gamble partly. But mostly, I thought it was solid.

"Will she recognize Breno?" I asked.

"What? Why?" Christopher asked.

"Will she?"

"She's never met him. But she's seen pictures of the twins. So she might make the connection," Christopher said.

"I have a plan," I said.

CHAPTER SEVEN

I watched the waves break against the shore in front of me. Just another lonely kid watching the waves in the moonlight. My sweatshirt hood was pulled up against the evening chill. It also conveniently hid the earbud I was wearing.

"Everyone in place?" Breno's voice came over the line.

"Ready to go," I said.

"Street is clear." Ryan.

"Beach is empty and neighbors on the south are watching a movie. Lights are out in the house to the north." I could see Reese in my peripheral vision. She was leaning against a lifeguard tower down the beach.

"Both houses are dark on the street," Ryan said.

"Getaway car is ready." Christopher had the getaway car. We didn't need it. Probably. But plan B was to run like hell.

"Where's Joan?" I asked.

"Kitchen," Reese said. "If you go now she'll see you."

"I'm going to start walking," I said.

I stood and turned south toward Joan's house. I kept to the shoreline. There was sand in my Chucks. It was annoying as hell. I could feel the small grains working their way into my socks, between my toes, shifting with every step I took.

"You can veer closer to the neighbor's house. Stop before you hit Joan's outdoor lights," Reese said.

"Gotcha."

I waited at the edge of the low picket fence. The wooden slats looked flimsy, but I knew they were sturdy. I'd tested them.

"Breno. Go now," Reese said.

"I am walking up to her door," Breno said.

I hear a distant doorbell from inside the house.

"Go, Coop. She just left the kitchen," Reese said.

I climbed the fence and balanced on it for a moment before reaching up. This was going to work in theory. But we were relying on my upper body strength. Maybe we should have thought it through more. Maybe I should have thought it through more. No one knew exactly what I was planning. I hadn't told them. And by the time they figured it out, it would be too late.

I grabbed the edge of the balcony above my head. Took a deep breath. Jumped and hauled myself up. I braced my foot against the side of the house. I felt a sharp pull in my bicep. Fucking stitches. Somehow, I was able to climb until I was standing on the edge of the balcony. After that, it was easy to get over the railing.

Breno's voice came over the line as Joan answered the door. I yanked the earbud out and let it dangle against my chest. Hopefully, he would be able to distract her for a minute. I opened the sliding glass door and walked into Joan's bedroom. In the near darkness, I skirted the edge of her bed and slid into the hallway. The next door was open. I could hear voices downstairs. Breno's sounded friendly. Joan's was cautious.

I went through the open door. Joan's daughter was sleeping on her back. One tiny hand was curled into her hair; the other was stretched out across the small crib. I leaned over and picked up the sleeping child. She made a small noise and burrowed into my shoulder. Weird. Downstairs, the door closed. Damn. There were footsteps on the stairs. I stepped out into the hallway as Joan reached the top. She gasped. I shook my head.

"Be quiet now," I said softly. "She's sleeping. Wouldn't want to wake her."

"Please."

"Let's just use our calm voices. Kids are so receptive to tone, you know what I mean?" I asked.

"Just please. Don't hurt her." Joan reached out and took an unconscious step forward.

"Stop." I reached under my sweatshirt and pulled a gun from my waistband. The silencer caught on my jeans for a second, but then it was free. "I don't want to use this. I don't want anyone to get hurt."

"Oh, God." Joan began to sob. "If you hurt her, I'll kill you."

"If I have to hurt her, I'll probably kill you too. So you won't get a chance to kill me." I smiled. "Let's just avoid killing altogether. Maiming too. I hate maiming. It gets so bloody." I kept my tone even and soft. It made me sound like Esau. It made me want to hurl.

"Is this about the money?" she asked. "I'll give it back. I'm sorry. Just, please, don't hurt her."

"I'm not going to hurt her."

"Then give her to me." Joan stretched her arms out.

"No. Go back downstairs. Turn off the alarm," I said.

"Why?"

"Because you have company."

"I don't understand," she said.

"You will. Let's go." I nodded at the stairs.

Joan turned and slowly descended. I followed her to the kitchen, watched her input the alarm code.

"Now what?" she asked.

In response, I lifted the earbud and put it back in my ear. It was hard with the gun in my hand, but I couldn't exactly let go of the kid or the gun. I needed reinforcements.

"We're clear. Come in, guys," I said.

"You're in?" Reese asked. "That was fast."

"Bro." Ryan.

"The front door is locked," Breno said.

"Go unlock the front door," I told Joan.

"Should I come in?" Christopher asked.

"Not yet," I said. There were still a hundred ways this could get fucked up. I didn't want Joan to know how many people were involved. Plus, a getaway car was always a good thing.

Joan went back through the house to the front door. When she opened it, Breno and Ryan were waiting on the doorstep. When she saw them together, she gasped as she made the connection.

"Hey, Coop." Ryan waved.

I laughed at him. So excited to not be sitting and waiting. He was going to be disappointed when he figured out we had a lot more sitting and waiting to do.

"Go let Reese in," I told him. "The kitchen door needs to be unlocked." He nodded and walked past me.

"How many of you are there?" Joan asked.

"Enough," I said.

"Take whatever you want and get the hell out."

"Happy to," I said.

"Hurry up. I want my daughter back," she said.

Reese and Ryan came in just in time to hear her last comment. Reese inhaled sharply. Ryan tilted his head and looked at me weird. Breno just stared.

"Breno, take Joan and tie her up somewhere. The bathroom upstairs doesn't have windows. That will probably be the best."

"All right."

"No. I'm not leaving Emma with you." Joan took a step away from Breno.

"Yes, you are. She's sleeping. She'll be fine. And you don't really have a choice." I held up the gun.

"Damn you." Joan clenched her teeth and turned to Breno.

"Here." Ryan handed Breno the small duffle he was carrying.

"Thanks." Breno cupped Joan's elbow and started to guide her up the stairs.

"And make sure you search her," I said.

Breno paused and patted her down. She was carrying a cell phone. He pocketed it. They continued up the stairs.

We heard the door upstairs close. Reese turned to me. She looked livid.

"Careful," I said. "Don't wanna wake the kid up."

"You're fucking psychotic," she whispered.

"Are you holding the kid hostage?" Ryan asked.

"I'm not going to hurt her," I said.

"But you kidnapped a toddler!" Reese was still whispering, but she may as well have been screaming.

"That's kinda fucked," Ryan said.

"But I'm not going to hurt her." I searched for an argument to defend myself, but came up empty. "I threatened her, that's all. Joan's a mom. She's not going to risk anything. It's simple and quiet and fast." I tucked the gun back into my waistband so I could switch the kid to my other side. My arm was getting tired.

"You're fucking psychotic," Reese said again.

I shrugged.

Breno joined us again. "That may not have been wise."

"It's not like you had any better ideas," Ryan said. Oh, now he was on my side.

"I am only suggesting that there may have been other ways. That said—"

"Back off; Ryan's right." Reese cut in. Now she was defending me?

"I was trying to say that it is quite smart," Breno said. "Even if there were better ways. This is expedient."

"Oh, great." Reese glared and walked away. No wonder I couldn't keep up with Reese's moods. She couldn't even keep up with them.

"Should we follow her?" Breno asked.

"No," I said.

"We need to figure out where she stashed the gold," Ryan said. "Speed this shit up."

"Totally."

"Shall I interrogate her?" Breno asked.

"Yeah, in a sec." I transferred the kid back to my other side. How did people carry these things around all the time? "Can we sit down or something? This kid is heavy."

"I'll take her." Ryan held out his arms.

"You're not gonna give her back are you?" I asked. I thought the question was justified. I'd worked really hard to take her hostage. I couldn't let their collective skepticism ruin it.

"Come on. I'm not stupid."

"Just checking." I handed her to Ryan.

"We can put her back in bed. As long as somebody is guarding her," Breno said.

"Yeah, that's probably smart," I said.

"On it." Ryan went up the stairs.

"You have a gun, right?" I asked his retreating back. In response, he lifted the tail of his shirt. A handgun was tucked in his waistband.

"Shall we find out where our money is?" Breno asked.

"After you." I indicated the stairs.

Joan was chained to the toilet. She looked pissed. When I opened the door and slid inside, she stopped struggling against the chains.

"Where is the gold?" Breno asked.

"Gone."

"Gone where?" I asked.

"I sold it."

"Then where's the money?" I asked.

"The remainder is in an account." Joan's eyes darted between me, Breno, and the door. Once, she shot a look at the skylight. It was high. I wasn't worried.

"The remainder?" Breno.

"I bought a house, a car, food, toys. Paid utilities and insurance. I have an eighteen-month-old. Life adds up." She shrugged. Her chains rattled.

"You're lying." I opened the door and Breno and I walked out. When we were out of hearing distance, Breno turned to me.

"How do you know she is lying?"

"I don't."

"Then why—"

"Chances are good that she is. Plus, this will make her sweat. We'll go back in a couple hours." I shrugged.

He nodded. "All right, then. We will go back in a couple hours."

❖

"How is Emma?" Was the first thing Joan said when Breno and I returned.

"Fine. She's still sleeping," I said.

"Let me see her."

"No." I wasn't going to give up my bargaining chip that easy.

"Please."

"No. The faster we do this, the faster you see her," I said.

"Okay. Unchain me."

"No." I perched on the edge of the counter and stared at her.

"What?"

"Are you prepared to tell us the truth this time?" Breno asked.

"Yes, fine. Just leave Emma and me alone."

"Where is the money?" I asked.

"In an account."

"I have heard this before." Breno had his daughter's uncanny ability to look utterly bored.

"Fine. In multiple accounts."

"Good. You can transfer them to us," I said.

"I will. Let me go."

"No. Tell us about the accounts," Breno said.

"There are three. They are based in the Cayman Islands. But it will take days to transfer the money."

"Why?" I knew why. I just wanted her to talk more.

"Because you can't simply close out accounts like that."

"Interesting. How much is in each account?" Breno asked.

"I don't know. I would need to look it up online."

"Roughly." Me.

"There is about ten million in one. The other two have a few million."

"Just those three accounts?" I asked.

"Yes."

"You have a debit card linked to an account in the Caymans with a few million in it?" I let my disbelief bleed into my tone.

"What? No. I don't—"

"You used a debit card at the grocery store. And in that small coffee shop," I said.

"You also used it when you bought clothing two days ago. And when you bought—is it Emma?" Joan nodded. "Yes, when you purchased books for Emma yesterday," Breno said.

"What? How long have you been watching me?"

I turned to Breno. "I think she's still lying."

"I agree." He made it sound like the worst possible offense. Worse than kidnapping babies.

When we filed out and shut the door, Joan started screaming. Mostly about how perverse we were. Not a good thing for the neighbors to hear. I opened the door and stuck my head back in.

"If you scream, it will wake Emma up. And she will cry for her mother, but we won't bring her to you. Do you want to listen to your kid crying?"

"You bastard."

I shrugged and closed the door. Joan was silent.

It was nearly three in the morning when we returned to Joan. She was sleeping awkwardly with her head against the wall.

I nudged her leg with my foot. She jerked awake.

"You ready to tell the truth?" I asked.

"Why the hell should I?"

"So you can get your kid back."

"Why? You won't let us live. The longer I hold out, the better my chances are."

"That is not entirely true." Breno shook his head.

"He's right. I don't like killing people. Especially kids. That's not cool," I said.

"So let us go."

"No. But if you play nice and transfer the money then we will let you and the kid go. We don't want to hurt you. And we're not afraid that you'll come after us. So there's no harm in letting you live. All you have to do is give us the money. We will go quietly away and you get to live. Win-win," I said.

"And if I don't?"

I sighed. "Lose-lose."

"What will you do?"

"We will kill you and Emma and dump your bodies in the Gulf of Mexico," Breno said.

"Thankfully, you have a boat," I said.

"All right. Fine. I'll walk you through all of the accounts."

"Good." Breno opened Joan's handcuffs.

"Can I see Emma first?"

"No," I said.

"I need proof that she is alive before I give you anything."

"Whatever." I grabbed Joan, pulled her tight against me, and put my gun to her thigh. "You make a sound and walking is going to be painful. You understand?"

Joan nodded.

Breno opened the door. We walked to the doorway of Emma's room. Ryan had his back propped against the leg of her crib. A game of solitaire was spread on the floor. He started to wave with his gun, then realized that was bad. He held up his free hand and waved. Behind him, Emma slept on. Her delicate breathing echoed through the room. Joan took a deep breath and nodded. We turned away.

Kidnapping was hard.

CHAPTER EIGHT

By five in the morning, Joan had walked Breno through all five of her accounts. I got bored fifteen minutes in, but I figured she was intimidated enough by Breno and his gun so I probably didn't need to sit there and intimidate her with my gun.

I should have gone to sleep, but I was dreading dawn. The kid was going to wake up. The whole waking up to a house of strangers was probably not going to go over well. I didn't know shit about kids, but I knew that much.

I sat on the balcony and watched the sun come up over the ocean. Which was just wrong. The sun was supposed to set on the ocean. It was confusing.

The glass door behind me opened. I didn't move.

"We need coffee," Ryan said.

I spun around. Fast. "What are you doing? The kid is going to wake up soon."

"No shit. Not my scene."

"You can't just leave her." I stood and started to go into the house.

"I didn't, dumbass. Reese is in there. She volunteered." Ryan grabbed me and shoved me back into the chair I'd been sitting in.

"And you trusted her?" I tried to get up. Ryan sat on me.

"And so will you. You don't, she's gonna flip."

"Shit." I stopped struggling.

"You cool?" he asked.

"Yeah."

"Good." He moved to the other chair.

"She didn't talk to me all night. I didn't even see her."

"You were interrogating that bitch and plotting with Breno half the night," he said.

"So?"

"She probably didn't want to be involved." He waited for that to sink in before saying, "Also she was asleep."

"Oh."

"Yeah, oh."

"Coffee?" I asked.

"That's what I've been saying."

We went inside. When we got downstairs, I could smell the coffee already brewing. There were voices in the kitchen. We followed them.

Joan was sitting at the kitchen table trying to smile and play nice. Breno was moving around making breakfast. Reese was playing with the toddler strapped into a highchair. Both Reese and Breno were wearing guns.

It was weird.

"There you are," Breno said. "Would you like some breakfast?"

"Dude," Ryan said.

"Whatcha makin'?" I asked.

"Waffles, eggs, and sausage. There is coffee, if you would like some."

"Dude," Ryan said again.

"Do not worry, Cooper. It is chicken sausage," Breno said before I could even ask.

"You rock."

The kid grabbed a fistful of oatmeal and aimed for her mouth.

"Hey, Emma. This is my brother Ryan and my friend Cooper," Reese said.

The kid smiled. "Hi." At least, I think she said hi. It was hard to tell through the oatmeal haze.

"Hi. You're Emma, right?" I asked.

She nodded.

"How you doing, Emma?" I pulled a chair up next to her and Reese.

She dug a hand into her bowl. Again.

"Awesome," I said.

"Emma, spoon," Joan said from the table.

"Nuh-uh." Emma slurped a handful of oatmeal. It dripped down her arm. She licked it. Appetizing.

"Breakfast," Breno announced.

I started to stand, but Ryan stopped me.

"I got it, bro."

"Thanks."

Ryan grabbed a stack of plates and tossed a couple waffles on each one. He added scrambled eggs and sausage to two of them. Mine and his. For Reese he found a second, smaller plate for eggs and sausage. She didn't like to mix her food.

"Joan?" Ryan asked as he set the plates on the table.

"Yes?" She was trying to keep her voice even, keep the hatred out of her tone. She wasn't entirely successful.

"Whatcha want? Waffles, eggs, sausage? The whole thing?"

"A waffle. And could you give Emma half a waffle and some eggs, please?"

"Eggs for the little one." Ryan got down another small plate and scooped eggs onto it.

"Use a fork to break them up. Otherwise, they will be too hot for her. There are plastic forks in the drawer," Joan said.

"Cool eggs for the little one." Ryan got a neon blue fork and broke up the eggs. He set them on the high chair tray.

Emma did a little dance. She ignored the fork and grabbed a handful.

"Fork, Emma," Joan said.

"Nuh-uh."

I was starting to see a pattern. And I so didn't want kids. One of the many reasons I was glad I was queer. No surprises. Well, I guess some queers ended up with surprise kids. Like Christopher. That would have kinda sucked.

Oh, shit.

"Uh-oh," I said.

"What?" Reese asked.

"We forgot Christopher. He's still waiting."

Breno said something in Portuguese. I'd finally broken down and asked Christopher what language they had been speaking. He had looked at me like I was stupid.

"I didn't forget him." Reese.

"Nope. Me either." Ryan.

"What? You guys just decided to leave him out there?" I asked.

Ryan shrugged. "Yeah, he's a dou—"

"Ryan," Reese cut him off.

"A dummy," Ryan finished.

I just shook my head and called Christopher. Breno and I waited to start eating until Christopher was inside the house. Reese and Ryan didn't. Joan lifted an eyebrow when he joined us.

"Hello, Christopher," she said.

"Joan, darling." Christopher squeezed in next to her.

"Welcome to the party, jerk."

"Well, if you weren't a lying thief…" He lifted one shoulder in a lazy shrug.

I got the distinct feeling they were choosing their words carefully. Jerk and lying thief sounded very tame.

"Mama?" Emma piped up.

"Yes?"

"Who he?"

"His name is Christopher," Joan said.

Christopher waved with his fork. "Hi, Emma."

She ignored him and went back to mixing her eggs and syrup.

"This isn't at all awkward," I said.

Every single person in the kitchen glared at me. Except Emma. She didn't really care.

❖

After breakfast, Ryan and Emma went to play in the backyard. Breno and Joan returned to the computer. Which left Christopher and Reese and me to clean up the kitchen.

"Thanks for letting me sleep in the car," Christopher said.

"You should thank me for not smothering you in your sleep," Reese shot back.

"Oh, still touchy I see."

"Still? Fuck you."

"Whoa. Let's not do this," I said.

"Do what? Be honest?" Reese asked. "I don't like him. I don't trust him. Why the hell should I pretend otherwise? I know you forgave him for being an asshole, but I'm not feeling forgiving."

"I didn't forgive him." I crossed the room so I was standing in front of her.

"And yet, here we are." Reese glared.

"It doesn't mean I forgave him. It means we need to do business. That's all. I still think he's an asshole."

"Hey, I'm right here," Christopher said.

"Why is that?" Reese asked. "Go the fuck away."

"No. I'm not taking this shit from you anymore." Christopher threw the pan he was washing back into the sink and dried his hands. "Look. I'm sorry I wasn't the world's greatest father, but you had it way better than a lot of people. So stop with the whole entitled thing."

"Oh my fucking God. You think I'm entitled? Because I call you on your shit? No, this isn't about your fucked up parenting," Reese was screaming now.

"Then what the hell is it about?" Christopher shouted back.

"Hey, both of you. Quiet. This is so not the time or place to scream at each other," I said.

"No, we need to do this," Reese told me.

"I agree. I'm tired of being the bad guy. What did I do that was so horrible?" Christopher asked.

"Seriously, dude?" I stared at him.

"What?"

"This." I cupped Reese's chin. She tried to jerk her face out of my hand, but I gripped harder. I turned her cheek to him. "This is what you fucking did."

"What?" he repeated.

"The fucking scar." I traced it with my free hand, trailing my fingertip across her cheek.

"Haven't I apologized enough for that? Christ, you would think I beat her all the time."

Reese finally broke free from my grip.

"You haven't apologized at all, you piece of shit," she said.

"Yes, I have. I told Cooper—shit." He actually looked contrite. But contrite wasn't going to cut it. "I…I'm sorry, Reese. I told Cooper I was sorry. I suppose I never told you, though."

"Gee. I feel all better now," Reese said.

"I'm sorry. I was angry and I lashed out and I shouldn't have."

"Fuck you." Reese pushed past him.

I followed her into the hallway.

"Leave me alone," she said.

"I can't."

"Why?"

Reese rounded on me, but her eyes locked onto something over my shoulder.

"What?" I turned. Breno was standing in the doorway to the kitchen.

"I am sorry, but I think we have a problem," he said.

"What is it?" I asked.

"Come into the kitchen."

Reese and I followed him. Joan was standing by the door. Christopher was back at the sink washing dishes. Reese sat down. I started to lean against the counter, but the gun at my back was digging into my skin.

That was when I made a mistake.

I took out the gun and set it on the counter, then leaned back.

"In order to transfer the money, Joan needs to go into her bank and sign a number of forms," Breno said.

I looked at him while he spoke. Just long enough for Joan to make a decision. She bolted for the door.

I lunged for Joan. I didn't get her arm like I wanted. Just a fistful of her shirt. That was enough. I yanked her back, grabbed her arm, and hauled her into the hallway. She stumbled and I threw her down. Her head glanced off the floor with a dull thud. She looked at me, panic in her eyes.

"I told you not to try anything, bitch." And then I kicked her in the side.

She rolled over and curled into the fetal position. I kicked her again.

"Stop. Please. Stop," she yelled.

"No." I pulled back to hit her, but Breno grabbed me.

"I'm sorry," Joan sobbed.

"I'll make you fuckin' sorry." I tried to push Breno off, but he held me tight.

"It is all right, Cooper," he said softly. "You caught her."

"Right. Yeah." I shrugged off his hands. He let me. "Get up," I told Joan.

"I can't." One of her hands was clasped to her side. The other was cupping the back of her head.

"Yes, you can." I reached down and took her arm.

"I think you broke my rib."

"It will heal. Get up. Now."

Joan slowly pushed herself upright. I dragged her to the stairs. I glanced back once and saw Reese staring at me openmouthed. Her eyes were gray and wet. This was going to be bad.

"What did you do with her?" Christopher asked when I walked back into the kitchen.

"Chained her to the toilet again." I pulled out a chair and joined them at the table.

Reese glared, but said nothing.

"As I was saying, Joan needs to go into the bank and sign some forms. Her bank is in the Caymans," Breno said.

"So you'll go with her and transfer the money," I said.

"And if she runs?" Christopher asked.

"She won't. She just tried and it didn't work. She won't try again," I said.

"It's true," Reese said. "That woman is terrified."

"Good," I said.

"If you keep Emma here, then I believe Joan will behave," Breno said. "But there's something else that might also help. It is your call."

"What is it?"

"Her accounts total nearly seventeen and a half million."

"Huh?" I'd been up all night. Coherent wasn't gonna happen. "She only stole fifteen."

"So, what? She already had two and a half mill in the bank?" Reese asked.

"No. Before she stole our money, she had six thousand four hundred eighty-two dollars and fourteen cents," Breno said.

Well, now I was extra confused.

"Joan is very good with her money. She invests well. When she has money to invest, that is," Breno continued.

"She made two million in six months?" I asked.

"More than two million. She also owns this home and two nearby vacation properties that she rents out," Breno said.

"And her boat," Christopher contributed. "And two cars."

"So what are you thinking?" I asked Breno.

"It is up to you guys and Ryan, as I said." I nodded. He continued. "I suggest that we let her keep her houses as well as the two and a half million. She will be able to live quite well on that."

"And she won't be all pissed off and shit," I said. It sounded smart. Not me, Breno's plan.

"I like it," Reese said.

"Agreed." Christopher.

"Should we ask Ryan?" Breno asked.

"I'll do it." Reese pushed away from the table and went outside.

"Cool." I stood. "I'm going to sleep. Leave Joan where she is."

"Wait," Breno said.

"What?" I really wanted to sleep. So I might have sounded pissed.

"You're bleeding again." Breno pointed to my arm.

I looked. He was right. "Fuck."

"Sit down."

"Shit." I didn't sit down. I didn't move at all.

Breno stood and led me back to the table. He rolled the sleeve of my T-shirt and peeled the tape off my bandage.

"You have really done it this time, Cooper."

"What?"

"Over half of your stitches are torn out." I decided to take his word for it. Looking at my wounds made them hurt more. "Stay here. I need to give you new stitches."

"No fuckin' way."

"You need to listen to Breno," Christopher said.

"I have plenty of stitches, I don't need new ones. Thanks. I'm going to bed." I started to stand, but Breno pushed me back into my seat. I didn't hear the door open.

"Hey, get the hell off her." Ryan crossed to my side.

"It's okay," I told him. "Breno just wants to give me stitches. I'm respectfully declining."

"Why?" Ryan asked.

"'Cause I don't want a needle shoved repeatedly through my skin."

"No, why do you need stitches?"

"She tore some out." Breno lifted the bandage away so Ryan could see.

"Fuck, Coop. Half your stitches are gone. That shit is gross."

Breno put the bandage back in place.

"She tore some in Vegas. The rest, I believe, are from the tussle with Joan. Although I don't remember this much damage. Did you do anything that would tear them since Vegas?" Breno asked.

I had. I'd fucked his daughter and lost two stitches. Then, when I climbed into Joan's house and carried her toddler around, I'd lost a couple more. But I'd just mopped up the blood and ignored it.

"Maybe when I climbed into the house."

"You hid them from me," Breno said.

"Not on purpose. I just didn't want more stitches," I mumbled.

"Too bad." Ryan sat at the table and put his hand on my shoulder. "Go get whatever supplies you need," he said to Breno. "I'll keep her here."

Breno nodded and disappeared through the doorway.

"Fuck you," I said to Ryan.

"Blow me."

Breno came back with a plastic first aid kit. He washed his hands. Spread a piece of gauze on the table. Started laying out instruments. I wasn't having this. Or maybe I was. Damn. He put on latex gloves. And pulled off a long strip of dental floss.

"What the fuck are you doing?" I asked.

"What do you mean?" Breno closed the floss and tossed the small container down.

"Yeah, what's with the floss?" Ryan asked.

"What did you expect me to use? Thread?" Breno asked. Then he and Christopher laughed.

"It's not like it's mint flavored," Christopher said. "It's sanitary. And it won't break off into little infectious threads."

"Damn." That sounded logical. I reached over and took Ryan's hand. He squeezed reassuringly.

"Want some booze?" Ryan asked.

"We'll see," I said.

"This will hurt," Breno warned me.

He was right. It hurt like a bitch.

❖

I don't know how long I had been asleep before I felt the bed dip as someone climbed in next to me. I grunted. It was the best greeting my sleep-drugged mind could come up with.

"I heard you smacked a bitch," Ryan said. "Not a tussle," he imitated Breno. "But straight up smacked a bitch."

"Uh-huh."

"Christopher and Reese talked. They only loathe each other now, instead of being mortal enemies."

"Good."

"You can go back to sleep now," he said.

"'Kay."

And I did.

I hadn't had the dream since I'd found Ryan. My subconscious had been blissfully quiet. I hadn't really thought about it either. It's strange how easily nightmares can be ignored when you don't want to face them. But they always come back. Always. Until you deal, I guess. I hadn't dealt, though.

It was the same as always. Blood seeping into my shoes, sucking at my feet, seeping between my toes. It climbed my body, weighed me down. I waded, swam, lunged for Reese. The gun. That fucking piece of shit gun. I pointed it at Tommy. It turned on Reese. She was silent. In death. In recrimination. Her cool gray eyes glaring even after the life had gone from them.

"Please, please, I'm sorry. Come back. I'm sorry."

"Coop, Coop. Wake the fuck up." Warm arms were around me. A muscled body pressed close. My tears streamed into a warm, soft shoulder. He held me close and rocked me. "It's okay. I got you. It's okay."

"Shit." I sniffled. My throat was raw. I must have been screaming.

"What the hell?"

"Fucking dream."

"Dream? What the fuck kind of nightmares are you having?" Ryan asked softly.

"They…It started in Mexico. After…"

"Tommy."

"Yeah," I said.

"Shit. What's it about?"

And I started to talk. Didn't even consider not telling him. It was time. I told about the first dream and how Reese ignored me. I told him about the pot farm in Mexico. How Marco had covered for me. How fuckin' terrified I'd been. How terrified I was of myself.

It started slow. A jumble of thoughts and images that made no sense. Then they began to take form. I found the chronology. I remembered the names of the men Esau had killed. I told Ryan how I had watched them slowly die, kept alive by the hope that they might make it through the night. But Esau didn't leave survivors.

Ryan didn't ask questions. He didn't need to. At that point, I was just spilling my story. Like blood falling to a cement floor. Tentative drips at the first cut, gushing by the last, until the heart ceases to beat and there is nothing left except a cooling body.

I stopped crying at some point, started again at another. Felt the tension begin to drain as my tears mingled with his sweat. He didn't stop me when he started to cry. He just rested his cheek against the top of my head and let my hair dry his tears.

When I told him about Alexis, he tensed up. By the time I got to the trafficking, his muscles were so tight it was like leaning against a wall. Good. I was glad someone else was as horrified as I had been.

This time when I told him about Christopher and Breno, I didn't gloss over details. There was no need to protect myself or them. I wasn't arguing for some relationship between father and children that would never come to fruition. 'Cause there was just me and Ryan.

We fell asleep like that. With the afternoon sun slanting across our bodies, warm in the aftermath of the truth.

CHAPTER NINE

I wasn't asleep long. The sun hadn't moved. Neither had Ryan. For the first time in a very long time, I was content. No, not content. Calm maybe. Everything had been drained from me. In a good way. It would come back. I knew it would come back. But I felt like Ryan had started a wall between me and the past. Maybe I could keep it at bay, let it slowly slip away until I was me again. Maybe.

I couldn't tell right away why I had woken up, but then I heard it. Soft breathing, hitched with tears. Reese.

She was somewhere. I could feel her now. I looked around the room. She wasn't there. The hallway. Carefully, I extricated myself from Ryan's grasp. Found the jeans I'd been wearing for two days. Pulled them on. The door creaked when I opened it. The small cracks seemed deafening as they echoed down the hallway.

Reese looked up when she heard the noise. She was sitting on the floor, her back to the wall. Her cheeks were wet.

"I...I'm sorry." She pushed herself up. "I wasn't trying to listen in." She turned and started to walk away. "I just heard screaming. And I...I swear I wasn't trying to listen in." Her voice was so low I could barely hear her.

"Wait."

She stopped but didn't turn. "I'm sorry."

"I'm not mad."

"You should be. You should be livid that we dragged you into this. Left you to those bastards. You should be so mad." Her fists were clenched at her sides. Her head down. "So mad."

"I'm not." I didn't know if I was lying. I'd yelled at Ryan only two weeks before for presuming to take my grief and anger.

"Well, I am."

"Come here," I said. She didn't move. "Just turn around, please." I could have gone to her, but somehow I knew that wouldn't be a good idea.

Reese glanced over her shoulder. Unclenched one fist. Held her hand out to me. "Come on."

"What?"

"Come with me."

I took a step forward and slid my palm against hers. She tugged lightly, pulled me down the hallway. We passed the open study. The computer on the desk was still on. We went into the kitchen. Christopher and Breno were playing in the living room with Emma. I could hear faint giggles. They didn't notice us. Joan was silent up in her small prison. Probably sleeping. Or nursing her bruised ribs. We went out the sliding door, through the backyard this time instead of over the fence.

"Where are we going?" I asked.

Reese didn't answer. Just led me down the beach. I didn't ask any more questions. I didn't know where we were going. I didn't care. We must have walked a mile before Reese broke her silence. Or maybe it just felt that way. Walking on sand is hard.

"I should have asked about the scars."

"What?" I knew what she had said. I don't know why I wanted her to repeat it.

"The scars. You're covered in fuckin' scars. I should have asked. I didn't."

"I wouldn't have told you," I said. "I didn't want you to know about them."

"I can't blame you. I wouldn't have told me either." Reese let go of my hand. I'd forgotten we were even holding hands, but I still felt the sudden loss.

"It wasn't about you. I didn't want you to worry."

She laughed. A hard, raw sound. "You thought I wouldn't care. Don't lie."

"No. That wasn't it." Even as I said it, I realized she was right. Sort of. I'd been afraid she wouldn't care.

"I don't blame you. After the way I treated you in Mexico."

I didn't respond. I didn't know what to say.

"Fuck." She turned and walked toward the water. "Damn it." And then she started to cry. Again.

"Hey, it's okay." I followed her. Put my hand on her shoulder.

"It's not okay. It's not."

It wasn't, but I lied anyway. "Really, it is."

Reese spun and stared me down. "Damn it, Coop. Stop trying to make me feel better. I knew you were all fucked up and I just left you to deal on your own."

I didn't know what to say, so I said nothing.

"There are a thousand things I could have, should have done. I didn't. So please don't pacify me," she said.

"What do you want me to do? Get mad? I did just as much damage to myself. You can't blame yourself for all of it." I was too damn tired to blame anyone anymore. It was easier to forget. Or maybe it was easier to acknowledge that it had happened like I had earlier with Ryan—and just move on. Yeah, that was it. I couldn't change the past. I couldn't change what I had done. But maybe I could let it go.

"What are you talking about? I dragged you into this shit."

"Stop it," I said.

"What?"

"You didn't drag me. I wanted to be with you guys. You couldn't have stopped me."

"I should have tried. You didn't know who we were going up against. I did." She clenched her hands at her side again.

"I knew when I went to Vito." As I said the words, I got mad. At myself. I'd known Vito was a douche bag. And I'd thrown myself on his altar. What the fuck had I been thinking? "I could have walked away. I thought about it every day. But I didn't. It was my damn choice. And I stayed. So all that fucked up shit I did and saw, that was on me." I stepped close to her. "Don't delude yourself, buttercup."

"Why the fuck did you stay?" she shouted. "Seriously. What the fuck were you thinking?"

I knew the answer to her question. It wasn't a good answer. Not for this conversation.

"Answer me, damn it." She kinda looked like she wanted to deck me.

"You."

"What?" She stepped back.

"I was thinking of you." I stepped closer again.

"Fuck you."

"I'm not blaming you. But I knew the only way to find you was to stay with Vito and wait for you to find me." I'd needed her to want me enough to come back, but I wasn't going to tell her that.

"Why?"

I only had one response. I pulled her against me and held tight. Reese put her hands on my stomach and tried to push me away. But I slid my arms around her and locked my arms until she stopped struggling.

It took a while. First, she let one hand drop. Then, the other. She turned so her shoulder was digging into my chest. I didn't let go. Finally, reluctantly, she relaxed into me. After a very long minute, she gave up and put her arms around my waist.

It had been so long since I'd actually held her. She felt good. Smelled good. And it wasn't just her. It was the way she pressed against me. Like we were supposed to be like that. She felt right.

Maybe we should have kept arguing. Yelled until we both felt better. But we didn't need to. I didn't think we needed to. It was as if when she finally let me hold her we just decided not to have that circular argument. Again.

"Should we go back?" Her face was buried in my neck so her voice was muffled.

"Probably. Where else would we go?"

"Well…"

"What?" I asked.

"I was gonna kidnap you and hide you somewhere until this shit was over with."

She'd tried before so I knew she was serious. I probably shouldn't have laughed. But I did.

"What?" she asked.

"How were you planning on doing that?" I let go of her. Only enough so I could lean back and look at her within the circle of my arms.

"Well…umm. I was going to take you to Joan's boat. Go somewhere else. Then I'd come back and wait till it was safe for you to join us."

"Really?" And I laughed again.

"What?"

I dropped my hands to her ass, squeezed a little. Then I felt her front pockets. Then I patted my own. "Neither of us have keys to the boat or any of the cars. And we don't have money or anything."

"So? I would have figured it out." She looked a little pouty.

"Peanut butter, I'm not even wearing shoes."

She started laughing. "Okay. Maybe I didn't think it through."

"Maybe."

"I don't think I like you." She dropped her arms and stepped back. But then she took my hand.

"Liar," I said.

"Maybe." She smiled.

Damn, I loved that girl.

❖

"Where'd you go?" Ryan asked when we got back. He was in the kitchen drinking a cup of coffee.

Reese smiled. Like really smiled at him. "We walked." She squeezed my hand.

"Cool." He glanced at our hands. Smiled big. "Breno wanted you to tell Joan she's only kinda broke," he said to me.

"Why?"

Ryan shrugged. "I dunno. Consistency?"

"All right. Where is he?" I asked.

"Breno?"

"Yeah."

"I think he's sleeping upstairs. Christopher is with Emma."

"I'm hungry," I said.

"Bro." Ryan.

"I'm sure we can find something to eat." Reese went to look in the fridge. We were still holding hands and I didn't want to let go so I went too.

"Pizza." Ryan.

"Yeah," I said.

"There's no pizza in here." Reese closed the fridge.

"Order it." Ryan.

"I don't know if we should order pizza." Reese was so smart.

"Oh, probably not." Now I was sad.

"But we can go pick it up," she said.

"Pick what up?" Christopher walked into the kitchen with Emma in tow.

"Pizza," I said.

"Pizza!" Emma yelled.

"Oh, sh—uhhh, shoot. Sorry."

"Way to go." Christopher scowled at me.

"What was I supposed to do?" I asked.

"Spell it. D-u-m-b-a-s-s."

"What? Bass?" I asked. Christopher gave me another death look. I repeated what he had said in my head. "Oh, got it."

I didn't know it then, but Christopher and Reese would take to spelling things in front of me. A useless code that gave them endless amusement. It always took me about five minutes to figure out what was going on.

"Pizza," Emma said again.

"So I guess we are going to pick up pizza," Reese said.

"Me and Reese can go get it," I said. Maybe I was a little too eager.

Christopher gave me a sharp look. "Okay," he said like it wasn't okay.

"I'll call it in," Ryan said.

Joan had a file of menus by her phone. It was all very organized. We waited while Ryan found the menu for a pizza place. Christopher was giving us dirty looks the whole time. I didn't get what he was so pissed about.

The entire time we were standing there, Reese was running her thumb slowly back and forth over my hand. It felt good. Like I wanted to crawl into a bed with her and not leave for a really long time. I also wanted to push her up against the fridge and kiss her until...just kiss her.

Maybe we could take the long route to pick up the pizza.

"Why are you all standing in the kitchen?" Breno asked from the doorway.

"Ryan's ordering pizza. We're going to pick it up," Reese said.

"Did you talk to Joan yet?" Breno asked me.

"Oh, no. Not yet."

"You should."

"Now?" I may have sounded a little whiny.

"Why not?" he asked. Because I want to hold your daughter's hand and then do dirty things to her. But I didn't say that. "Go now. Ryan can go with Reese to pick up pizza. They will be back by the time you are finished."

"Fine." I fought the urge to roll my eyes.

I walked out of the kitchen. Reese walked with me. We weren't letting go till we had to. Breno shot a look at our held hands and scrunched up his eyes a little. Not in a judging way. Not yet. More in a curious way.

We stopped at the foot of the stairs.

"Have fun getting pizza," I said. I felt like we were saying good-bye. We weren't.

"Don't have fun talking to Joan."

"I won't." I grinned.

"Okay."

"Reese, you ready to go?" Ryan had crept up behind us.

"Yeah, I just…yeah." Reese took a step back. Started to let go of my hand. I pulled her toward me and kissed her lightly on the lips.

"See you in a sec," I said.

"Yeah." She smiled.

❖

When I opened the door to the bathroom, Joan scooted back against the wall. She couldn't go far.

"What do you want now?" she asked.

"Calm down. I'm not going to hurt you." I leaned against the counter.

"Screw you."

"What is wrong with you?"

"My head is bleeding and my ribs are broken." Joan tried to kill me with a look.

"If they were broken you wouldn't be able to sit there. They're probably only cracked."

"Thanks, I feel much better now."

"Fuck you. I came here to play nice," I said.

"No, you came here to kidnap my child and rip me off."

"You ripped us off first." She didn't have a response to that. "Here's the deal. Apparently, you're good with money. Like, two point five mill in six months, good."

"And?" She scowled at me.

"And we're not monsters."

"Sorry, what? My concussion must be disrupting my hearing."

"Fuck this. Maybe we'll just take Emma and leave you to rot, bitch." I pushed off the counter and opened the door.

"You can't do that!"

"Yes, we can."

"No, please. Please, Cooper. I'm sorry."

I closed the door and leaned against it. "Are you done with the snarky, bitchy shit?"

"Yes. Please, just let us go. I'll give you all the money."

"That's what I wanted to talk about," I said.

"What?"

"The money you made. And the houses. The car, the boat."

"What about them?" she asked.

"We're going to take fifteen million. You get to keep everything else."

Her eyes got big. "Why? What's the catch?"

"We call it even. You don't try for revenge. You don't follow us or come after us. 'Cause I really, really never want to see you again."

"That's it? Call it even?" she asked.

"Yeah, we'll call the broken ribs payment."

"Deal."

"Awesome."

"Will you unchain me now?"

"Yeah. And Breno will check out your head if you want." I leaned down and unlocked the cuffs. As a gesture of trust, I unlocked and unwound the series of chains and padlocks Breno had woven around the toilet. No wonder Joan was bitchy. Breno had done some Boy Scout shit on that. The chains were so tight I was surprised she had even been able to sit up.

"Thank you." It sounded forced, but at least Joan was faking pleasantries.

"No problem." I heard the front door open. "Now come on. We're havin' a pizza party." I held out my hand. She took it and slowly stood.

・110・

DIRTY POWER

CHAPTER TEN

D inner was just as awkward as breakfast. Joan was all stiff. Probably from being chained up for the last twenty-four hours. Also the broken ribs. Those might have contributed to her discomfort. But she pretended nothing was wrong. I didn't know if that was out of pride or just to keep Emma calm.

Christopher kept shooting looks at me and Reese. But mostly at me. I guess he wasn't too happy with us being together again. Breno started to ask a few questions, but every time he started, Christopher would look pointedly at Joan, and Breno would shut up. That was probably smart. We didn't want to give her any more information about us.

Ryan was stoned. I was pretty sure of it. Reese must have let him smoke when they got the pizza. Breno had no idea Ryan was high. Christopher knew. I could tell by the dirty looks he was giving Ryan.

Maybe Christopher was just pissed off at everyone.

Reese didn't seem very interested in pizza. She did seem very interested in the seam of my jeans. Or I figured that was what she was interested in because she kept running her fingertips up and down the inside of my thigh. Which made me also uninterested in pizza. Tease.

I abandoned my pizza so I could rest my hand on Reese's thigh. She just kept talking to Ryan. As I trailed my hand higher, her breathing sped up. Good. I didn't want to be in this state alone.

• 111 •

I squeezed her cunt through her jeans for a brief moment. Then I started eating my pizza again. Reese glared at me. I smiled.

After we ate, Breno led Joan off to tape up her ribs. She insisted she was fine. But we could all see that she was lying, so eventually, she gave in.

"So, uhh, we're going to go for a walk," I said once Breno and Joan left the room.

"Yep." Reese stood and took our plates to the counter. "We'll be back soon."

"Yeah, kinda soon." Not too soon, I hoped.

"A walk?" Christopher asked.

"Yeah. We need to talk." Reese came back to the table and set her hands on my shoulders.

"Right now?" Christopher wasn't liking that idea.

Reese started digging her thumb into the base of my neck. It felt really fucking good.

"It's important." I had to fight to keep my voice even.

"Really important." Reese.

"We don't even need to walk. We can just go upstairs and talk," I said.

Ryan shook his head and hid a smile.

"That's fine, but Breno just set up our accounts. He and I need to go over them with Reese." Christopher had no fucking clue what Reese and I needed to discuss. He was just that clueless. For someone so perceptive he could be really dense.

"Can we talk while you're waiting?" I asked. I was really hoping for some marathon nakedness, but I'd settle for heavy making out.

"No, he and Joan will be done soon. Breno needs to get to sleep. He and Joan are leaving for the Caymans early tomorrow morning. So he needs to walk Reese and me through this first."

This man was going to kill me. Okay, maybe not literally.

"Can you guys go over them with Ryan?" I asked, desperation bleeding into my tone.

"I think it's best that we tell Reese. Honestly"—he shot an apologetic look at Ryan—"I think she is the only one of you who will retain it. And you guys need this information."

We couldn't really argue with that.

"It's fine. It'll be fast." Reese squeezed the back of my neck one last time. It took everything in me not to moan out loud.

"This blows," I whined.

"What blows?" Breno asked as he came back into the kitchen.

"Nothing. Where's Joan?" I asked.

"I cuffed her to the headboard in the guest room upstairs," he said.

"Kinky," Ryan said.

Breno's eyebrows drew together and he cocked his head to the side.

"Ryan," Christopher said.

"What?" Ryan giggled.

"I think Joan is quite happy that she isn't chained to a toilet." Breno decided to forge ahead. "I put her in the guest room because there are better curtains in there. Her room has too many windows."

"Neat." Reese.

"Whatever." Me.

"Dude." Ryan.

"I'm telling you because that means we have fewer beds." Breno looked at us expectantly.

Which gave me an awesome idea. "Maybe we should just take off then. Get a room for the night." I was nonchalant as hell.

"No, you don't need to do that," Breno said. "I will take the couch. Besides, Joan and I leave very early tomorrow. Christopher may need help in the morning with Emma."

"We don't mind getting a room somewhere," Reese said.

Ryan giggled again.

"Breno is right. You guys don't need to leave," Christopher said.

Damn.

"Fine," I said. This sucked.

Christopher stood. "We should look at those accounts."

"Yes, let's," Breno said.

Reese rolled her eyes. "Whatever."

"We will be fast." Christopher and Breno left the room.

"Hurry," I told Reese.

She smiled. "Yeah." Then she leaned down and kissed my neck. There was tongue involved.

"You're killing me," I whispered.

"You're killing me," Ryan didn't whisper. "Gross."

Reese rolled her eyes and followed Christopher. I watched her walk away and started imagining all the things I was going to do with that perfect ass of hers.

"My God, Cooper. She's my sister. Can you at least pretend you aren't eye fuck—umm." Ryan glanced at Emma wriggling in her high chair. "Can you not look at her like that?"

"Bro." I tried to sound apologetic. I wasn't.

Ryan rolled his eyes. "Gross."

Christopher lied. It took them two hours to go over the convoluted string of accounts Breno had set up. By that time, I was ready to run a marathon or go ten rounds. Or fuck Reese. Running is lame.

Instead of that, we got stuck putting Emma to bed. Kids take work. Lots of it. There were stories to read and teeth to brush and bath time and pj's to put on. Christopher was exhausted so he made us do it. We weren't really sure about the rules of bathing a kid, but we figured that it wasn't a Ryan job. So Reese and I got stuck on make-sure-the-kid-doesn't-drown duty.

When we finally got her clothed and read to and asleep, Reese and I left Ryan playing cards by himself on the floor of Emma's room. We crept out into the hall and Reese pulled the door shut halfway.

"Are we done?" I asked.

Reese didn't answer. Instead, she pressed me back against the wall and kissed me. I cupped her ass in my hands and pulled her against me. She groaned into my mouth. I slid one hand up under her shirt and stroked the smooth skin of her back. Reese fisted her hands in my shirt and held me still as she stuck her tongue in my mouth. I let her.

I had some reservations about making out in the hallway with a sleeping kid in one room, a hostage in another, and Christopher down the hall. But those reservations disappeared when Reese started unbuttoning my jeans. She slid inside and stroked me over my boxers.

"I need you bad," I whispered.

"Mmm-hmm. Me too." Then she went back to kissing me. And stroking me. Fuck. She was going to make me come without actually touching skin. Girl was magic. And sexy. I wanted her under me. I wanted her in me.

I did not want Christopher's door to open.

Reese and I broke apart. She looked guilty. I probably did too. Reese tugged her shirt back into place and stood in front of me while I buttoned my jeans.

Christopher came out of the master bedroom. He looked at us and shook his head.

"Umm, we got Emma to sleep. Ryan is guarding her." Reese nodded at the half-closed door.

"You have got to be kidding me," Christopher said.

"Uhh, what?" I asked ingeniously.

Ryan stuck his head out of Emma's room. "What's going on?" He looked at me and Reese, then back at Christopher. "Oh, that. Get a room." Then he went back into Emma's room and closed the door.

"Look, congratulations. I'm glad you two worked it out." Christopher crossed his arms over his chest. Then re-crossed them the other way. Then went back to the first way. "But you guys can't make out two feet away from our sleeping hostages. One of them is a child."

Like a champ I said, "We weren't making out."

Christopher gave me a bad look. "Don't revert to being fifteen. You were an obnoxious fifteen-year-old. Just go downstairs or something. I'm trying to sleep." He waved at the stairs.

Reese and I shuffled to the stairs.

"And...also, that's creepy. I'm your stepfather. Ryan is in the next room. Breno is downstairs. Don't you two have any restraint?"

Reese glared. I rolled my eyes.

Christopher shook his head. "I hope you two have kids. And I hope they're hellions."

With that, he went back into his room. Reese and I went downstairs as fast as we could without running. She held my hand again as we went through the kitchen, down the hallway, and to the bedroom next to the office.

I stopped Reese before we went in. "Wait," I whispered.

"What?" she whispered back.

"Breno's in there."

"What? Why?"

"I told him he could have the bed. Sorry." I shrugged. I was an idiot.

"Shit."

"Couch?"

Reese grinned and pulled me back to the living room. We fell onto the couch. Reese tried to take off my shirt, but we were kissing so she only got it off of one arm. I started laughing. She raised her thigh so it was tight against my crotch. That made me stop laughing.

"We have to be quiet," Reese whispered.

"Fuck that. I've been wanting this all day. No, all week. No, wait since I was fourte—" Reese kissed me again. It was good way to get me to shut up.

Reese twisted her leg around mine and pushed up, and suddenly, I found myself on my back with Reese stretched on top of me.

"Smooth, honey. Maybe you should have been a wrest—"

"Cooper, shut the fuck up." And then she wrapped her tongue around my nipple. I decided to stop talking.

The heat and warmth of Reese's mouth against my skin seemed to spread from my chest out to every inch of my body. With every gentle lap and hard suck, I got wetter, more needy. Her hands were at my hips holding me still. Her fingertips dug into my flesh.

I wanted to push up, to put her under me and thrust until I came. But I didn't. I couldn't. I just let her kiss down to my bellybutton and back up to my lips. Her hands never moved. It wasn't until I groaned into her mouth that she smiled and unbuttoned my jeans again.

"Please, Reese," I whispered.

"Shhh, soon, sweetheart."

Just the sound of her voice made my heart pound. I knew the promise of that tone. I'd missed the sound of her voice when she was getting ready to take me. How easy she made it to let her.

She started to kiss me again. Her tongue traced my bottom lip, the inside of my mouth. It was distracting. But not distracting enough to draw my attention away from the subtle vibration as she unzipped my jeans. I lifted my hips so she could tug my boxers down. She scraped her fingernails up my thigh, down the other, teasing me, promising me. I whimpered when she finally slid between my folds. Her now slick fingers dragged through my heat.

Her mouth never left mine. Even as my breathing got rough. Everything, every sensation in my body was reduced to the glide of her fingers over my clit and her lips against mine. She edged my boxers further down, pressed two fingers low enough to enter me. But then she waited. I lifted my hips and pushed against her hand.

When she went inside me, I moaned. Loudly.

"Oh God, you feel so fucking good," Reese murmured.

"Don't stop. Please." She eased out, then back in. "Oh, fuck. Harder, please, harder."

Reese moved her hand faster. I could hear the wet sucking sound of her fingers buried in my cunt. I grabbed the back of her neck, pulled her closer. Her mouth was at my throat. The rush of her breathing filled my ear.

I spread my legs wider, arched into her thrusts.

"Reese, I'm gonna come."

She just groaned and kept fucking me until I came. I felt the tremble and pull of my muscles grasping her fingers as she nursed every small contraction from me that she could until I shuddered and she slumped on top of me. Her weight felt good, right.

"I missed you."

Reese nodded against my shoulder. "Same here."

ASHLEY BARTLETT

I fell asleep with her still inside me.

❖

Breno and Joan left the next morning for the Caymans. They'd only been gone for a few hours when Christopher gathered us all in the kitchen.

"Where's the kid?" I asked.

"Nap time," Christopher said. He'd taken over Emma watch. We didn't want to do it. And he was oddly good with her.

"So what's up?" Ryan asked.

"We need to figure out where to go from here," Christopher said.

"I vote Italy or Spain. Maybe Portugal," Reese said.

"Spain," I said. They all looked at me. "What? I can't speak Spanish, but at least I sort of understand it when people talk to me."

"Spain it is. We need to go, buy a house. My associate will meet us there…" Christopher kept talking, but I tuned out. Apparently, Reese and Ryan did to. We just nodded along. "Are any of you listening to me?"

"Uhh." Me.

"Sort of." Ryan.

"Not at all." Reese.

"Why?"

"I just realized something," Reese said.

"What?" Christopher asked.

"We're not coming with you," she said.

An awkward silence fell over the room. For some reason, I knew exactly what she meant. Christopher looked a little hurt.

"If that's how you feel, I understand. Just tell me where you want the money sent," Christopher finally said.

"No. Well, maybe. But that's not what I meant. We'll probably meet up with you in Spain. But Coop and I are going on a trip."

"Where?" Christopher asked.

"It doesn't matter where," I said. "But the two of us need a vacation." Reese and I hadn't discussed it. We didn't need to. 'Cause we both just knew that we needed time away from all of them. I reached under the table and took Reese's hand.

"What about Ryan?" Christopher asked. We all looked at Ryan. He shrugged.

"I'm guessing he's going to need a Eurail pass and a big backpack," I said.

"Yep," Ryan said.

That was it. Just yep.

"When you and Breno are settled, just let us know. We'll show up at some point," I said. Reese squeezed my hand.

"Okay." Christopher nodded. He probably didn't understand. But he didn't need to.

CHAPTER ELEVEN

I'm totally serious."

"Sure." Reese glared. Okay, she was wearing sunglasses so it was hard to tell. But I was pretty sure there was a glare in there.

"Dead serious."

"Idiot."

"I could do it," I said.

"Live off wine and bread and honey? It's not possible." More glaring.

"I'm sure it's like biblical or some shit. I could probably start a foundation. People would pay me to eat biblically."

"Yes, what a wonderful philosophy." Reese turned away to stare at the ocean.

"I'm just sayin' it's that good."

"I thought you hated wine."

"That was American me. That bitch was dumb. Turns out, wine is good," I said.

"And biblical, apparently."

Why did her indifference turn me on so much? "The bread makes it biblical."

"Sweetheart, maybe you shouldn't speak so often."

"Oh, I see how it is. You want me to take you out to dinner and fuck you, but not talk." I pretended to be offended.

"Exactly." She smiled and pulled out a slim cigar.

"Deal." I dug around in Reese's beach bag until I found her cigar cutter. I held it out in one palm, while searching through the bag for her lighter.

"Thanks." Reese clipped the end of her cigar and tossed the cutter back into the bag. When I found the lighter, she leaned over to catch the flame I held. She puffed on the cigar and blew rank smoke into my face.

"Bitch."

She just smiled at the ocean. But I knew the smile was for me. This was what happiness felt like. My girl and sunshine and a pretty ocean.

❖

We were in Corsica. In an old port town. Like actually old. Not El Dorado Hills old. And I wasn't lying about the wine and bread and honey. I could probably live off that shit. And cheese. And fish maybe. The food there was insane.

We'd spent a week in our hotel room before going outside. I hadn't managed to get pants on the entire time. I hadn't tried. But after that first week, we ventured out a little. And then went back to the room. Naked Reese was way better than an old town.

We wandered. We held hands. We drank wine and sat on the beach. Bought bread that had been baked that morning. We weren't the only tourists. It was a tourist town. But at our little hotel, we were the only Americans. At first.

Reese saw them before I did. I don't know how long they had been staying at our hotel. Maybe they were really good and had been there the whole time. That lost week kind of stripped away all awareness of the world around us. Reese noticed them at a little café over the water. Then again on the beach. And then at our hotel the next morning.

They could have been tourists just like us. But they weren't. Something about her posture was too hard, too defined. That was what gave them away.

"How sad." Reese tilted her wineglass ever so slightly in their direction. We were in that first café staring at the ocean.

"What?"

"You think that dude knows his wife is a dyke?" Reese smiled behind her glass.

I stretched and not so subtly checked them out. Then I laughed. "No, he doesn't have a clue. But does she?"

"Come on, the cropped, peppered hair. Khaki cargoes. Columbia shirt. You don't buy Columbia unless you know you're into women."

"So sad."

We laughed in our smugness. Poor dyke trapped in a marriage to a dude. Made us want to help her. But not enough to do or say anything. Being twenty one and having seven years out of the closet breeds a special brand of arrogance.

Later on the beach, we saw them again. She was still wearing a T-shirt. He wasn't. Odd. Most couples sport the same level of public nudity. Reese and I did.

"Seriously, look at their body language." Reese tilted her chin at them.

"I know. Arms crossed." The dude. "And she is leaning in close."

"But when she touches him it's with the back of her hand," Reese said.

We watched as the woman finished the story she was telling her partner. She nudged his leg with the back of her fingers. Second time she had done it.

"Like, they know each other really well," I said.

"Yeah, intimately, but not with intimacy."

"That was hella deep."

"Shut up."

But it wasn't until the next morning when we went downstairs in the very late morning. Too late for a normal couple to be drinking coffee. And there they were. Drinking coffee.

"They're staying here?" I asked.

Reese shrugged. We started walking. There was a place with perfect coffee, according to Reese. We'd gone there for the last few mornings.

They got up and followed us.

After that, we couldn't shake them. I wouldn't have even seen them if I hadn't been looking. Except I was definitely looking. They split up partway through the day. He took the afternoon shift.

That's what it was. Shifts. Those two were cops. And they were following us.

❖

"We need to get the fuck out of here," Reese said the second we got back to our room.

"No shit. Pack your stuff."

"Leave it. If it won't fit in here, it doesn't matter." She tossed her beach bag and my daypack on the bed.

"Good call." After eight months on the run, we knew that favorite T-shirts and books were replaceable, but decent socks could save your life.

"How are we doing this?" Reese asked.

"What do you mean?"

"You want to fly or take a ferry?"

"You're the exit strategy person. I was the carry the bags person."

"Dumbass. I researched both. I'm asking if you would rather be trapped on a plane with the cops or trapped on a boat with the cops."

"Boat." Easy choice.

"Same here. And that means we can take another small bag. Story is we are doing a night in Livorno. Then we're coming back here. We'll book a return ferry for good measure."

Reese pulled out her passport. In the back was a cleanly folded sheet of paper. I glanced over her shoulder. Bastia, that was where we were, but the rest of the cities on the list—Livorno, Ancona, Patras—I'd never heard of.

"How does that make any sense?"

"The arrows." Reese drew her finger down the line of arrows that linked the city names.

"No, the list under each city."

"Hotels, hostels, bars, restaurants. Addresses for all of them. Shit like that. So we know where to go in each city."

"Plan much?" I was giving her shit, but at least she had a decent plan. It was kinda hot.

Reese rolled her eyes. "I'm thinking Livorno to Ancona. Then take a ferry to Greece. Backpack through there. From Athens we can fly to Vienna. If we can't lose them in Italy, we'll definitely lose them in Greece. Then catch a train to Munich, where we'll hook up with Ryan and go back down to Spain."

I shrugged. It sounded complicated as fuck, but that was probably a good thing. If I could barely keep up, the Feds would have an even harder time.

It was dark by the time we arrived in Livorno. We went to a small hotel for the benefit of the cops following us. The guy had managed to get his "wife" to the ferry in time to follow us. Not a travesty. At least we knew where they were. And this way they wouldn't know we were running until we were already gone.

They stopped in a small restaurant across the street from the hotel. Watched as Reese pretended to book a room. Instead, she offered fifty euros for an escort through the back entrance of the hotel. It's amazing what people will allow in exchange for a decent tip.

From there we found a bar. One from Reese's list. Filled with twenty-something-year-old foreigners. Reese left me to make friends and headed for a nearby hostel.

It didn't take me long to get invited to sit with a group of kids. I wasn't above buying friends, so I offered to get them a round of drinks. I used one of the crumpled euros that Reese had stuffed in my pocket. Not one of the crisp, clean bills in my wallet. Reese had been very specific about how to flash money.

"So you're American?" one of the girls asked me. Caitlin. I was pretty sure her name was Caitlin. She was Australian. Or that's what her accent suggested.

I shook my head. None of them were from North America so I figured I could lie. Which was good because my passport was definitely not American.

"Canadian. British Columbia," I said. The girl wrinkled her eyebrows. "I know." I smirked like I got that a lot. "I lived in the States until I was fifteen. Moved back to B.C. Then back to California for college."

"Oh." Caitlin nodded and smiled like that made sense. "We were traveling with a guy for a while. He had the same deal. Except he was from Saskatchewan."

I nodded politely. Where the fuck was Saskatchewan? Reese would know.

The other girl in the group spoke up. Her name was Sheer or something. She said it was a popular name in Israel, but I'd never heard it. She was the one who had invited me to sit with them. Which I was guessing was directly related to the amount of times she had cruised me since I'd walked in. She was super hot, but not my type. Not Reese.

"What about that girl you walked in with? The pretty one." Sheer was setting herself up for failure.

"Oh, my girlfriend? She's from B.C. too. But she came to the States with me for college," I said.

"Oh." Sheer's face dropped. "So you guys have been together a while then?"

I laughed. "Not really. Her brother is my best friend. But Reese and I only started dating a few months ago."

"Ohhh, your best friend's sister. Really?" Sam asked. He was Caitlin's brother. Or maybe boyfriend. I wasn't sure.

"Yeah. He's mostly over it now. But he was pretty pissed," I said.

"So where is he? Back in the States?" Caitlin asked.

"No, he's traveling with us. But we ditched him in Ireland. Reese wanted to do Italy. He wanted to do the Netherlands. So we split. What about you guys?"

"We hooked up in Spain." Sam nodded at Sheer.

"I was tired of traveling alone," Sheer said. "Getting hit on by drunk American boys is really annoying. Sam never hits on me, and he doesn't mind when I flirt with Caitlin."

They all laughed.

"So where did your girlfriend disappear off to?" Caitlin asked. "Reese, right?"

"Yeah. She went to get our bags."

"Alone?" Sheer asked.

I shrugged. "She wanted to e-mail back home too. It'll take her forever."

They nodded like that was normal.

"You guys staying nearby?" Caitlin asked.

"We were. I dunno. The hostel we were at was a little sketch. I want to find a different one," I said.

"Come back to our hostel. It's great. Clean rooms. The guy who runs it is really nice. And I think there are a few rooms available," Sam said.

"Serious? That would be awesome." And it was exactly what I was hoping he would say.

We chatted for another hour. Caitlin and Sam were sociable types. Sheer was more quiet. But she got over her crush pretty quick. By the time Reese showed up they were all excited to meet her. Perfect.

"Hey, babe." Reese dropped the not so heavy backpacks she was carrying.

I didn't know how she had managed it. The bags were worn and the zipper was jammed on one of them. They looked like they were filled with clothes, but I was guessing she had stuffed them with newspaper or something. I shouldn't have been surprised. She told me she was going to get backpacks so we would fit in. And she did.

"Hey. Meet Caitlin and Sam. And this is Sheer. Guys, this is Reese." Reese shook hands with everyone. Repeated names. Smiled that Reese smile. They were hooked. "Sam said we should come back to their hostel with them. He said it's really cool."

"Awesome. That place we were in was a hole."

"For real."

I'd managed to find a group of kids and a hostel. That was my task. And it took me forever. Reese got them to invite us to travel with them. She even suggested a route—her route—and it only took her fifteen minutes. The girl was magic.

CHAPTER TWELVE

Hitchhiking is hard with a group of five people. Like seriously.

When Reese suggested Greece, Sheer had gotten all excited. She'd shoved Sam's shoulder and grinned triumphantly. He started laughing and nodding.

"All right. All right. You win."

So we were walking through this valley in Greece. It was all farmland. Everyone had given up on hitchhiking except Caitlin. Every car that passed she would valiantly stick out her thumb and start praying. It wasn't working.

I had settled on annoying Sheer.

"Why couldn't you get us a ride?"

"Because my cousins don't have Internet access. So I don't have any way to contact them," Sheer said.

"How is it remotely possible that they don't have Internet?"

"If you haven't noticed, we're in the middle of nowhere." Sheer gestured grandly at the olive trees on either side of the road.

"It's cold," I said.

"It's warm considering it's March," Sheer said.

"That isn't comforting."

"It's not raining. The sun is out. Enjoy it," Sheer said.

"But—"

"Coop, shut up," Reese cut me off.

"I like this weather," Sam said.

"Tool," I said.

"Oh, oh, guys." A truck was coming. Caitlin jumped closer to the road and stuck out her thumb. The truck didn't even slow down. "Fuck."

"It's only a few more miles to town. We can get a ride from there," Sheer said.

"Miles?" I hated walking. I hated exercise.

"Walking is cheaper than anything else." Sheer shrugged.

Oh, yeah. I forgot we were supposed to be broke college students. Not millionaire thieves on the run from the cops.

"Oh, another. Look." Caitlin stuck out her thumb again.

Reese rolled her eyes at all of us. Took a single step closer to the road. Smiled at the truck driving toward us. It stopped.

"Why didn't you do that an hour ago?" I asked her. She just arched an eyebrow.

The driver of the truck got out and said something. I didn't understand him. No one else did either. He and Caitlin had an exaggerated conversation with hand gestures. Sheer told him the name of the town we were heading to. He smiled and nodded and waved us to the back of the truck.

Reese took one look at the dirty truck bed and glared at me. I shrugged. This was her plan, not mine. Everyone climbed in. Sam and I leaned against the wheel wells so the girls could line up against the back window of the truck. There was no tailgate. Hopefully, this guy wouldn't go too fast. I stretched out my feet. Sam did the same. Seat belts are so overrated.

❖

The farm that Sheer's cousins lived on was old school organic. Like they served wine with lunch that was made from grapes grown on the farm. Actually, most of what they served with lunch had been grown on the farm. It was kind of cool. They belonged to some organization where traveling kids could work on organic farms in exchange for food and lodgings.

But it was spring and they mostly had olive trees, so nothing was ripe. Which meant no traveling kids. They put up Sam and

Caitlin and Reese and me in two small apartments built above their barn. We offered to help around the farm, but there wasn't much to do and five extra people to do it.

The first full day we spent the morning clearing brush from the paths around the olive groves. That afternoon, we just hung out in the sunshine and talked. I really wanted running away from the cops to always be this awesome.

But it didn't last.

The next day was Saturday. We all piled into a pickup truck and went into town. There was a farmer's market set up in a big parking lot. Sam and Caitlin wandered off. Sheer dragged Reese and me around to find cheese. Which was cool. Cheese is good.

We were at this little stall tasting whatever it was that Sheer pointed out when Reese got very, very still. I wanted to look around to find what had spooked her, but I didn't.

"They're here," she whispered. "To your right. Don't look. Don't look. Okay, look now."

I glanced to my right. The dyke cop was a couple stalls over. She was picking out produce, but somehow I suspected she wasn't really interested in kale.

"Where's the dude?"

"I don't see him."

"Here, mizithra. Try it." Sheer handed me a bit of cheese.

I popped it in my mouth. "Oh, yeah. That's really good." I did my best to pretend I was interested.

"Hey, Sheer. When we're done is there anywhere we can check e-mail? I want to check in with my brother. He's supposed to e-mail me," Reese said all casually.

"Yeah. I should do the same. Lunch, then e-mail?"

We nodded. Sheer didn't notice because she was pointing out the various cheeses she wanted to buy.

The cop followed us through the six other stalls that Sheer stopped at, but when we ducked into the small restaurant, she disappeared. Two minutes later, the guy cop walked through the door and took a seat.

Reese and I did a decent job of feigning casual conversation. Mostly, that meant asking Sheer about Israel, where she was born, and Argentina, where she'd grown up. That kept her talking and let me watch the guy watching us.

After a lunch that I didn't taste, we went into a small Internet café. Sheer let us use the one open computer first.

Reese checked into one of the anonymous accounts we had set up. Sheer and I sat across from her. I watched the door. The chick cop was sitting across the street. Neither cop had followed us in. That was good.

"Oh my God," Reese said.

"What?" I asked. Even though I knew she was just going to lie her ass off.

"Ryan broke his arm."

"What?" I got up and walked around to look at the computer. As if there was an e-mail up. There wasn't. "Oh fuck."

"Your brother broke his arm?" Sheer asked. She was very concerned.

"Where is he?" I asked.

"Sweden."

"We need to go get him."

Reese opened up a new e-mail. She told Ryan that we were very worried about his broken arm and on the way to Sweden to meet him. Which meant that he would meet us in Germany. Codes are easier when everyone knows what they mean.

"Fuck. I can't believe him," Reese said.

"How did he break his arm?" Sheer asked.

I looked at Reese. Yes, darlin', do tell how he broke his arm.

Reese responded without hesitating, "Hiking. He fell. Dumbass."

"Why the hell is he hiking? It must be freezing." I figured I should point out the obvious before Sheer did.

"It's Ryan." Reese rolled her eyes and shrugged.

"Good point."

"There should be a train out of here tonight. If we leave now, there should be time to get your things and come back into town," Sheer said.

"Yes, if it isn't too much trouble," Reese said. We headed out to the street.

"We really appreciate this," I said.

"Don't worry. I just hope Ryan is all right."

"He'll be fine. He may be stupid, but he's pretty indestructible." Reese smiled.

We walked past the lady cop on the way back to the farmer's market. I smiled at her in a polite, but absentminded way. She almost fell out of her seat.

❖

Maybe I shouldn't have smiled at the bitch. Or maybe they were just afraid of losing us again. But the entire flight to Austria they were stuck to us. Same on the train to Germany. I wondered why they didn't just arrest us. That had to be why they were there. Maybe they just wanted to talk. Probably not. Reese thought they were waiting until we met up with Ryan to make a move.

Once we got to Munich, we did a half-assed James Bond to lose them in the train station. We wanted them to follow us, but we wanted a little distance, a little time. Reese and I split up outside of the train station. We figured that if they were waiting until Ryan showed up to arrest us, they wouldn't be able to move in if they found Ryan but one of us was in the wind.

I got to the hotel room fifteen minutes after Reese.

"Were you followed?" Ryan asked as he opened the door.

"Yeah, the chick is posted up across the street." I dropped my backpack on the floor.

"Fuck." Reese pushed past Ryan and hugged me. "Let's not split up anymore. That was the worst."

I nodded and held her tight. She smelled really good. How could I have missed her after only an hour?

"All right. Break it up. Gross." Ryan nudged me with his shoulder.

"Tool," I said. Reese just glared.

"So how are we doing this?" Reese asked.

"You aren't going to like it," Ryan said.

"Why?" Reese asked.

"Because I think we should split up."

"No." Reese.

"Yes." Ryan.

"Just split up?" I asked. That didn't sound so bad.

"No. I think Reese should go solo. In disguise, obviously. I'm thinking she should keep rocking the dirty backpacking look. And you and I are going to be a couple."

"Drag?" It had worked before, but not great.

"Uhh, sort of. That's the part you really won't like."

"Why?"

Ryan didn't answer. Instead, he broke eye contact and walked to the bed. "I got supplies," he mumbled.

"Why are you being weird?" I asked.

"I think you should dress like a chick." Ryan cringed and held up a pack of barrettes. They had bows.

"Fuck you," I said.

Reese started laughing.

"It'll work. I think. We'll be a couple. Honeymooning, maybe. I think we'll be wealthy. I'm in technology. You're my wife. They won't be looking for that. I know it sounds insane, but..." He shrugged.

Reese laughed some more. "It's genius."

"I hate you." This was going to blow.

❖

"If Ryan can walk in heels, you can." Reese held up a pair of shoes.

"I'm wearing a fucking skirt. I can't do heels too." I crossed my arms over my chest, but it didn't work. Reese had done some weird magic with a push-up bra so I had mad cleavage.

"They're not that high."

"They're high enough." I sat on the bed and tried to pull on my dirty, bloodstained Chucks. But the skirt I was wearing went almost to my knees and was really tight. So my legs weren't bending the way they were supposed to. "Fuck."

"Don't even try." Reese took my Chucks, tossed them in a suitcase, and threw the heels at me.

I caught them and stared at the straps. They were even more complicated than the bra. "You're fucking with me, right? These aren't real shoes."

"At least they're clean," Reese said.

"My Chucks have character." My day was already long and fucked up. I was not in the mood to defend my shoes.

"I'm throwing them out." Reese looked serious.

"I'll leave you." I managed to sound almost serious.

Reese rolled her eyes. "Coop, you're gonna end up wearing the heels. Stop stalling."

"She's right." Ryan was standing behind Reese laughing his ass off. "You need the heels."

"Shut up, J.Crew."

"What? You don't like khaki?" Ryan tugged at his slacks. "Country club is totally a good look on me."

"Mock now. You're getting a hair cut." I dropped the heels to the floor.

"What?" Ryan laughed. "No, I'm not."

Reese pursed her lips and stared at the floor. "Uhh, yeah. You are."

"What? No! I'm not cutting my hair."

"Country club boys don't have shoulder length hair. Sorry," I said

"Blow me."

"We don't need to cut it all off. Just most of it," Reese said.

"Fine. But Coop has to wear the heels." Ryan scowled at me.

"Obviously. And she needs to learn to walk." Reese knelt on the floor and started strapping on the heels. I gave up and let her.

When she was done, Ryan offered me a hand. I stood. And realized that high heels are the worst invention ever.

"Ouch."

"They're not that bad," Reese said.

"For you. You've been wearing them for years." I took an unsteady step.

"Hey, I wore 'em," Ryan said.

"Don't lie. You've worn them for years too." I let go of Ryan and made a go at walking across the room. I probably didn't look very graceful, but I made it. "Fuck this." I leaned against the wall.

"See? You totally got it," Reese lied. "Keep practicing. Ryan, haircut time." She grabbed his arm and dragged him to the bathroom.

Ryan looked like he'd just lost his puppy, but he followed her.

I walked back over to the bed, then back to the wall. I wasn't doing well. But it sounded like Ryan was crying in the bathroom, so I was doing better than he was.

❖

"All of this to drive to the airport and sit on a plane." I leaned close to Ryan as I said it. He cocked his head to listen to me and smiled.

"It's working," he said low enough so only I could hear him.

We were on a plane to Portugal. First class. Our matching suitcases had been checked, but I was carrying a purse. It was stashed at my feet as if I cared about the contents. I really just wanted to throw it so I would have room for my feet. Which were killing me.

Ryan was right about the plan working. I knew because our cop friends had been stationed across the street from our hotel. Reese left about five minutes before we did. The guy took off and followed her to the train station.

The dyke stayed in place and scoped everyone who left the hotel. She barely even glanced at Ryan and me when we walked out and got into the waiting car. I didn't blame her. We were unrecognizable. Ryan had on a cropped wool coat with a pale blue cardigan. His belt had dancing flamingos. And his shorn head looked fucking weird.

I was wearing a fucking skirt. Plus, a shitload of makeup and brown contacts. And there was a little barrette in my hair. This was some weird twilight zone shit.

So we were pretty damn sure no one had followed us. Now Reese just had to lose her tail. I wasn't worried about it. I was worried about pretending that sitting in a skirt was comfortable. Also the top. It was all low-cut and flimsy, and I was pretty sure it was just going to fall apart at any moment. Or maybe that was me. Maybe I was going to fall apart. I'd never felt so naked in my life.

Chapter Thirteen

Ryan rented a car at the airport in Faro. I smiled and
pretended it was charming when he insisted that it be a
luxury car. I even managed to look smitten when he demanded a
stick shift. Apparently, his masculinity required it.

We dropped the façade once we got to the car. It was late.
Almost midnight. The garage was empty. We both climbed in the
backseat. I stripped off everything I was wearing. Ryan got down
to his boxers. Which was a problem when we realized that our bags
were in the trunk. I pulled on the coat Ryan had been wearing and
pouted until he put his pants and loafers back on and got our clothes
out of the trunk. I was naked, he had underwear, it just seemed
logical that he had to step up.

It was three in the morning when we passed through Seville.
Ryan had gotten lost, so that was an hour out the window. I took over
driving. We hit the coast about four in the morning. Which meant
Breno and Christopher were really surprised to find us pounding on
the door at five a.m.

"Why the hell are you here so early? I thought you were going
to call when you were ready," Christopher said.

"Is everything all right?" Breno asked.

"You guys know it's a little weird to answer the door together,
right?" It was a little homoerotic too because they were both only
wearing their underwear. Small underwear. I didn't tell them that
'cause I figured Christopher had dibs.

"Totally." Ryan muscled past them with our bags.

"What's going on?" Christopher asked.

"Reese and I had company in Corsica. They followed us all the fuck over Europe. We ditched them in Germany," I said.

"What?" Christopher.

"Where is Reese?" Breno.

"Are you sure you weren't followed here?" Christopher.

"Who was following you?" Breno.

"Whoa. Dudes. Ease off with the questions," Ryan said.

"Yeah. Is there any food? I'm starving," I said.

"And could you guys put some pants on?" Ryan asked.

They stared in response.

I rolled my eyes. "Fine. Ryan and I weren't followed. Reese led them on a merry chase through central Europe to get them off our tail. She should have lost them by now. And they seemed like cops. Definitely not mob enforcement types."

"Now can we have breakfast?" Ryan asked.

They didn't let it go so easily. But at least they put on pants before quizzing us. Which was good because Christopher made omelets while we outlined the details. Cooking in your underwear has got to be dangerous.

"So what you're saying is that twenty-four hours from now, Reese will be hitchhiking on a main road in northeastern Spain?" Christopher asked.

"Alone," Breno said.

"Well, yeah." Ryan shrugged and took a bite of omelet.

"Why did that seem like a good idea to you?" Breno asked.

"We didn't say it was ideal." It was too late to change the plan. So I didn't see what they were getting all worked up about.

"And you want us to drive up there and pick her up?" Christopher asked.

"We can't," Ryan said.

"Yeah, if the cops are still following her, then they'll recognize us. But you guys are probably unknown entities."

"Probably?" Christopher shouted.

"Yeah, probably." I shrugged.

"That isn't very reassuring," Breno said.

"Well, I checked the FBI app for wanted fugitives and you guys weren't on it," I said.

"There's an app for wanted fugitives?" Christopher was so stupid.

Ryan started laughing, then started choking on his eggs. "Mmm-hmm. The app where criminals can chart their progress. You know, to see how far ahead of the cops they are."

"Yeah." I was laughing too. "The Feds and CIA and US Marshals and Secret Service. They all link into it. It's awesome."

Christopher and Breno did perfect versions of Reese's glare. Ryan and I laughed at them.

"What?" I asked when five minutes went by without a break in the glare.

"I'm amazed that you two ever made it to adulthood," Christopher finally said.

"Yeah, well, our plans work better than yours. So get your asses in gear." I pointed with my fork.

They seemed very unimpressed with being ordered around by me. But they went and got ready for a long-ass road trip. Bonus points to me and Ryan.

❖

Ryan and I slept most of the day. When we woke up, we started exploring our new digs. The house was a massive improvement from that ugly monstrosity in EDH. It was still huge, bigger than the last place. Like way bigger. But it was built before the twentieth century and we thought that was pretty cool. We decided immediately that the second floor was haunted. Not actually. We decided to rig it to make Breno think it was haunted. He seemed gullible enough to fall for that.

There were two secret passages leading off the kitchen and winding through the back of the house. Probably for servants. So they weren't exactly secret. But Ryan and I had a habit of reverting to the ten-year-old versions of ourselves whenever possible. We may have played hide-and-seek. In the dark. For an hour.

There was a shitload of land surrounding the big house. Our nearest neighbor was probably a couple miles off. It was cold as fuck outside, so we layered on every long sleeve shirt and pair of socks we could find, and ran through the orchards. There was a vineyard too, but vineyards smell like ass so we stayed upwind.

Late in the evening, we opened a few bottles of wine and sat outside staring at the stars. When we couldn't feel our fingers anymore, we went in. The bottles of wine made us think that sliding across the floors in the main hall was a good idea. Ryan's socks were more slippery so he ate it first. Cracked his head on a wall. After that, we figured sliding in socks was a bad idea.

It was well after midnight when we crashed. I hadn't been out that long when the door to my room opened. Reese. I don't know how I knew, but I did.

"You can turn on the light," I said.

"You're awake?" Reese asked.

"Sort of." I rolled over as she turned on the light. Fucking blinding.

"Sorry."

"It's okay. How did it go?"

"Surprisingly well. Christopher and Breno just went to bed. They're exhausted."

My eyes finally adjusted so I could see her. Her hair clearly hadn't been washed in a few days. The beanie tucked in her back pocket explained that. She was wearing a pair of my jeans. They were baggy on her. Her face was clean, but there was a light patina of dust on her neck and ears. And the jacket she was wearing looked like it had been lived in for a year.

She was the sexiest thing I'd ever seen.

"Is it weird that I think you're really hot right now?" I asked.

"Yes." She smiled. "I'm going to take a shower."

"Can I—"

"No. I'm washing every inch of myself before I get in bed with you." Reese stripped off the jacket and kicked off the jeans.

"I'm really good at washing every inch of you."

The smile got bigger and her eyes went gray. "Be patient. And take off your clothes. I'll be right back."

I couldn't really argue with that.

Reese wasn't in the shower very long. I managed to wait until the water was shut off. But then I went into the bathroom. She was bent over slightly to towel dry her hair.

"You're staring at my ass aren't you?" Reese asked.

"Totally."

"Stop it." She straightened and shot me an unconvincing glare.

"Make me." I grinned.

Reese tossed the damp towel at my head. I ducked and caught the towel. She laughed.

"Move. I need clothes." She tried to skirt past me. I grabbed at her, but she got away.

I chased her back into our room and tackled her onto the bed. She tried to scoot out from under me, but I held her in place.

"Hey, did you know that you're naked?" I asked.

"You're very observant."

"Yeah, I went to college. I'm smart."

"Oh, yeah?" Reese laughed. "They taught you that in college?"

"Yep. I can identify colors too." I grabbed her arms and pinned them above her head.

"I'm very impressed." Reese raised her head up to kiss me. "How about counting? Can you count too?"

"Girl, I can count so high. Like to ten." I kissed her again. "One, two, three..." I forgot what came after that because Reese started kissing my neck. The slight pull of her teeth and the warmth of her tongue made thinking real hard.

"What's the matter, sweetheart?" she asked between kisses and bites. "Can't go higher than three?"

"Nope. Don't care what comes after three." I captured her mouth and kissed her long enough and hard enough that I was pretty sure she couldn't make it to four either.

As we kissed, Reese edged her thigh between my legs. She thrust up against me. Slowly.

"Fuck, I missed you."

"You better." Her lips trailed up my neck to my ear.

"I was worried."

Reese stopped kissing me so she could pull back and look into my eyes. "About what?

"You. What if they caught you?"

She laughed. "That's fucking hilarious."

"Why?"

"Because I just got this image of you pacing and waiting for me. Please tell me you weren't doing that."

I started laughing too. "No. Ryan and I got drunk and played hide-and-seek."

"That's more like it."

Reese twisted her wrists out of my hands and dragged my T-shirt over my head. Or tried. I sat up and pulled the shirt the rest of the way off.

"You are epically bad at undressing me sometimes."

"I've never had to before." She grinned up at me.

"Huh?"

"Have you seen me? Women's clothes usually just fall off around me."

"Not anymore." I traced my hands over her ribcage. She arched and stretched.

"What do you mean?"

"If any chicks start stripping, I'll have to knock 'em out. You're mine, peanut butter."

Reese's eyes went completely gray. "Yeah, I guess so."

"Damn right."

I leaned down and kissed along her ribs, following the trail of my hands. Reese lifted her hips, a quiet plea that I ignored. I wanted to kiss her until I was the only one she remembered. Until all that she knew was me.

Her fingers traced patterns in my hair, along my ears, over my neck as I kissed her shoulders, her collarbones. When I lowered my mouth to one nipple, then the other, and back again, Reese's fingers tightened. She gasped when I sucked hard on her nipple. She lifted her hips into me. But I wasn't going there. Not yet.

I cupped her ass with one hand. Squeezed it slowly as she arched against me. Reese caught my eyes and smiled. She traced the edge of my jaw with a fingertip. I kissed her finger then licked it. She moaned softly and her eyes rolled back. I sucked her finger into my mouth, bit it a little. She pulled me close to kiss me. Just kiss me. Softly, slowly. I was so distracted I almost didn't notice the way she started thrusting against my leg. Almost. I moved my leg away and grinned.

"Not yet."

"Come on."

"Nope." I moved my lips to her throat. Kissed a line to her bellybutton. Dipped my tongue in and around it. Reese squirmed and tried to scoot higher on the bed. I planted my hand between her breasts and held her still. She fell back, her hips still jerking. The scent of her arousal hit me suddenly. It made my mouth water. So I hooked my arms under her thighs and slid down the bed.

Reese sighed when I kissed her. I licked the length of her and her breath hitched. I smiled against her cunt.

"Damn it, you teased me enough." Reese gripped my hair and tried to push me down. But I was stronger.

I licked around her clit, lingering in the spots where she was most sensitive. She sobbed my name. When I finally sucked her into my mouth, a rush of wetness coated my chin. Her thighs tightened and she arched off the bed. I sucked her hard, letting her clit roll over my tongue again and again. The sweet tissues in my mouth throbbed as she came. But I didn't stop sucking her.

Reese held my head in place so she could keep fucking my mouth. Her hips were in the air, keeping a constant rhythm against the jerk of my tongue.

"Oh, oh God. Coop." Her fingers tightened, pulling my hair, as she came again.

We collapsed to the bed.

I lay there with my head pillowed on her thigh, not even trying to control my ragged, satisfied breathing. Reese tugged my hair lightly until I moved up next to her. She turned and burrowed her head into my armpit. One lazy hand traced patterns on my stomach. I rubbed the bare expanse of her back as her breathing slowed.

"Told you I missed you," I said quietly.

She smiled and kissed my side. "Yeah, I guess I missed you too."

"You better," I mimicked her.

"Whatever."

"Tired?"

"Sort of. Tired of being on a train." She walked her fingers up my stomach. Not like she was trying to start anything. Just playing.

"So where did you lose them?" I asked.

"Slovenia."

"Where the hell is that?"

Reese raised her head up to stare at me. "Were you stoned all through high school or just in class?"

"Umm, mostly just the last two years."

She shook her head, grinned, and lay back down. "It's below Austria. I caught a train in Munich that took me to Ljubljana, which is in Slovenia." She poked me in the side.

"Ouch. Fine. I'll learn some geography."

"Good. I got to Ljubljana really early in the morning. They followed me to a very leisurely breakfast. I read the paper, enjoyed my coffee. It totally drove them crazy. The dude looked like he wanted to approach me, but the chick stopped him."

"So you decided to lose them?"

"Well, yeah. They were getting antsy. I figured that we'd fucked with them enough."

Smart girl. "How'd you do it?"

"Walked through the city. Ditched them long enough to steal a car. Drove it back—"

"Wait. You stole a car?" This was a whole new side of Reese.

"Uhh, yeah. I hotwired it."

"You can hotwire a car?" A really sexy side.

"Well, yeah. I learned last year. When I was working for my grandfather."

"Why?" I asked.

"I don't know actually. I think he thought it would be fun to teach me. Introductory course to a life of crime or something." She shrugged a little like she was embarrassed.

"I can't see Lawrence DiGiovanni teaching you to hotwire a car."

"I know. It's weird, right? He had one of his guys bring in an old car. His whole garage is filled with these identical luxury sedans, all dark and masculine. And a couple sports cars that I've never seen him drive. And then there was this beat-up baby blue Toyota pickup. We were both crammed under the dash for about thirty minutes before I got it right. He was super excited."

"It was fun?" I guessed.

"Yeah. I know that's weird. But it's one of the few times he actually spent time with me." She gave another embarrassed shrug.

"Maybe you could teach me sometime?"

"Okay. Yeah. I could do that." She pressed her lips against my skin again. "So anyway. I drove back to the train station. Caught a train to France."

"You went back to the same train station?"

"It's massive. Almost like there are five train stations all crammed together. Once I was on the train, I changed my outfit and shit. Put on the beanie to cover my hair. Flirted with some boy for the last hour. We left the station together. Then I ditched him and came south. You know the rest."

"Babe."

"What?"

"You're a badass."

"I know."

CHAPTER FOURTEEN

Eighteen Months Later

I woke up to a half-naked Reese sprawled next to me. One foot was off the bed. The other was playing footsie with me. She had her hand under my ass. Like she'd put it there and fallen back to sleep. It was a common occurrence.

She was wearing a pair of boxer briefs and nothing else. The boxers were tight on her ass and thighs and looked sexy as hell. She was sexy as hell.

I leaned over and kissed her cheek. Then her ear, down her neck, and across her shoulders. She murmured in her sleep.

"Morning, peanut butter."

"Mmm-hmm." And she was out again.

I climbed out of bed and found a T-shirt. My pj pants were tangled on the floor with our blankets. Also a common occurrence.

I padded down to the kitchen. There was a carafe of coffee on the counter. I poured myself a mug and wandered out back. Christopher was reading the paper. Breno was on his laptop.

"Morning," Christopher called.

"You guys want more coffee?" I asked.

"Please."

"Sure."

I went back in and brought the carafe out with me. Christopher held his mug aloft without taking his eyes off the paper.

"Thank you." Breno smiled at me as I filled his cup.

"Whatever." I put the coffee on the table between them. Then I snagged the chair opposite Christopher.

"Reese still asleep?" Christopher asked.

"Yep. Ryan?"

"Of course," Breno said.

"So today's the big day?" Christopher asked.

"Yeah, Ryan said he picked up the—" I stopped talking when the door opened.

"Is the coffee out here?" Reese asked. An empty mug dangled from her hand.

"Yeah, sorry." I nodded at the carafe.

"Cool." She sauntered out barefoot. Her hair was all messy and sexy. She'd thrown on a pair of her shorts and one of my hoodies. I was guessing there was nothing under the sweatshirt and I really wanted to find out.

Christopher pulled out a chunk of the newspaper and handed it to Reese as she sat down.

"Thanks." Reese poured some coffee and blew across the top of her mug. Then she opened the paper and proceeded to ignore me for the next thirty minutes.

"Are you guys about ready for breakfast?" Breno closed his laptop.

"Mmm-hmm." Reese was still reading the paper.

"I'm down. You want help?" I asked.

"Just go wake up Ryan."

I rolled my eyes and followed Breno inside. He set down his computer and the empty coffee carafe.

"Should I make more coffee?" he asked.

"Please. Or I'll never get him out of bed."

"Tell him I'm making waffles." Breno started measuring out more coffee.

"Got it." I headed back upstairs.

Ryan's room was dark. I pulled open the curtains and he groaned.

"Why do you hate me?" he asked from beneath a pile of blankets.

"I don't hate you. The sun hates you."

"Go the fuck away."

"Are you talking to me or the sun?" I asked.

"Please, Coop. Fuck off," he whined.

"You don't have a girl under there, do you?"

"No. Close the curtains."

"Nope. Gotta wake up and shit."

"Why? I have absolutely no responsibilities." The mound of blankets shifted a little and Ryan's head poked out.

"Breno told me to wake you up."

"There better be coffee."

"And waffles," I said.

"Fine. I'll get up. But I don't like you today."

"Sure you do. We're gonna be family today."

"You're such a fucking tool." Ryan started giggling. "And she still has to say yes."

"Oh, she'll say yes."

"Just because you're all excited to face the day doesn't mean I have to be."

"Good point. But if you sleep, you will miss waffles."

"Damn you and your waffles."

"Whatever." I found a pair of sweats on the floor and tossed them at him. "Your loss."

"Okay, okay. I'm getting up." Ryan sat up and grabbed the sweats. "You excited?"

"Yes. But I'm trying to be cool."

He laughed again. "Let me know how that works out."

"Fuck off."

"Want to smoke?" Ryan leaned over and opened the drawer on his bedside table. He pulled out his cigarette case and chose a joint.

"Nah, man. I'm cool. Don't light the blankets on fire."

"Please," he scoffed.

"I'll see you downstairs, okay?"

"Sure."

I went back down to the kitchen. Breno was stirring his waffle batter.

"Is he awake?"

"Sort of."

"Christ. He's smoking isn't he?"

"Umm…"

"I told him. If he's going to smoke, he needs to do it outside." Breno sighed.

I didn't know why he cared. He'd told Ryan not to smoke in the house almost every day since we'd moved in. Ryan hadn't listened once.

"I'm sure if you ask him just one more time, he will listen."

"Do you think?" Breno looked up from his heating waffle iron.

"Totally. The first five hundred times he probably just misunderstood you, but five hundred and one, he will totally get the message."

"You are messing with me again, aren't you?"

"Dumbass." I shook my head and turned to go back outside.

"You don't get waffles today," Breno said.

"Sure I do." I grinned. "Dad."

Breno fought to keep his scowl in place and lost miserably. "Damn it."

I laughed at him. "You're a sucker, you know that?"

He didn't seem to mind.

"Hey, Cooper?"

"What?"

"In case I don't get a chance later, I just wanted to say good luck tonight."

"Thanks." I smiled at him and went outside to get Christopher and Reese for breakfast.

❖

"Don't screw it up," Ryan said.

"Fuck you. Where is it?" I asked.

"Calm down. Your ring is right here." He tossed me a little wooden box. "But don't screw it up."

"I got that the first twenty times you told me." I turned back to the mirror I was preening in front of. Why did Ryan's room have a better mirror than mine?

I had on a pair of jeans and a blazer over a T-shirt. The jeans were black. That and the blazer were my nod to propriety. 'Cause I was never putting on a suit again.

"You look fine."

"I want to look more than fine."

Ryan grabbed my shoulder and spun me around. He pulled me into a massive hug. Which totally messed up my jacket and probably my hair.

"Get off. You got me all messed up."

"Well, clean, shiny Coop is weird. Reese'll know something is up."

"Something is up."

"Dude." He straightened my lapels, tweaked the front of my hawk just a little more to the side, and smacked my cheek. "Don't screw it up."

"Yeah, yeah. Thanks, Ryan."

"Love you," he said.

"Same here."

"Your ass looks amazing in those jeans."

"I know."

"Go get her." And then he smacked my ass.

I scowled at him. He grinned back. I opened the door and went downstairs to meet Reese.

She looked fucking perfect. Standing there by the front door with the early evening light slanting through the windows onto her nearly bare shoulders.

"I don't know what you guys are up to, but I don't trust it," she said.

"Keep your pants on." I could have lied, but she would have known. "No, wait, don't. Take 'em off."

"I'm not wearing pants. This is a skirt, sweetheart. And we have dinner reservations."

"Oh, yeah. That."

"Come on." She held out her hand.

"Have fun." We turned and Breno was standing there grinning like a tool. Christopher was behind him doing the same thing. They'd probably been lurking in the hallway waiting.

"Don't wait up," I said.

Reese rolled her eyes and pulled me out the door. I brushed my hand over my jacket pocket. Ring was still there.

"Seriously, what is with all of you?" Reese asked.

"It's not really a surprise if I tell you."

She rolled her eyes again and got into the car. As we drove into the city, I tried to focus on the road, but it was difficult. Reese was like super hot. And she smelled really good. Driving was hard.

❖

We were a course and a glass of wine in when I started to panic. After my second glass of wine, I calmed down a bit. I could do this. We'd finish dinner, take a walk, go to that park we loved. And I'd get down on one knee and ask the girl to marry me. No big.

I did another subtle check for the ring. Still there.

Reese smiled at me. Oh, yeah. I could do this. I was so going to marry that girl.

We were debating dessert—well, Reese was debating, I was nodding along—when I glanced away from her. Only for a moment. There were tons of people passing by on the street. It was a warm summer night. But one girl seemed to stand out, maybe it was the way she walked, or the way she brushed her long hair back from her face. I don't know. But I knew it was her.

"Oh, fuck."

"What?" Reese turned to see what I was staring at.

"I'm sorry. I'll explain later. But I got to go."

"What do you mean?"

"I have to go. I'm sorry." I dug my wallet out of the inside pocket in my jacket. It caught on the ring box and I had a moment of pure terror. "Fuck. Really, really sorry."

"Cooper, what is going on?"

"I'll explain later." I tossed a bundle of cash onto the table and vaulted over the railing onto the sidewalk.

She was a block and a half ahead of me already. I dodged around pedestrians, practically running to catch up. My legs were still longer than hers. It didn't take long.

It probably wasn't even her. It wasn't her. It couldn't be. How the fuck had she found me? No, she hadn't found me. It was a freak occurrence. And it didn't matter, 'cause it wasn't going to be her. It was dark and I was seeing shit.

Reese would be pissed. I would tell her all about it and she would be pissed. But we would laugh about it later. This was what would make the story of proposing tellable. I was halfway through the night when I ran away. Ha ha.

But it was her. She turned a corner and I saw her face. Fuck. I kept going, overzealous stalker style.

What the fuck was Ade doing in Spain?

She crossed the street. It was darker here. Fewer streetlights. Fewer people. It was the only chance I'd get.

We passed an alley. I grabbed her and pulled her back into it. One hand clamped over her mouth, the other holding her tight against my body. She arched her back and tried to break my grip, but couldn't.

"Shhhh, it's okay. It's me, it's V."

Ade stiffened. I let her go, but kept my hand on her arm. She turned around slowly, then threw herself into my arms.

"We thought you were dead."

"No, no. I'm so sorry."

And then she was crying.

"You disappeared. We looked everywhere," she said. Her voice was so low it was practically a whisper.

"I know. I'm sorry."

"Ryan, Reese. Are they okay? Are they with you?"

"Yeah. I was having dinner with Reese just now. We live about thirty minutes from here."

"What?" she screamed. "You asshole. Do you know what we went through? Do you—no, of course not. You don't give a fuck do you?" And then she punched me in the chest. I took a step back.

"No, that's not it at all. I swear."

"You fucking disappeared. Like gone. And I find you in Spain having dinner with Reese. You asshole." She punched me again.

"Let me explain, okay? There was a lot going on."

"Fuck you."

"Seriously, Reese is a couple blocks back." I pointed. "Let us explain."

"Fine." Ade marched out of the alley and turned back the way we'd come. I caught up to her and threw my arm around her shoulders.

"I missed you."

"You're a dick." She sniffled and wiped her face, but she didn't push me away or punch me.

"I know." I figured it would be bad to linger on that detail. "So what are you doing here? In Spain, I mean."

"I decided to do Europe before I start college in a couple months. Mom and Dad wouldn't let me go before I turned eighteen."

"Shut the fuck up. I can't believe you're eighteen now."

"Fuck you," she said again.

"Where are you going to college?"

"Davis."

"Really? Damn. Smarty-pants. Congratulations."

She shrugged. "Didn't get into Berkeley."

"No one gets into Berkeley as a freshman." I squeezed her shoulders.

"You have got to be fucking kidding me." At the sound of Reese's voice, I looked up. She was standing down the street with her arms crossed. She looked livid. "You literally ran away from proposing to me to chase some girl. Fuck you." Then she turned and took off the other direction.

"Reese, wait." I let go of Ade so I could chase after Reese. This night was so not going the way I planned. "It's not some girl. It's Adriana. It's my sister," I called.

That made her stop.

Ade caught up with us just as Reese was spinning around. Ade threw herself into Reese's arms and they hugged for a long, long time. Like, turning in circles, long time.

"Wait. You knew I was going to propose?" I asked.

"Don't ever play poker, sweetheart."

They spun in another circle while I stood there grinning like an idiot. But then I saw something that made me stop smiling, stop breathing, stop everything. High on Adriana's back, between her shoulder blades, I could see the outline of a small box.

The bitch was wearing a wire.

Reese had her arms around Ade's waist, which was pulling her top tight. That was the only reason I saw it.

I forced my smile back in place. "Can I get another hug like that?"

"I'm still pissed at you." Ade let go of Reese. "But yes." She launched herself at me again. I hugged her tight, tugging at the material of her shirt. Reese was watching us and smiling. I frowned and looked pointedly down. Reese was confused, but then she saw what I was looking at.

"Shit," Reese said.

"What?" Ade asked.

"Nothing. Just I guess we have some explaining to do." It was a cheap lie, but Ade fell for it.

"Damn right." Ade let go of me.

"There's a bar not far from here." I nodded down the street. "Let's go there. Sit and talk."

"But I want to go see Ryan," Ade said.

"I'll text him to meet us, okay?" Reese lied again.

"Cool."

Reese pulled her phone out of her purse. She fell back a step to text Ryan. I didn't need to see what she was typing to know what it said. Plan C.

Ryan wouldn't show up at the bar. In under ten minutes, he, Breno, and Christopher would be out of the house and on the way to an apartment an hour away from here. Plan C: Run like fucking hell.

A few blocks later, we stopped outside a very noisy and very popular club in downtown.

"This place is kinda loud. Should we go somewhere we can actually talk?" Ade asked.

"We can go upstairs. It's quieter there." I pointed at the upper floor.

She nodded and followed us in.

"Back stairs are this way." Reese led us to a dark hallway that did not, in fact, lead to the back stairs.

Two girls walked out of the bathroom ahead of us. I nodded as we let them pass. A moment later, we were alone in the very loud hallway. I clamped my hand over Ade's mouth and grabbed her hands. Reese reached under Ade's shirt and peeled away the leads for the wire. Ade started to scream, but I pinched her cheeks until she stopped struggling. I doubted the sound would be picked up. That was why I'd chosen this place.

Reese left the wire and battery on a wide ledge on the wall. It would buy us a few minutes before they—whoever they were—realized that no one was attached to them anymore.

I yanked Ade down the hall, past the bathrooms, and out the back door.

"What the fuck did you do, Ade?" I asked as I pulled her down the back alley to the street.

"I'm sorry. I...they just want to talk to you. Help you out. Let me go." She tried to pull away, but I tightened my grip on her wrists.

"Keep moving," Reese said.

"Who?"

"What do you mean?" Ade asked.

"Who sent you?"

"The FBI. They just want to talk to you, I swear." Ade was crying now. "You're hurting me. Let go."

"No. Keep walking or I'll carry you." It was another lie. I couldn't carry her. But she didn't know that.

"Why did they send you?" Reese asked.

"To help bring you home. Mom and Dad didn't want me to come, but I had to. Those people, your family." She shot a look at Reese. "They're going to kill you guys."

"If they find us they'll kill us, but they couldn't find us, Ade. Until you led them here." I shot her a look of my own.

"No, they don't know I'm here. They couldn't know."

"Why do the Feds want us?"

"To help bring the DiGiovannis down. That's what they told me."

"Be quiet for a minute," Reese said. We were at a street now. Reese looked around until she found what she was looking for. An old car, windows down. Too rusty and pathetic to bother stealing. Reese climbed in the driver's seat. She reached back and popped the locks.

"Get in." I shoved Ade forward.

"What? But this isn't your car."

She couldn't know that. Except she did. How long had they been watching?

"How long have they been following us?" I pushed her into the backseat. She scooted over. I climbed in next to her, still holding her wrists.

"I don't know."

"How long have you been following us?" I asked.

"I haven't been."

"You're a shitty liar." She always had been.

"A couple weeks. They just want to help. I just want to help."

"Fuck," I said.

"Shit." Reese had her hands so far under the steering column that I could barely see her head.

"Are we stealing this car?" Ade asked.

"Trying. Will you be quiet?" Reese asked. She had half the wires out of the dash now. After a few unsuccessful attempts, the car came to life. Limping, coughing, dying, but life. We took off.

"Please, guys. This isn't who you are. You don't steal cars and hurt people. Just come talk to Agent Ogilvy. She can help straighten this whole thing out. You can come home."

"We don't live there anymore," Reese said. She was weaving in and out of traffic. I didn't bother glancing back. I pretty much always figured someone was following us. Reese would lose them. She was good at that now.

"But you can come back."

"Sorry, not happening. It's not our home." Reese sounded pissed. She should have been. We'd found whatever peace we could. And Ade had just destroyed it.

"What do you mean? It's home. It'll always be home."

"You wouldn't understand," I said.

"Oh, right. Of course not. You sound just like Mom and Dad. When the Feds showed up they were all happy you guys were alive, and then they wouldn't help bring you back. It's fucking bullshit."

"And you turned eighteen and jumped on a plane, right?" I asked.

"Damn right."

"You couldn't just let me live, could you?"

"I want you home. Why is that bad?"

"Because I'm not going home."

"Yes, you are. That's why I'm here," she said.

"Listen, darlin'. If they catch me, I'm going to prison. Not back to EDH. Is that better? You can visit me. I'll always be somewhere you can find me. Behind fucking bars. Is that what you want?" I finally let go of Ade's hands. She wasn't going anywhere. And I didn't want to touch her. Or be anywhere near her.

"It's not like that. Those DiGiovanni people want to kill you. The Feds will protect you."

"They lied," Reese said. "They don't want to help us. They want to help themselves."

"Screw you. I'm not some naïve fifteen-year-old. I know how this works."

"You're a naïve eighteen-year-old, and you're going to get Coop killed," Reese said.

"That's it. Let me out of the car. Fuck you guys," Ade said.

We were on a curving country road. It was late. There was no one behind us and no one ahead of us. Reese pulled the car over.

"Okay. Get out," Reese said.

"What? Here?"

"Out now."

Ade looked at me, desperation in her eyes.

"You have a cell phone?" I asked.

"What?"

"Cell phone?" I leaned over and checked her pockets.

"Hey!"

But it was too late. I'd found the phone. I tucked it back into her pocket, leaned over her, and opened the door.

"You heard Reese. Get out."

"But you can't do this." More tears.

I pushed her until she climbed out of the car.

"Ade, I love you," I said as she slammed the door.

"Fuck you!" she shouted one last time as Reese drove away.

CHAPTER FIFTEEN

F"uck!"
   "Yep," Reese said.
"Fucking stupid bitch!"
"Breathing, Coop."
The therapist I'd seen for our first six months in Spain had been all big on breathing when I got angry. Instead of beating on people. I hadn't been big on breathing. But Reese still thought it was helpful.
"I don't want to breathe," I said.
Reese shrugged. "We need to contact Ryan."
"Yeah, cell phones are in the kitchen."
We were in a studio apartment about thirty miles away from the larger safe house where Christopher, Breno, and Ryan were. There were two such apartments in Spain because we lived close by. Another was in Sweden. And a fourth in Ireland. We also had a big ass house in Brazil. But only Christopher and Breno had been there. Reese and Ryan and I hadn't visited it yet. There were two apartments near that place too. Each had supplies in case we needed to run.
Apparently, we needed to run.
We had ditched our stolen car a few blocks away and walked here. By the time they found the car and tracked down this apartment, we would be gone.
"Got 'em." Reese walked back into the small room. She tossed me a box and started tearing into a second one.

I left mine on the table and went in search of clothes.

"Hey." Reese wasn't talking to me so I didn't respond. Instead, I pulled out jeans and a T-shirt for Reese. Then I found a sweatshirt for each of us. My sweatshirt had SFU written across the chest. It was some university in British Columbia. Breno had ordered it online and washed it about a thousand times. Authenticity, he had said.

"No, her sister showed up," Reese said.

"Fucking stupid bitch," I said again. But Ryan couldn't hear me and Reese wasn't listening.

"Yeah. We'll be there in a few." Reese hung up the phone. Keep it short. Just in case.

"Disguises?" I asked.

"I can't believe I'm saying this, but we need to color your hair."

"Probably smart." I didn't want to shave it off like last time. Hadn't worked anyway.

"Strip and get in the kitchen."

I did as I was told. Reese joined me with another box. This one was store-bought hair dye. Awesome. She spent way too much time reading the box. How hard could it be?

"You know I'm only wearing my underwear, right?"

"Yes, it's distracting." She didn't look away from the box.

I smiled. "I mean, it's cold."

"Sorry. I've never done this before."

"Liar," I said.

"Huh?"

"Senior year. You died Carson's hair blue when he was super drunk and he couldn't stop you."

Reese started laughing. "I was trying to give him more school spirit."

"Bitch."

"Yeah. Now shut up. I'm trying to read."

Reese opened the box. There was a lot of crap in there. She put on the disposable gloves, then mixed some shit together in a squeeze bottle.

"Sit down and hold still."

"Gotcha." I sat in the only chair in the kitchen—furnishing hadn't been a big priority—and bowed my head forward.

Reese started squeezing the contents of the bottle onto my head. It was cold. But then she started massaging it into my hair. Which felt good.

"Shit."

"What?" I asked.

"I got it on your ear. Do you think that's bad?"

"Probably. Wipe it off."

"Let me finish. Then I'll clean you up."

It didn't take her long to finish. My hair was short. She peeled off the gloves and tossed them into the sink. Then she used a damp towel to wipe off my neck and ears.

"That feels good," I said.

"Shut up."

"It does." I lifted my head and stared into her eyes. They went gray. So I kissed her. She smiled against my lips.

"This isn't supposed to be fun, you know?"

"But I'm with you. So it's fun already." I grinned.

"Liar."

"Hey, Reese."

"What?"

"Marry me?"

"Shouldn't you be on one knee, wearing clothing, and not covered in hair color?"

I laughed. But the girl wanted it, so I slid off the chair and knelt. "Now will you marry me?"

Reese leaned down and kissed me. "Yes."

"Are you just saying that 'cause I'm not wearing a shirt?"

"Yes." She kissed me again.

"Good enough." I stood and pulled her into a hug.

"Get off." She pushed me away. "I don't want dye all over me."

"Fine. But you're gonna marry me?" It seemed like I should make sure.

"Yes, Coop, I'm going to marry you."

"I win," I said.

Reese rolled her eyes. "We're on the run now. Try to be serious."

"All right. I'll pretend to be serious." I sighed like it was a big deal. "So, seriously, you're gonna marry me?" Reese rolled her eyes. "Fine." I sat in my chair. "How long do I have to keep this crap on?"

"Ummm." She picked up the box again. "Like ten more minutes."

"This is totally how I envisioned the night going."

"Such a romantic."

"I know."

Ten minutes later, Reese washed my hair in the sink. Soapy dye kept running down my face. It collected in my ears and dripped off the end of my nose. I didn't like it. So I shut my eyes and tried to breathe through my mouth.

When I straightened, Reese toweled my hair dry. She was all sexy and concentrating. I kissed her. For real this time. Nibbled on her lower lip, tasted the tip of her tongue. I pulled her close. She dropped the towel and kissed me back. Her hands fell to my shoulders and slid down my back.

"Wait. We can't." Reese pulled away.

"Yeah, we can. I'm chemical free." I backed her against the counter.

"No, we need to get out of here. Like an hour ago."

"An hour ago we weren't even here."

"Exactly," she said.

"Damn."

"Whoever the hell is after us could be here anytime."

"Okay, let's go."

I put my pants back on. Reese lost the skirt and I lost my resolve. But then she gave me a scary look so I let her put some jeans on. Reese exchanged her top for the T-shirt I'd pulled out. We pocketed our new phones. Reese grabbed a set of keys from the kitchen. After studying the street out the windows for a full five minutes, we went out the door. Reese was in the middle of locking it when I stopped her.

"Shit, wait."

"What now?"

"Your ring. I got you a fuckin' awesome ring. It's inside. In my jacket pocket."

Reese managed to glare and laugh at the same time. But she opened the door back up. I ran in, grabbed the little wooden box, and ran back out.

"Do I know how to propose or what?" I asked.

"Yeah, you're really suave."

"I know."

"You're driving." Reese tossed me the car keys.

"Okay, why?"

"Because I want to stare at my new ring."

"It's awesome."

"Did they all help pick it out?" Reese stared at the box skeptically. She hadn't opened it yet.

"I let Breno pick out the box. Christopher helped pick out the ring. Ryan got to pick it up."

"Thank God. Ryan's taste is…not great."

"For real."

We climbed in the car. I didn't see anyone around. And no one followed us. It was getting late. Any tail would have been obvious.

"I think we're in the clear."

Reese didn't say anything. I spared her a glance. She was cradling the ring box and it looked like she was crying.

"Are you crying?" I asked.

"No." Yes. "Pull over."

I did. Reese popped both our seat belts and climbed into my lap.

"I guess you like it?"

"Shut up." And then she was kissing me. Fingers twisting in my damp hair, tongue in my mouth, tits pressed against mine, ass grinding into my lap, kissing me.

We could ditch the cops later.

I pulled her into the backseat with me. We fell so my feet were still in the front seat and her tits were in my face. Reese laughed and pulled her shirt over her head.

"Smooth, sweetheart."

"I know." I started unbuttoning her jeans. There was some fumbling and an elbow to my stomach, but we managed to get both our shirts off and her jeans halfway down her ass. She yanked my jeans and got them and one shoe off.

"So fucking romantic," Reese said.

"Wait till you see what I planned for the honeymoon."

And then we were both laughing and kissing and I really, really didn't give a fuck if someone wanted to arrest us. Reese pressed her leg between mine. I arched up to meet her thrusts. Her hands were tangled in my hair, holding me close.

"You know it's kinda hot, right?" Reese asked.

"Huh? No talking. Kiss me." I captured her lips again.

"Your hair," she said against my lips. "You're kinda hot as a brunette."

"You're hotter." And then I slid my tongue into her mouth and she stopped talking.

Reese wrapped her arms around my shoulders, lifting my face closer to hers. I pulled her hips close until I could feel her skin everywhere. Just everywhere.

"Touch me, Coop. Come on."

So I pushed my hand between our bodies. She gasped when I slid my fingertips around her clit, lifted her hips so I could slip inside her. The warm grasp of her muscles pulled me in. She moaned into my mouth.

I so loved this girl.

"Come with me?" Reese asked. I could only nod and stare into her eyes. Fuck, she had beautiful eyes.

When Reese squeezed my clit, I thought my head was going to come off. And my heart was just going to beat right out of my chest. As I fucked her slow, then hard, and slow again, she just kept rubbing my clit. Too slow to come. Fast enough to keep me waiting, begging on the edge.

Her lips left mine, trailed down my cheek to my ear. Her warm breath tickled my neck. She bit a spot, sucked hard. She was going to come. Soon.

She picked up the pace, increased the pressure on my clit.

And then we were coming. Her hips jerked in my lap. Her fingers twitched on my clit. I lost myself in the feel of her clenching around my fingers. She gasped, moaned in my ear, and collapsed into me.

We stayed like that. I don't know how long. I kissed her hair. Played my hand over her bare back. She kissed my neck, softly, slowly. Like she was falling asleep. But she wasn't.

"It's really pretty."

"Huh?" I was always articulate after sex.

"The ring. It's really pretty."

"Good. I'm glad you like it."

"Yeah." Reese kissed my neck again and started to sit up. "We have to go."

"No."

"Yeah."

"Fuck."

"I know." She started pulling her jeans back up. I found her bra and handed it over.

"Have you seen my other shoe?" I'd managed to get my pants back on, but the shoe was gone.

"Uhhh." Reese climbed into the front seat. I smacked her ass when she reached down to the floorboards for my shoe. "Not helping."

"Or am I?" I asked.

"No." She threw the shoe at me. "Not helping."

Five minutes later, we were back on the road. Fully clothed and everything. Being on the run sucks.

❖

"Holy fuck." Ryan yanked us inside and shut the door. "They're here," he called. And then he pulled us into a group hug.

Breno and Christopher came into the room. They waited until we were done hugging Ryan, then they hugged us too.

"What happened?" Breno asked.

"My sister showed up. We were having dinner and I looked up and she was walking down the street. So I followed her."

"But why did we need to run?" Christopher asked. "She's only a kid."

"She's eighteen now. Not a kid. Feds sent her in. I saw the wire when she hugged Reese. I need coffee. Do we have coffee?" I moved past them into the small kitchen. There was a pot of coffee waiting. I poured a mug. When I turned around, Christopher, Breno, and Ryan were all crammed into the doorway. Ryan was practically vibrating.

"Why the hell would the Feds send in an eighteen-year-old?" Christopher asked.

Not a question I wanted to answer. Really, really not a question I wanted to answer. I had a pretty good idea of why the Feds would resort to the fuckin' low move of sending in my baby sis. She was a risk. A child in a foreign country betting on a familial tie that might be dead.

After France, they probably figured she was their last shot. But the guys didn't know about that weird weekend on the Mediterranean.

Reese and I had figured we didn't need to tell them. It was in Marseille that we had figured out how the cops were following us. So we hauled ass home and suggested that everyone get new passports. Christopher called his guy and he came through. No big. It had been six months since the last time we were followed on one of our little vacations.

We thought we were in the clear. Apparently, we were wrong.

Reese was standing behind the guys. I caught her eye and she gave me a brief nod.

"Remember when Reese and I went to France a little while ago?" I asked.

"Yeah, what about it?" Christopher asked.

"And when we got back we suggested that everyone get new passports?"

"That was when we decided to have safe houses," Ryan said.

"Yeah. Well, Reese and I kinda didn't mention something."

"What do you mean?" Breno asked.

"We were being followed in Paris," Reese said from behind them.

They all spun to face Reese.

"What the fuck?" Ryan.

"Why did you not tell us?" Breno.

"Damn it." Christopher.

"Also in Nice," I said. They turned back to stare at me. "And Marseille."

"What the hell is wrong with you?" Christopher.

"My God." Breno.

"Shut the fuck up." Ryan.

"How could you not tell us that?" Breno asked.

"We didn't want you guys to worry," Reese said. They spun comically. This was getting ridiculous. Reese pushed through the doorway and perched on the counter. I poured her a cup of coffee.

"We thought it was a fluke in Paris. We were in this weird little town. What was it?" I asked Reese.

She shrugged. "It was pretty." Well, that narrowed it down.

"So we were in this town and it was like touristy, but not American touristy. And it was just like what happened in Corsica. This American couple started following us. Different couple than last time, but it was a small place, hard to miss, you know? Then we went south and they were there too."

"I am going to kill you two," Breno said. Then he started muttering in Portuguese. I'd picked up enough to know he was pissed.

Reese rolled her eyes. "Cut the dramatics. It happened before. This time we just dealt with it solo."

"Yeah, we figured out it was our passports tipping them off. So everyone got new ones. And none of us have been followed since. Chill," I said.

"Chill?" Christopher didn't seem to want to chill. "If it was your passports, then they were able to tell every damn time that you disappeared in Spain. You led them to us."

"Fuck off. Spain is big. Needle in a haystack." Reese waved him off.

Breno started cursing in Portuguese again. Ryan and Christopher started cursing in English.

"Guys, calm the fuck down," I said.

"She's right," Christopher said. Breno and Ryan looked at him like he'd lost it. "We can yell later. Right now we need to leave the country."

Breno sighed. Loudly. "Brazil?"

"Yes. You and I will travel separately," Christopher told Breno. "The kids will use their new passports"—he glared at me and Reese—"and fly out from here."

"Did Adriana give you any useful information?" Breno asked.

"Yeah, what'd she say?" Ryan asked.

"Well, she wanted to see you," I said.

"Damn, girl, I know that. I'm hot as fuck," Ryan said.

Reese, Christopher, Breno, and I all sighed and shook our heads. When we managed to overcome that statement—which took a while—Reese and I launched into the story. We stopped telling it at the part where we got to the apartment. They didn't need to know all the details.

"The Feds have been watching us for weeks?" Breno asked.

"I guess." I shrugged. "Sounded like it."

"So they know what Breno and I look like and that we are involved?" Christopher asked.

"Shit." Reese.

"Fuck." Ryan.

"And they also know by now that we left. They may have even followed us. They could be outside right now." Breno pointed at the front door.

Ryan's eyes got wide. "Fuck that." He ran back into the living room, grabbed his backpack, ran back to the kitchen, and started to muscle the window open. We were on the third floor. Not smart.

"Ryan, stop." I grabbed him and pulled him away. "Don't be a dumbass."

"No, Coop. We gotta go." He pushed me aside and started to shove his bag out the window.

I pulled the bag back out and body slammed Ryan into the wall. "They didn't follow you."

"How the fuck do you know?"

"Because if they followed you they would already be in here arresting our asses."

"Oh." He thought about that for a second. Then he closed the window. "My bad."

"I'm assuming you guys left out the back and took the long way to the backup car. Like I told you too," Reese said.

"Yeah. Okay, you're right. I'm dumb," Ryan said.

"We still need to get going," Christopher said.

"Yes, the longer we wait, the better chance they have of catching us," Breno said.

"Which airport?" Reese asked. "They're probably waiting at Jerez."

"But if we drive too far, there's a chance they will have alerted the authorities to stop us," Christopher said.

"I think Seville is our best bet," I said.

"What about Málaga?" Reese asked.

"That could work," Christopher said.

"I agree." Breno nodded.

"Málaga, then." I didn't give a fuck where we flew out of. I just wanted to be gone.

"Bro." Ryan picked his bag back up.

Christopher and Breno nodded. In five minutes, we had grabbed our bags and were on our way.

Christopher and Breno dropped us at the front of the airport, then left to park the car somewhere else. They would take a cab back to the airport. We weren't as worried about them being followed, so they were going to catch a flight directly to Brazil.

Reese and Ryan and I were supposed to fly to somewhere in South America. Wherever we could get the soonest flight to. Ryan and I hung back, pretending to get our backpacks in order. It was a ruse. The bags just had clothes. Breno had all the important paperwork for our bank accounts. We had destroyed all the documentation that would screw us if it were found. So all we had were our real passports and the passports we would be using.

Reese scanned the flights until she picked the best one. It stopped briefly in London, and from there would take us to Bolivia. If we thought anyone was following us, we could lose them in Bolivia before crossing the border into Brazil. Thank God Reese knew her geography.

Everything went just like it was supposed to. At first.

Reese bought our tickets with a credit card that routed through about eight accounts or something. Breno assured us it was untraceable. They checked our passports. Gave us the tickets. In an hour, we were seated on a flight to London.

For the stopover, we decided to stay in our seats, obviously. The passengers who were leaving got off. The passengers who were getting on got on. It was the middle of the night. The flight was relatively empty.

And then the flight was delayed. Technical difficulties. We waited thirty minutes.

When four guys in uniform got on the plane, we knew we were fucked. Ryan and I slouched down in our seats as if that would help. Reese held her head high. She knew we weren't getting away this time.

They were very polite as they led us off the plane and delivered us in handcuffs to a waiting group of cops.

That was when they separated us.

CHAPTER SIXTEEN

Sometime late the next evening, I was taken back to the airport by more Interpol agents than I thought was necessary. I was cuffed to a not-very-talkative FBI agent before boarding the plane. She looked like she could keep me from running with very minimal effort. So I thought the cuffs were a little bit much. I was also wondering what her plan was if either of us had to pee. That questioned was answered when her partner joined us. He was even less talkative.

I slept for most of the flight. I hadn't gotten much sleep, and I like sleep. Plus, I wasn't sure how comfy prison beds were, but I was betting this plane was better than that. Better to get as much sleep now as I could. At least here I was protected by guard dogs. I didn't think I was going to do very well in prison.

At the airport, I was taken to a waiting undercover cop-type car. It looked very similar to the cars Vito was so fond of. American, big, dark. I thought that was a little ironic.

They didn't book me, but they gave me a change of clothes from my bag. And a toothbrush. I thought that was nice of them. But I still didn't like them very much. I really didn't like them when they put me in an interrogation room. The chairs were uncomfortable. And it smelled funky. Stale, like old sweat, which didn't bode well for me. Also faintly of fast food. Which made me hungry and nauseous at the same time. There was a massive mirror facing me. I thought they only had those in cop shows, but apparently not. I turned my chair to the side to give 'em my gorgeous profile, and shut my eyes.

I must have fallen asleep because when the door opened, my back felt like it was bruised from the chair and my foot was numb and tingly. A cop tossed in a fast food bag. I decided to be cool and sit up slowly. There was a burger and fries inside.

"What? No ketchup?" I asked.

The guy shut the door.

I was starving. I seriously considered eating the burger. But I figured after nearly a decade of not eating beef, it would probably make me sick. So I pulled out the patty and had an awesome mayo and lettuce sandwich. Yum. After two bites, I poured my cold fries onto the bun. Much better.

Some time went by. I didn't know how long. Long enough to know I really didn't like interrogation rooms.

The door opened again. It was a woman this time. She was in a suit. A nice suit. A guy's suit tailored to fit her slightly muscular frame. She was old. Or what I considered old. Maybe in her late forties. Short hair. No makeup.

Smooth. Send in a dyke to get the little dyke to talk. That had to be a new method. How progressive.

"Hello, Vivian. I'm Agent Ogilvy." She sat across from me.

"Cooper," I said.

"Excuse me?"

"My mother is the only one who calls me Vivian."

"All right, Cooper, then." She smiled like we were going to be friends. Bitch. "The boys were wondering what was wrong with the burger? Your friend did the same thing."

"We don't eat beef."

"Ahh. Are you still hungry?" She turned to the mirror and made a gesture.

Was this good cop? I didn't like good cop. I was thinking I really wouldn't like bad cop.

"I don't really care about food right now. I'll grab something once I get the fuck out of here."

"All right. Just answer my questions and that can be arranged. I would like to come to an agreement. You help me, I help you."

"I don't really feel like talking."

"Why not?"

I imitated Reese and glared.

"Your friend Ryan is singing right now." Ogilvy raised her eyebrows as if she had just given me an awesome reason to talk.

I smiled. "I bet he is. How do your guys like the Buddy Holly songbook?"

It was brief. The smallest break in her smiling façade.

I started laughing. "Darlin'"—she really didn't like it when I called her that—"you may as well let us go."

Ogilvy made a sad face. "I don't see that happening anytime soon."

"Sure it will. You haven't charged me with anything. So I'm thinking you can't hold me for that long."

"Would you prefer I charge you?"

"With what?" Not a question I should have asked.

She stared me down. Hard. Fuck. This bitch was good cop and bad cop. Scary.

"I would like you to answer some questions." This was the not good cop asking.

"No shit. I want a lawyer. Then I'll answer your questions."

"All right. That can be arranged." Ogilvy stood. She made a little signal at the mirror again. Guess I wasn't getting any more food.

The door opened and a guy in a suit came in. Same dude who had stared me down on the flight. He was carrying a box.

Ogilvy waited until he set it down. Then she lifted out a laptop. She clicked some shit and turned it to face me. Guard dog pulled out some other shit. My old Chucks in an evidence bag. He set those on the far edge of the table. Then he set out three photos. Mug shots. On the other end of the table, he set five stacks of photos. Each from a different folder.

Ogilvy hit enter on the laptop and they left.

Left me with a video of myself shooting a guy. It was back in Vegas. The parking garage where Vito had tried to kidnap the twins. I'd lost my temper and shot Vito's guy in the knee. Fuck. I couldn't even remember the guy's name.

The video was on loop. I tried to be cool like I didn't give a fuck about the pictures. But I was curious. And if the rest of their evidence against me was half as good as this, I was so fucking screwed.

The mug shots with my shoes were all dudes I had watched Esau kill. I didn't know if that was good or bad. I hadn't killed them. But I'd watched them die. I was guessing the Feds had pulled their blood from the shoes. Why the fuck did I keep those things? What else had they found in the house in Spain?

I decided not to worry about that. They had blood from some dudes who were missing. Esau didn't leave corpses. So the dudes were just missing. Maybe I got in a lot of bar fights. Maybe those guys liked to bare-knuckle box and I had a weird gambling problem. There were a lot of maybes. I'd commit to the lie when I needed to.

The other stacks of photos weren't great either. But they weren't horrible. Alexis DiGiovanni and her merry band of thugs. Also me. I was really happy right then that Alexis managed to stay so far away from her own illegal dealings. By default, the photos only showed us and a bunch of thugs in weird locations. And I was pretty sure they couldn't put me away for having sucky friends.

The video was the worst part. But assault in Vegas. That was like jaywalking anywhere else. Probably only got you a ticket.

Okay, maybe not. But I wasn't going to sweat this shit. Decent lawyer could probably spin it as self-defense.

I was feeling pretty decent about my self-defense, bare-knuckle boxing addiction, bad friends excuse. So good that when Ogilvy and her thug came back in, I smiled at them.

"Ready to let me go?" I asked.

"As soon as we get these questions answered." Ogilvy spun the laptop and did some more clicking. Thug boy packed up the photos. Then he started putting out new ones. Oh great, time for a repeat. This time there were more evidence bags. And they all had bullets and shells. I wasn't liking the look of this shit.

"Why are you showing me this? I'm fucking bored. Where's my lawyer?"

"I'm showing you this to entertain you until your lawyer arrives." Ogilvy smiled. It was a good smile. Mocking and kind of sexy. Which pissed me off even more. "Of course, we can make this all go away if you answer a few questions."

I rolled my eyes. Ogilvy hit enter. They left.

It wasn't a video this time. It was an audio recording of a 911 call. I listened to myself report a body count and a series of GPS coordinates.

I had well and truly fucked myself.

I didn't need to look at the photos. The details of that night were immortalized in my fucking nightmares. I felt a little bad about Vito's guys. We hadn't meant to kill the one who'd bled out. And I'd heard that Gino's shoulder never totally recovered. He still didn't have his full range of motion.

But Tommy I didn't give a shit about. Hell, I was glad I'd killed him. The fucker needed to be put down or locked up.

Not that it mattered. I'd killed two men. Not that they could necessarily link me to them. Maybe I'd just been walking and I'd stumbled across them. Thought it was my civic duty to report it.

No. That sounded thin, even to me.

And if they couldn't pinpoint the actual shooter, they still had three suspects. All of whom were in custody. I couldn't let the twins go down for this shit.

"Hey, Ogilvy," I shouted to no one. "Fuck the lawyer. I'll answer your damn questions."

She kept me waiting. I didn't shout again. I'd made my move. I wasn't going to beg for an audience. Time started doing that weird thing again where I couldn't tell how much of it had passed. When the door finally opened, I had to fight every instinct that told me to run, to fight my way out of there.

"You said you wanted to speak with me?" Ogilvy asked.

"Yeah, I'll answer your questions."

She smiled. One of her minions came in and packed away the evidence. Then left me in that airless room with her.

Ogilvy sat down. Folded her hands on the table. "I would like you to tell me everything there is to know about the DiGiovanni family."

"That's it?"

"Yes."

"You'll let me go?"

"I didn't say that."

Bitch. "Yeah, you did. I answer your questions I get to leave."

"If you only answer my questions, then I can arrange for some leniency in your case."

"Blow me." I crossed my arms, shut my eyes, and reclined in my chair.

"The DiGiovannis want you dead, don't they?"

"The DiGiovannis want everyone dead." I didn't bother opening my eyes. This wasn't earth shattering information.

"If we arrest you, put you in lockup, how long do you think you'll last? Will you even make it to trial?"

I opened my eyes but didn't sit up. "Have you seen this face? I'm fucking hot. Someone will want to keep me alive."

"That's it? Pretty people get farther in life?"

"It's worked so far." I was bluffing. Obviously. I didn't really have much leverage. Just arrogance and a pretty face. But I was thinking Ogilvy wanted something else from me. Whatever it was, I would give it up.

"I can arrange to make this all go away, but I'll need more than information."

"Darlin', just tell me what you want," I said with a sigh.

"I want to put the DiGiovannis out of business. If the information that you have is enough—which I doubt—then you can go. But if I need more, then I want you to go back to the DiGiovannis. Gain their trust. And bring me enough to take them down."

I thought about that. There was only one slight problem. "I go back, Vito will kill me."

"Not if we give you something to make them trust you."

"There's nothing that will make them trust me," I said.

"Are you aware that Lawrence DiGiovanni has put a contract on his grandson's head?" she asked.

"Not really surprising. He hates Ryan."

"All we need to do is release reports that Ryan has been killed and that you are sought for questioning. You go to the don and demand payment."

"You're fucking insane," I said.

Ogilvy smiled. "What do you say?"

"I want immunity."

"That can be arranged."

"And I want to see Reese and Ryan." Even though Reese would probably kick my ass.

"I'll think about it." Bitch.

"They get immunity too." I thought about that, then added, "For anything they might have inadvertently done."

"That's reasonable."

I reached across the table and offered my hand. I didn't know if she had any honor, but I did. It was all I could offer. Ogilvy shook my hand.

What the fuck did I just get myself into?

CHAPTER SEVENTEEN

A cop led me into a conference room of sorts. Reese and Ryan were already seated. Ogilvy and three other Feds sat across from them.

"Fuck." Ryan jumped out of his seat to hug me, but Reese moved faster.

I wrapped my arms around Reese, and Ryan wrapped his arms around both of us.

"Did they give you guys immunity?" I whispered.

"Yeah," Reese said. Ryan nodded.

"Let's do this."

We let go, but as soon as we sat down, they each grabbed one of my hands.

"Are we ready?" Ogilvy asked.

"Yep," I said. The twins nodded.

"This is Agent Eudora." Ogilvy pointed to the only other chick Fed. She was kinda hot in that angry, straight girl way. Like she knew more than she was supposed to about the world. "And Agents Goldberg and Florence." The two guys. Goldberg was big and muscular, but pretty. As if he thought brawn might make up for having girly eyes. And Florence was homely, but he was the only one who smiled at us. It was a reserved smile, but at least it was a kind one.

All of them had pads of paper to take notes, which seemed a little pointless because they were videotaping the interview.

"Please, state your names for the record," Eudora said.

I was feeling less than forthcoming so I smiled and said, "I'm Cameron Roberts. And of course you know Blair Powell." I nodded at Reese. Both Reese and Ryan started laughing so hard they nearly fell out of their chairs. "And Mac Phillips." I nodded at Ryan. He stopped laughing.

"Hey, I wanna be Stark. Way more badass."

"Mac's kind of badass," Reese said.

"Stark is way more badass, though," Ryan said.

The agents looked really not amused.

"I'm sorry, I'm sorry," I said. "This is Lord Henry Wotton." I nodded at Ryan. "And Basil Hallward." Reese. "And I'm Dorian Gray."

Ryan started howling again.

Reese smacked me with the back of her free hand. "Hey, that means you kill me. Jerk."

"Oh, my bad."

"May I remind the three of you about the seriousness of this situation?" Ogilvy said.

I tried to force my face to make a serious expression. It didn't work. Ryan failed also.

"Okay, we're sorry," Reese said. "For the record…" The agents seemed to lean forward collectively. Dumbasses. "I'm Stella, this is my husband Stanley Kowalski, and my sister, Blanche Dubois."

"Great, now I'm a rapist too," I said. Ryan giggled.

Ogilvy stood. "This is not a joke. If you refuse to help us, you will be in violation of the immunity agreement that all of you signed. And I will take pleasure in booking you myself." She wasn't shouting. She didn't need to. There was something terrifying and honest in her gaze.

I sighed. Ryan did too. Reese glared.

"My name is Vivian Cooper."

"I'm Ryan DiGiovanni."

"Reese DiGiovanni."

I was a little surprised that Reese and Ryan said their own names instead of each other's.

The interview got really fucking boring after that. Ogilvy had a big board with pictures of the DiGiovanni club. We got to go through the whole thing so Reese and Ryan could clarify familial connections. Then the Feds wanted to know all about DiGiovanni's lieutenants. He had three: Michael Acconci, Vito Serra, and Alexis DiGiovanni. I'd never heard of Acconci. And all Reese and Ryan knew was that he was like a cousin removed about four times.

We moved on to Vito. It wasn't very exciting. Reese and I gave our portrait of him. Psycho, control issues, blah, blah.

We learned a few things the Feds knew that we didn't. His wife Madge had given birth to two kids way before Reese and Ryan were born. Both the babies died before they were a year old. Vito started moving up the ranks of the DiGiovannis really fast after that. I guess if you can't have kids you throw yourself into work. I didn't know why the Feds knew that. And I really didn't get why that was relevant.

I told the Feds that Madge was well aware of her husband's business dealings. They got all excited, but then I told them she would never turn on him. Less excited.

We were happy to testify to Vito's multiple attempted kidnappings of the twins. And his threat to murder Ryan. But that didn't seem to rock anyone's world. In fact, they seemed a little bored. Maybe it was because they already had a video of Vito kidnapping someone at gunpoint. And that video ended with me shooting Vito's assistant.

We took a fifteen-minute break. I decided I should really take up smoking. Ryan looked like he wanted his own brand of cigarette. Tough.

The rest of the morning was dedicated to Alexis DiGiovanni. Apparently, she was a big deal or something.

I told them about the night I'd been stabbed. They found that very, very interesting. But they were pretty pissed that I couldn't pinpoint which of Alexis's men had actually killed someone. But having a witness inside a massacre was gold.

Beyond that, I only had one thing to contribute. "Alexis is a fucking sociopath."

Florence shot Ogilvy a pointed look.

"Yes, we've considered that," Ogilvy said diplomatically.

"No, really. Psychotic motherfucker," I said.

"Total cunt too," Reese said.

"For real. Major asshole. And she's crazy as fuck," Ryan said.

"She also has a very shrewd business sense," Ogilvy said. "Florence is our Alexis expert. So I'll let him give you the background that we know. Hopefully, you can fill in a few details."

"Thank you." Florence nodded to Ogilvy. "As you know, Alexis comes from a long line of—"

"Dude, are you really going to give us our family history?" Ryan asked. He was bored. Time to pick a fight.

"Sorry, I was going to say that Alexis has deviated quite a bit from the way her predecessors conducted business," Florence said.

"Hmm." Reese cocked her head to the side.

"What?" I asked her.

"He's right. She broke all the rules."

"Whoa. Yeah." Ryan nodded. "Tricky bitch."

"What do you guys mean?" I asked.

"Our family runs drugs. Our great-grandfather got his start during prohibition. When prohibition ended, he used the contacts he had to expand into the drug business. The DiGiovannis were small time then, but by the sixties, my grandfather had made a name for himself. But it was always in drugs." Reese shook her head.

I stared at Reese. Damn, the girl could write a history book on her family.

"But now we run guns, girls, and who knows what the fuck else," Ryan said. "Douche bag fucking cunt."

"That doesn't even make sense," I said.

"I know. That's the problem. Alexis has moved into territory that doesn't belong to us," Reese said.

"No. Douche bag fucking cunt. Is she a cunt who's also a douche bag? Or is she a douche bag who fucks cunts? Wait. Maybe that would make sense."

"Coop." Ryan.

"Seriously, Cooper." Reese.

"Let's focus." Ogilvy.

"Please." Florence.

"Sorry," I said.

"Alexis has moved into new territory, as you say." Agent Florence tried to get the conversation back on track.

"But she managed to do it without incurring the wrath of those who own the territory," Goldberg said.

"How?" Reese asked.

"Planning," Florence said.

"No shit," I said.

"I mean, since she was a teenager, at least in her early twenties."

"How do you know?" Reese asked.

"In college she took Russian and Ukrainian. She also appears to have a working knowledge of a handful of other Eastern European languages. About ten years ago, in her early twenties, she made friends with the Russians. She gained their trust, did very civil business with them."

"But she barely works with the Russians now. I mean, I went to a lot of meetings with her where they spoke Russian, but I always got the sense that they were working for her," I said.

Agent Florence wrote that down. Must have been interesting. "We thought as much."

Eudora spoke up. "There was an incident about six years ago. We never got all of the details, but the head of the local Russian mob and all of his lieutenants were at a private party. The food was poisoned. Eight men dead. As well as a dog. We never got any leads."

"How do you not get any leads when eight dudes are killed?" I asked.

Eudora got even angrier looking than before. "Very few witnesses. All of whom either disappeared or turned up dead. And the little evidence we did have all pointed to a different, much smaller crime family. Most of them are still serving time for the killings. Those who aren't in prison are dead as well."

"Alexis took out the competition in one fell swoop. Well, we believe it was Alexis. She was vacationing in the Caribbean at the time," Florence said.

"Your cousin is fucking crazy," I told the twins.

"Let's pretend we're not related to that bitch," Reese said.

"Totally," Ryan said.

I was really not looking forward to going back to face Alexis DiGiovanni again.

❖

We broke for lunch. Goldberg actually asked what we wanted this time. It was the first real meal I'd had in two days. It was the best meal of my life.

The rest of the afternoon was a detailed look at the guys from the morning. That evening was dedicated to Alexis. Again. I was so tired of that chick. What the Feds really wanted was some sort of confession. They had circumstantial evidence to tie her to a handful of crimes. If we could manage a little more evidence on any of those crimes, it would be enough to put her away.

Lawrence DiGiovanni was only afforded an hour. I was pretty sure the Feds knew they would never take the don down. So they weren't even trying. Besides, it sounded like he wasn't running the show much anymore. His lieutenants handled the business. Actually, Alexis handled the business. The don was just there for ring kissing. Someone had to wear it.

I knew it was going to be a long-ass night when I said something that made all the agents tense up and made Reese and Ryan look at me funny.

"When are we going to be done here? This isn't getting your investigation anywhere so I know you're sending my ass to Chicago. I'm tired of waiting." That was when the room went still.

"Chicago?" Reese asked.

"Uhh, yeah. We haven't given them any earth shattering information. And that was the agreement." I realized as I was saying it that Ogilvy hadn't shared the entire agreement with Reese and Ryan. This was going to be bad.

"The agreement was information for immunity," Reese said. She looked at me, then Ogilvy, then back to me.

"You didn't tell them about the deal you offered me?" I asked Ogilvy.

"Why would I?" she asked.

"What the fuck is going on?" Ryan asked.

"The deal Ogilvy offered me was contingent on enough information to arrest the don's lieutenants. Alexis and Vito would be ideal, but Acconci would work also."

"Shut the fuck up." Reese.

"Stupid bitch." Ryan. It was directed at Ogilvy, not me. "You're going to get Coop killed."

"She is not going to Chicago. They'll kill her." Reese.

Ogilvy used the same line on them that she used on me. "Are you aware that the don put out a contract on Ryan?"

Ryan laughed. "I'm not surprised."

"What the fuck?" Reese screamed. "We were fine. We were far away from those assholes and you dragged us back here. What happens when they realize we are in the country? They will kill Ryan and probably Coop for good measure."

"Reese." I put my hand on the back of her neck. "It's okay."

"No, it's fucking not." She shrugged my hand off.

"I didn't have much of a choice. If they arrest me, I'll get killed in prison. It won't take Vito long. This way I at least have a chance."

"What fucking chance? Please don't kill me, let's be friends. Oh, and can I please have some incriminating evidence?" She had a point.

"Yeah," Ryan said.

"We aren't going to send her in with nothing," Ogilvy said.

"Oh, yeah. Put a wire on her too. That will help." Reese crossed her arms and turned away.

"We're going to release reports that Ryan has been killed. Cooper will go to the don and demand payment. It will build trust and demonstrate loyalty," Ogilvy said.

The room went silent for an entire minute.

"Well, fuck me," Ryan said.

"If she dies, I'll fucking bury all of you," Reese said.

She was implying their credibility and jobs. But I was pretty sure that if I died she would actually bury all of them. Like six feet under.

"Noted." Ogilvy.

❖

"How could you not tell me?" Reese asked.

We were in a hotel suite. It was a huge improvement from the jail they'd been holding us in. Even if there was an FBI agent stationed in the main room.

"Seriously, Coop," Ryan said.

"I swear, I thought you knew." I sat on the bed. Ryan sat next to me and crossed his legs. Reese stayed standing.

"Why the hell would we agree to that?" Reese asked.

"I don't know. It's the best option."

"Not if they kill you." Somehow, Reese managed to scream under her breath. Wouldn't want the nice Fed to come in here.

"They know I killed Tommy and that other guy in Vegas," I whispered. "They'll send my ass to prison. Even if Vito doesn't have me killed in there, I'm not going to last long."

"Fuck this. Let's get out of here." Reese marched to the window. It was sealed. "Damn it."

"Babe, we're on like the twentieth floor," I said.

"I'll make it work." Reese tried to open the window that didn't open.

Ryan started laughing. "Reese, chill."

"Don't tell me to fucking chill." She put her shoulder to the window and pushed.

"Peanut butter, it's not happening." I walked over and pulled her away from the window. "Besides, where would we go? We don't have passports or money. Or clothes, even."

"So what? We stay here and wait until they ship you off for your death sentence? Fuck that."

"Vito isn't going to kill me," I lied. I didn't know if he was going to kill me. It was about sixty-forty at this point. But forty percent chance of not dying was looking pretty good.

"She's right," Ryan said.

"How the hell would you know?" Reese asked.

"You didn't see him in that warehouse. When Coop started to cut me loose, Vito looked like he'd lost his favorite puppy."

"So?" Reese asked.

"So he likes Coop. A lot. He was really upset that she chose me over him. This way he'll think she finally chose him."

"So we're pretty much banking on Vito's sentimentality. I'm so reassured. Thanks."

"Seriously. Alexis told me once that Vito considered me his kid or something. I mean, he's obviously deranged, but I think he will want to believe that I chose him," I said.

"I'm still not sold on this shit." Reese.

"For real." Ryan.

"But we agree it's the only viable option, right?" I asked.

"Whatever." Ryan.

"Yeah." Reese.

"Any chance we can go to sleep now? I really want to sleep in a real bed."

Reese nodded and kicked off her shoes. "Are you sleeping in here or your own room?" she asked Ryan.

"I don't know," he said.

"Go to your own room."

"Why?"

"Because I'm about to strip."

"Whoa. Going. Chill." Ryan put one hand over his eyes and held the other out in front of himself. "Night, kids. No loud sex. It's creepy and I don't like the look of that Fed."

Reese and I grinned but managed to keep from laughing out loud. Ryan was a freak.

CHAPTER EIGHTEEN

The story broke when I was in the air. When I got off the plane at O'Hare, it seemed like my face was plastered on half the TVs. Thankfully, Americans don't give a shit about the news, so no one was paying attention. Also, the Feds had released my blond, green-eyed passport photo. No one noticed me with my boring brown hair.

I caught a cab and had the guy drop me about a mile from Vito's house. It was early evening. Still hot as fuck. The Feds had wired up a leather jacket. It had video through one of the buttons on the collar. A different button was a mic. All the wires were sewn to the seams inside the lining. I'd tried to find them, but I couldn't. Neither could Reese and Ryan. Good enough for me. The problem was, it was way too fucking hot to wear a leather jacket.

I also had a disposable cell phone. The kind that someone on the run would buy for twenty bucks in a drug store. The kind I'd been carrying for two years. It was wired too. Just audio. And GPS. I knew there were about five Feds and twenty local cops glued to my ass monitoring the wires, but I couldn't see them. Hopefully, Vito wouldn't be able to either.

I wanted to linger outside of Vito's house. Take a moment to breathe before walking into a death trap. But I was playing the part of nervous fugitive so I went up and knocked on the door.

Madge opened it. She made an angry face. And her face was already ugly as fuck so it wasn't a good look.

"Hey."

"Get in here, now." To facilitate my entry, Madge grabbed the strap of my backpack and hauled me inside.

"I...I didn't know where else to go."

Madge didn't say anything. And she didn't let go of my backpack either. She dragged me upstairs to one of the guest bedrooms and made me sit on the bed.

"Stay."

I stayed. "I'm sorry. I know you guys don't want me around, but—"

"Be quiet." Madge pulled out her cell phone and dialed Vito. Or I assumed she was calling Vito. "Your bastard son just showed up here."

A code. This one didn't require an answer key.

Madge ended the call. "Strip."

"Huh?"

"I can search you, or Vito can. You can decide."

I glared at her, but it didn't seem like she was going to let this one go. So I threw my backpack at her feet. The jacket tumbled out of the straps. Then I yanked off my shoes and tossed those to her. My T-shirt was sweaty. I hoped it grossed her out. Same with my socks. I emptied the pockets of my jeans onto the bed before dropping my pants and kicking those to her.

"Happy?" I asked.

"Underwear too," was her response.

I scowled and took off my boxer briefs. I threw them at her. She caught them, held them up for inspection, then dropped them on the floor. She could have given them back, but no. I had to stand there buck-ass naked while she very thoroughly searched my clothing, felt the seams of my jeans and jacket, took the lining and laces out of my new Chucks, upended my backpack and combed the contents, took the battery out of my cheap phone, and finally made me spin in a circle to make sure there wasn't a wire taped anywhere on my body.

It was humiliating. Which was exactly what she wanted it to be.

"You broke his heart when you left," she said.

"That's dumb. I've already got a father."

"Get dressed. I can't look at you anymore."

Gee, and I was so enjoying standing here naked. I pulled on my clothes, put my wallet and cell back in my pocket, and sat on the bed.

"So what now?" I asked.

"Are you hungry?" She sounded like she was being nice, but the face was still angry.

"Starving."

"Come on."

I followed Madge back downstairs. She pointed at the kitchen table. I sat down. Then she brought me a beer—they kept them in the fridge for company—and pulled out the makings of a sandwich. I remembered why I liked Madge.

A year and a half had gone by since I'd been in this house. But Madge remembered that I liked turkey and Swiss. No tomato. Avocado, onion, and lettuce. Pepper, but no salt. She used the good mustard, the kind reserved for Vito, and not offered to anyone else. That meant she still liked me. She even found a stockpile of Cheetos. I also warranted a scoop of her homemade potato salad. Maybe this undercover thing wouldn't be so bad.

A door slammed somewhere.

"Where the hell is she?" Vito shouted.

"If you're gonna kill me, can I finish this sandwich first?" I shouted back.

Vito stomped into the kitchen. Madge set a second sandwich on the table. Then gave Vito a look that made him sit down. He ate the first half of his sandwich without breaking the death stare he was giving me. For the second half he looked everywhere except at me.

When we were done eating, Vito stood and grabbed the collar of my shirt. I snagged my beer and let him drag me to my feet.

"Wait," Madge said.

"Not now." Vito twisted my shirt so it was choking me a little.

"You need to know—"

"Not now!" Vito hauled me into the study. "What the hell are you doing here?"

"Where the hell else am I going to go?"

"I don't care where you go."

"I got nothing, Vito."

"That is not my problem."

"Just help me out a little, okay? I need somewhere to hide. I need some way across the border. Help me, please," I was begging. I was giving him the power. He liked power.

"No. You made your choice. The DiGiovannis will not help you. Now get out of my house." Vito pointed toward the door.

"Fine. Pay me and I'll go." I didn't stand. I just took a drink of my beer.

"Pay you? Pay you what?"

"Don't play dumb. It was a stupid fucking accident, but I still deserve to get paid. You owe me that at least."

"What the hell are you talking about?"

For a moment, I thought he was just covering his ass. It's not a good idea to admit that your associates put a contract on someone. But then I realized that he actually didn't know.

"Oh my God."

"What?"

"You don't know."

"I don't know what?"

And that was when his phone rang. He grunted some mono-syllabic words, glared at me, grunted some more, then hung up.

"Stay here."

I waited all of sixty seconds before following him to the TV.

"...crime of passion. The agents in charge of the investigation report only that the murder was brutal, the victim stabbed half a dozen times, before the suspect fled the scene. The suspect, Vivian Cooper, aka Cooper Wells, is thought to be armed and should be considered dangerous. Reese DiGiovanni, the victim's sister, is also sought for questioning; however, the police maintain that she is not a suspect in this case."

Vito turned off the TV and slowly turned to look at me.

"You killed Ryan."

I spun and walked back to the kitchen. I left my empty beer bottle by the sink and grabbed a fresh one. After a fruitless two-minute search for a bottle opener, I sat cross-legged on the floor, and stared at the beer that I couldn't open. Vito took the bottle out of my hands, popped the top with an opener that was stuck to the side of the fridge, and handed it back. I drank half. Burped. Hiccupped.

"She was going to leave me," I told my beer.

"Reese?" Vito asked.

"Yeah. I was going to propose and she decided to leave me. I bought a ring and everything. When I showed Ryan, he told me not to do it. The bastard knew. He knew she was going to leave me. They were going to take off with the money and leave me with nothing. After all I fucking did for them." I looked up at Vito. "After all I fucking did for them," I shouted. "Now I got nothing."

"Come on." Vito held out his hand. I took it and let him pull me to my feet. "Do you have a change of clothes? We are going to see someone."

"I have a clean T-shirt." I shrugged.

"Okay, go change." Vito tried to take the beer, but I wouldn't give it up.

I went upstairs, changed into a less funky shirt, and put my shoes back on. I remembered to grab the jacket. Hopefully, it would cool down enough for me to wear it.

Vito was waiting downstairs. He was on his phone. I waited until he ended the call. He clapped a hand on my shoulder and led me out to the car.

I realized as I climbed in the passenger seat that this might be my last car ride. Which was fucking depressing so I ignored that particular thought. Vito was a pretty easy guy to read. When he was pissed, he let you know. And when he was feeling kind, he showed it. He had opened my beer. That was nice Vito. Nice Vito didn't want to kill me.

I was placing all my bets on someone opening a beer. Not a great move.

I didn't pay much attention to where we were driving until I realized that we were in a familiar neighborhood. Alexis's neighborhood.

"What the fuck, man?"

"Excuse me?" Vito asked.

"You're taking me to Alexis. She will kill my ass for sure."

"Alex won't kill you. She may not like you very much, but she isn't going to kill you."

"The bitch is psycho," I said.

"Hey, watch your tongue. She could have killed you a hundred times and she didn't."

"Great, that makes me feel all better." I rolled my eyes. "If I die, it's your damn fault."

"Calm down." Vito parked in front of Alexis's house.

"I'm having trouble staying calm in general. This is not helping."

Vito got out of the car and waited for me on the sidewalk. Reluctantly, I got out. For good measure, I pulled on my jacket. It was getting dark. Good enough. By the time we got to the door Alexis was waiting. She looked not happy. We followed her inside. Sal and Bobby were waiting inside. So was the don. Shit. Fuck.

DiGiovanni, Alexis, and Vito went into another room, leaving me with two angry looking thugs.

"Hey, guys."

Nothing. Sal rubbed his shaved head. Bobby made absolutely no expression. This was going to be fun.

"You want something to drink?" I turned to go into the kitchen.

"Sit down," Sal said.

"Fine." I fell onto the couch. As far as they knew, I'd done them a massive favor. They could at least be cool about it.

We spent an awesome ten minutes in silence. Sal and Bobby were trying to have a staring contest with me. I made just enough eye contact for them to know I was aware of it, then pointedly, disinterestedly, looked away.

When the don and his lieutenants returned, Sal and Bobby sat up straighter. I did not.

"Cooper," the don said.

"Mr. DiGiovanni." I figured if we were saying names.

"I understand that I owe you a debt of gratitude."

"Whatever."

He stepped closer to me. From behind him, Vito gave me a hard look that made me get off my ass. As I stood, the don held out his hand. I shook it. He smelled like lavender, but with something musky underneath it. And cigarettes. The faintest aroma of smoke clung to him. My grandfather didn't smell like this at all. He smelled like soap and newsprint and pine trees. I remembered sitting on my grandpa's lap when I was a kid. He was always so warm. And he would always adjust his newspaper or book or whatever he was reading so he could see the pages and still have room for me.

Reese and Ryan didn't talk about their grandfather much. From what I'd heard about him, I didn't blame them. He was angry and self-obsessed and an all-around arrogant douche bag. And a fucking tool. A tool who smelled like lavender. Very odd.

The don gestured to Alexis who handed him a small duffle bag. Then he gave me the duffle. It was lightweight and a little bulky. Cash.

"For taking care of the problem," he said.

"Huh?"

"My bastard of a grandson. Thank you for taking care of him."

I looked in the bag and estimated. "Killing your grandson is only worth ten grand? So you're cheap, in addition to being an asshole."

He laughed. "You're right, Vito. She is a spitfire." Vito laughed too, but I could tell he was nervous.

"Alexis and the boys will escort you to a safe house. In a few days, we will have arranged for new identification and safe passage to Canada." He expected me to fall at his feet and thank him. Fat fucking chance.

"Hell the fuck no."

"Excuse me?" People probably didn't tell him no very often.

"You leave me alone with Alexis and her boys"— I nodded in their hostile direction—"and I'll be dead in an hour."

Alexis smiled. "I have assured my uncle that I won't kill you unless he tells me to."

"Comforting."

"Cooper, this is the safest option for you. On the street it will only be a matter of time until you are arrested."

Not exactly true. But he didn't need to know that a small faction of Chicago's finest were trailing my ass with the Feds to make a fake arrest if this thing went south. More importantly, I hadn't gotten enough information. Unless being an evil asshole was a crime. Which totally should have been.

I guess I was too quiet for too long because Vito said, "Cooper?"

"What?" I jerked a little when he said my name.

"Are you all right?"

"Uhh, yeah. I was trying to think of decent leverage to keep me alive, but I got nothing. So, please don't kill me?" I realized after I said it that it was exactly what Reese had said. She was smart. Hopefully, she wasn't prophetic.

The don leaned back and stared at me. He seemed to be vacillating between amused and disturbed. I'm not sure which emotion won because he blinked, shook his head a little, and stepped back.

"I recommend South America. You will like it. Or find a small island that does not extradite criminals. Good luck, Cooper." He shook my hand a final time, then left faster than someone of his age should have been able to.

"Tell me when the car is ready." Alexis spun on her heel and left the room.

Sal nodded in my direction. I followed him.

The safe house they took me to was in a suburban neighborhood outside the city limits. It looked like a lot of other suburban neighborhoods I'd been in. Sal pulled the town car into a garage. When the big door finished closing, Alexis let me climb off the floor where I'd been hiding.

Sal led me inside the house. I was given a room on the second floor and told to keep away from the windows. Bobby took the room across the hall. Sal took the one next to mine. Alexis claimed the master bedroom, obviously. But she left soon after we arrived. Bobby went out to get us some dinner.

We tried to watch TV, but the news kept mentioning me and that was weird. I gave up and went to bed. Which just gave me time to stare at the ceiling and think. Not a good idea. But it was better than sitting between two dudes who wanted to kill me. I heard Bobby go into his room around eleven. Sal waited until Alexis came back before going to bed as well.

I tried to sleep, but that's a hard thing to do when there are people waiting to kill you. It seemed that Alexis had killed a number of people her uncle did not tell her to kill. Why would I be any different?

That was the lovely thought I fell asleep to.

❖

The next morning, I fell out of bed and pulled my jeans back on. I remembered at the last second to grab my phone and pocket it. Wouldn't want to forget my wire.

Bobby had retrieved my backpack from Vito's. But I hadn't packed much so I only had one more clean T-shirt. I wasn't going to waste it when this one only had half a day and a night on it. I wasn't too concerned with appearances.

There was coffee brewed downstairs. After opening every cabinet in the kitchen, I found the mugs. Fortified against everything except bullets, I went to find my keepers. Or guards. Or saviors. I wasn't sure yet.

Bobby and Sal were playing Xbox. Cards were so passé. They barely acknowledged me, which I was fine with.

"Am I allowed to go out in the backyard?"

Bobby grunted.

"Keep the door open so we can hear you. And don't let the neighbors see you. So no looking over the fence or anything," Sal said.

I saluted them with my coffee and went out back.

It was nice out. Warm, not hot. Kind of sticky, but I didn't mind it. I'd grown up in dry, hot heat. Sacramento was like that. So humidity was a novelty to me instead of straight up annoying.

I wondered where Alexis was. Only briefly. Then I realized that if she wasn't giving me shit or beating the crap out of me, I was happy. Of course, the more she gave me shit, the easier it would be to piss her off and make her slip. If I could just get her to say something stupid, then I could get the fuck out of here. Go home, wherever that was. I'd never have to see these assholes again. Except maybe in court. That would be ideal. Actually, it would be ideal if they all just killed each other.

The only good thing this family had ever done was make Reese and Ryan. I'd thought once that the twins were my salvation. Maybe they were. In a weird, codependent sort of way. But like a healthy codependence. It was a little sad that the don never realized that the twins could save him too. Carry on a legacy that wasn't built on hatred and fear.

That was his legacy. Alexis, in her depravity, was exactly the legacy he had created. Maybe that would be his undoing. If you build your life, your world on tradition, at some point all you're left with is a dying regime. Alexis had changed the game, expanded it, but her foundation was crumbling. It didn't matter how much she updated it. Something, somewhere was going to break.

I realized then, in that sunny moment on the porch of a mob safe house, that I had to win. Not just for my safety or that of the people I loved, but because the DiGiovannis needed to be taken down. Maybe some new crime family would take their place. I couldn't control that. But this was something I could control. Maybe they would kill me. Maybe I'd be a footnote in Ogilvy's case file. But I would do everything I could to change the outcome of this contest. Simply because it was the right thing to do.

Ryan would probably knock up some girl. Maybe one day I would knock up Reese. And maybe my actions would make this world a safer place for them to grown up in. All I had to do was survive the next week.

CHAPTER NINETEEN

A door inside slammed. I knew somehow that it was Alexis. She stopped and spoke with Sal and Bobby. I could hear their voices, but I couldn't really hear what they were saying. I didn't give a fuck either. I just drank my coffee and enjoyed the sunshine.

I wondered where Reese and Ryan were. Probably in that same hotel room driving each other and all the Feds crazy. Thinking about them must have made me reach for my necklace because, when Alexis stormed outside, she found me dragging the charm back and forth across the chain. She stared at the necklace and looked like she might hurl. For a devious bitch, she was surprisingly bad at hiding certain reactions.

"I thought you should know that you'll be out of here in two days," she said.

"Okay."

"Shouldn't you be happy?"

I shrugged. "I find very little to be happy about."

Alexis rolled her eyes. "He was a useless little shit. Let it go." My hands started to shake. I tried to hide the tremble, but she saw it. "Oh God. Why did you even like him? He was a pansy ass stoner. He didn't have a single redeeming quality."

"Fuck you." I stood to go inside.

"What's the matter, Cooper? Don't like hearing about how pathetic your little friends were?" She was trying to piss me off. Hell, if she wanted to pick a fight I was cool with that.

I spun back to face her. "They weren't just my friends. They were my family. They were my whole fucking world."

Alexis laughed. "What a sad little world. Trust me. You did us all a favor. The only thing you could have done better was kill Reese too."

I was suddenly furious. "Shut the fuck up. I don't want to hear any more of your shit."

"Maybe I should just do you a favor and kill Reese myself."

I bitch-slapped her. Hard. I'd like to say I wasn't proud of slapping Alexis. Violence wouldn't solve my problems. But it was one of the most satisfying things I'd ever done.

In an instant, Sal had me locked in an iron grip. I didn't know where he had come from, or how he had gotten there so fast. I decided not to fight his hold. Wouldn't get me anywhere.

Alexis stared at me with something icy and terrifying in her gaze. Every inch of me was suddenly very, very cold. She slid close to me. I started to squirm in Sal's grip. I didn't know what was coming, but I knew it was bad. Alexis twined her fingers into my hair and yanked until my ear was pressed to her lips.

I expected to her whisper. She didn't. She didn't yell either. I think she just wanted to touch me as she delivered her threat. As if forced intimacy would make it more threatening. It did. "You pull that shit again and I will kill your precious Reese." With every sentence, she tugged on my hair. "I'll get off on it." I tilted my head to take off the pressure. "I'll track her down and watch her die." She pulled hard enough to bring tears to my eyes. "Just like I did to her mother."

I was suddenly filled with a sort of pure happiness. Followed by utter panic. Alexis had just told me she was a murder. Would that be enough to put her away? Was she making shit up just to get to me? Would I live to testify?

I didn't know.

Almost as an afterthought, I realized that Alexis had killed Carissa. That the warm, vibrant woman who had taught me to swim, and played endless games of hide-and-seek, and given me hugs when I fell was deliberately taken by the fucker standing in front of me.

All of my quips and clever threats escaped me. I felt such emptiness that I couldn't breathe. I went completely slack. Sal let go of me and I crumpled to the ground. They left me like that.

❖

Bobby got takeout for lunch. I couldn't eat. I didn't try. I just sat outside, wishing I could run away. When I had enough, would the Feds pull me? Why hadn't they done so already? Maybe Alexis's confession hadn't been enough. Maybe there wasn't evidence to back it up. Maybe someone else had killed Carissa. Maybe no one was even monitoring my wire.

That night I couldn't sleep either. But when I finally crashed, I crashed hard. Blissful, dark sleep. That was probably why I didn't notice Alexis coming into my room. It wasn't until the next morning that I realized that something was off. Literally.

I rolled over, sat up. And something was missing. A slight weight on my chest. Its comfort had followed me from Vegas to Spain. My hand went to my throat, as if the act of reaching for it might bring it back. It didn't. The necklace was gone. I didn't know how she had managed to get it off me while I was sleeping, but I knew Alexis had taken it. Why would Sal or Bobby have any use for it, any need? But Alexis required a trophy of some sort. A tie to her family. A severing of my own tie to her family.

But that St. Christopher was mine. And I was getting it back. I was so pissed about what she took, I didn't even think about what else she might have done.

I ran downstairs. "Alexis!" No response. "Alexis, where the fuck are you?"

"She went out." Sal met me at the bottom of the stairs.

"Get her back here. Now."

"She'll be back," he said.

"Now, God damn it."

"Sorry." He walked away.

I realized I didn't have my phone. Or pants. So I booked it back to my room. I punched in Vito's number with one hand and pulled on my jeans with the other.

"Hello?"

"It's me."

"Why are you calling me?" he asked. At least he recognized my voice.

"Alexis took my St. Christopher. I want it back. Fucking now."

"Why would she do that?"

"You really want me to speculate on that?" I asked.

"No. I'll make some calls. Stay there." And he hung up.

He sounded pissed. It was probably stupid to call him. But he was my best chance. And I was getting that necklace back.

Alexis was a stupid motherfucker.

❖

It was late when Vito finally showed up. Well past dark. He was alone.

"Come with me," was all he said.

I didn't hesitate. Just grabbed my jacket and followed him. Probably shouldn't have. If a mobster orders you to do something, do the opposite. Also, run.

The car ride was oppressively silent. We didn't go to Alexis's house like I expected. We ended up somewhere downtown. It was Thursday night. Warm enough and close enough to the weekend to be busy. People were out. Going to dinner. Hitting the clubs. I remembered being one of those people. Simple, in a way. Unencumbered. I didn't want the weight I now carried. Like some sort of grotesque interpretation of adulthood.

Instead, I was here. With Vito. Wearing two wires and praying that this time, this conversation, would be enough to put him away, would be enough to keep the twins and me safe.

Vito pulled into a parking garage and drove to the top floor. It was empty. Except for two cars filled with Alexis and Vito's guys. Bad sign.

"Uhh, Vito, what the hell is going on? Why are Lorenzo, T, and Georgie here? And why did Bobby and Sal and Alexis meet us? Why didn't they all just go to the safe house?"

I didn't need to list off all their names. And I had a decent idea of why we were there. I wasn't going to live through this night. Unless the Feds were listening to my list and following my GPS. They needed to haul ass, because no one else was coming to save me.

Vito didn't answer me. Instead, he carefully pulled the car in next to the others so they formed a loose triangle. They thought I was going to run. They were right. I tried to open the door before Vito stopped, but the locks were engaged. We stopped. Bobby waited until Vito popped the lock and opened my door. He hauled me out with an iron grip on my arm.

"What the fuck, man? Let me go," I shouted. Where the fuck were the Feds?

Bobby put his hand over my mouth and held tight. Georgie yanked my jacket down my arm. Bobby pulled me back against his chest so I couldn't get away while Georgie worked the jacket off my other arm. I squirmed and twisted and kicked, but Bobby was bigger than me. Way bigger. Alexis sauntered over and patted down my pockets. She took out my cell phone and handed it to Georgie. He walked to the edge of the building and tossed the jacket and phone over the chest high cement wall. Bobby let me go.

"What the fuck?" I shoved Alexis out of the way and ran to the edge. I planted my hands and hauled myself up to look over. The wires were gone. Five useless stories below me. "God fucking damn it. Why the fuck did you do that?" I shouted. There were people down there. Maybe they could help me. "Help. Please I'm being—" I was going to say kidnapped. It felt dramatic, but it was true. I didn't get to finish though because Bobby and Georgie grabbed me and pulled me from the ledge. Bobby clapped his hand back over my mouth. They carried me back to cars and set me down.

"You walked into my house with a wire," Vito said.

"What the fuck did you expect me to do?" I asked.

Vito punched me. In the stomach. I doubled over. Shit. I'd been here before. It wasn't pretty. But maybe if I took the beating, it would give the Feds time to show up and arrest their asses.

"You stupid bitch." Alexis.

The second I straightened, she punched me in the face. Right below my eye. My cheek got warm. It was going to swell. Or was it? Would they execute me before I had a chance to show the evidence of this beating?

"We need to move this," Vito said.

Alexis nodded. She and Sal climbed into one car. Bobby picked me up and shoved me in Vito's trunk. I started screaming. He closed the trunk. It was dark. I heard car doors slam and engines start up. I stopped screaming.

I was going to die tonight. I felt around the trunk, but there was nothing in there. No weapons. Not a damn thing. Vito probably had experience transporting people in the trunk of his car. He probably knew to empty it when he was planning on putting in a body. Or at least the live ones.

So I did the logical thing. I started screaming again and kicking, punching, beating on the top of the trunk. Maybe someone would hear me. Maybe they wouldn't.

After what felt like a really long time, but was probably only ten minutes, I stopped yelling. My throat was raw. My hands hurt. More bruises that would never come to fruition. I started to cry. This was not what I wanted. I'd never really had a plan for my life, but that didn't mean I didn't want to live it.

I remembered that last summer before Reese and Ryan and I left home. I wanted ten more of those summers. No, forty more. I wanted camping trips. And beer and darts. I wanted that feeling back where I looked at Reese and my stomach dropped. I wanted to return to the airport in Sacramento and tell Reese to get back on that plane and graduate from Yale. I wanted nights of six-hour movie marathons with Ryan. I wanted to dance with Austin and have him mock me. I wanted to be Derek's wingman. I wanted to play football with Carson. I wanted all of the meaningless things we did to fill time. All of the silly entertainments that make a community. Our group was small and it was arbitrary, a collection of kids who didn't quite fit in with the other first graders, but it was ours.

I missed my mommy and daddy. I still kind of wanted to slap my little sister, but I also wanted to hug her. Hold her tight and tell her that this wasn't her fault. I was going to die tonight, and she would carry that forever. Are there support groups for that? Sending your sister to the grave. Would Mom and Dad forgive her? Would they forgive themselves? My grandparents were going to have to attend my funeral. No grandparent should bury their grandchild.

More than anything, I wanted to tell Reese I was sorry. I wanted to give her a lifetime. And all I'd offered was a year and a half. I should have told her in second grade that I was madly in love with her. I should have told her in twelfth grade that I wanted to grow old with her. I should have given her a decent proposal. Had I showed her that I loved her? I'd tried to show her. I had never told her. I'd told Ryan I loved him. I'd told Ryan I loved Reese. But I'd never actually told her that I loved her. I wanted to so bad and now I never would.

I wanted it all back and it was gone.

The tears ran down my face and collected in my ears. Snot ran down the back of my throat. I coughed and choked.

Was this how I would die? Sobbing over my own demise? Shot in the back of the head by a thug? Reese would have to identify that body. That faceless sack of meat.

No. Fuck that. I wasn't done yet. I was going to get out of this. And if I couldn't, I would die trying. I wouldn't die waiting and dreading a bullet.

I turned onto my side to do a second survey of the trunk's interior. A pressure eased from the center of my back. That was when I remembered the spare tire. In most trunks they were under the mat. I felt along where I'd been laying. There was a small ring. I scooted back as far as I could and pulled up. The mat was attached to a piece of board. From where I was, I couldn't reach around it to get to the juicy insides. So I kicked the board. It jerked out of my hands. I pulled it back up and tried again. After about twelve kicks, it started to bend. With some effort, I managed to get it folded down a bit. Just enough to reach over it. There was a spare tire. I could feel a toolbox of sorts beneath it. I had to get to that toolbox. But no matter what I did, I couldn't lift out the tire. Not from this angle. I just didn't have the leverage.

The road we were driving on got bumpy. Like it hadn't been paved in a while. It probably wasn't noticeable while driving, but from the trunk, it was very apparent. I gave the tire one last-ditch effort and failed. The car stopped and the engine turned off.

There was a series of car doors slamming before the trunk was opened. I heard Vito's rumbling voice, but couldn't understand what he was saying. I couldn't see him because I was barricaded behind the now bent floorboard. The board was jerked down. Two hands reached in to grab me. I kicked out and connected with an arm.

"Fucking bitch," Bobby yelled.

He reached in again and I kicked again. My kick pinned his hand against the edge of the trunk. He screamed and yanked it out. The third time he tried someone else was ready. When I kicked at Bobby, two hands grabbed my leg and pulled. It was Georgie. Lorenzo reached in and grabbed my other leg. Then Bobby took my arms and pulled me out. Bobby threw me on the ground and kicked me in the side. I started to retch, but held it in. They waited for me to get up. I got onto my hands and knees, spit a little, and looked around.

It was some sort of industrial area. There were a couple abandoned looking buildings. Two close by and a mass of others in the distance. We were in a parking lot with shitty lights that cast everything in shadow. Bobby was standing to my right. He was cradling the hand I had kicked. I hoped it was broken. Vito was behind him. Lorenzo and T were on my left. Sal was in front of me with his arms crossed over his chest. He was grinning like this was fun. Alexis was behind Sal. She looked so damn happy that I wanted to knock the bitch out.

Vito pulled out his gun. This was happening. He nodded over me at T. T came forward and kicked me again. Really, wasn't the kick from Bobby enough?

"Get up, Cooper," Vito said. He was the only one who didn't look gleeful. He seemed sad. And really pissed.

"I can't." I coughed and focused on breathing like I'd had the wind knocked out of me.

"Get her up," Alexis said.

Sal stepped forward. Good. He was the one I wanted to take on. I took off like a runner from blocks and hit Sal full force. As we connected, I kneed him as hard as I could in the junk. He made a high-pitched noise and dropped. Alexis moved to stop me, but I elbowed her in the face. There was a loud crack and she stepped back. A broken nose for my broken nose. I didn't stop to see the blood pouring from her face. It would have been satisfying, but it wasn't worth dying for.

I'd killed two of Vito's men. Helped kill a third. But I wasn't going to let my life balance the score.

I ran as fast as I could for a couple yards, then started weaving. I left the dull glow of the streetlight. I just had to get far enough away to make it hard to shoot me.

A crack, an explosion of sorts, rang out. The bullet hit my back and I stumbled. On the right side, down low. In the squishy good parts. I needed those parts. I knew that I had been shot, but somehow didn't quite process that fact. I didn't let myself process it. I just kept sprinting.

The second shot hit the back of my thigh. That one took me down. I wasn't going to let them win though. I couldn't. I forced myself to stand up. Fire burned up my leg. The kind of searing pain that can't be ignored. I took two more steps before my leg collapsed. I wouldn't be walking anywhere.

I could feel the warm, wet rush of blood soaking my shirt. The bullet must have gone straight through my stomach because the entire bottom half of my shirt was sodden. I clasped my hand ineffectually over the wound. More out of a sense of duty than to stop the bleeding. I knew that I was going to bleed out. If they didn't kill me first.

I tried to push with my elbows and good leg. A sort of backward crawl. I got about an inch before I heard the crunch and rasp of loafers on the crumbling pavement. As I collapsed onto my back, Vito stepped into my sightline. He stood over me, a look of pity on his face. Then he pointed his gun at my head. A shot rang out. The world went dark.

CHAPTER TWENTY

If this was hell then they'd done a damn good job. But this wasn't hell because I didn't believe in that shit. Or heaven. Or God. Just me. I believed in me. And I was in pain. And darkness. That was the part of hell they'd done a good job on.

I couldn't think straight. Or not straight. I couldn't think at all really. But I could hear. Footsteps. Voices. Maybe this was purgatory. I didn't know anything about that except that it was somewhere between heaven and hell. Which would make sense. I could hear my mom. That was heavenly. Not a far off voice either like she'd been for two years. But close and real. Except I knew she wasn't real.

Maybe the hell part was that I could hear her and I knew she wasn't real. As if this parade of voices of people I loved was there to torture me. Seemingly real, but so sad that I knew they weren't. My mommy had never sounded so sad. And I'd never heard my daddy cry. Or ask me the things he was asking me. This wasn't real. This wasn't life. They weren't here.

Reese and Ryan and my parents. Austin and Carson and Derek. For a moment, I even thought I heard Christopher and Breno. Which was insane because I didn't know where I was, but I knew they couldn't be there.

I'd done things to survive. I'd committed other sins out of pure rage. And there were things I had watched when I should have stopped them. Stopped them or walked away. Esau's executions were on my hands. I knew that. I knew that when someone had witnessed as many murders as I had, that they couldn't be clean. So whatever dirty place this was, I knew I was alone. My family didn't belong here.

Was this all that death offered? A vague sense of regret that couldn't be articulated, but couldn't be escaped either?

No. Because this wasn't death. Because I didn't believe in an afterlife. Did that mean that this was real?

❖

I woke up two days after I'd been shot. I didn't know that it was two days later. I just knew it was a long, long darkness later. When I woke, I was alone. My dreams had been playing cruel tricks on me. There was no family here. Only a woman in scrubs that I didn't know. She went off to bring back someone else in scrubs. They asked me questions. I answered them. I had questions, but I didn't ask them. I was pretty sure no one could answer them.

But then Derek walked into the room. And I was so surprised that I thought I was dreaming again.

"Well fuck me. Vivian Cooper, you dumb bitch."

That was when I knew it was real.

"Derek?"

"Yes, it's me. You asshole." He sat next to my bed and grinned at me. "When you get out of here, I'm going to punch you so hard, you'll have to come right back to the hospital."

"Okay." I smiled. I don't know why I smiled. It felt wrong. Also right.

"Fuck. I better go get everyone. They'll kill me otherwise."

"Is everyone here?" Those three words were really hard to say. Like pushing shards of glass into an emotional void.

"Everyone and their mom." Derek stood. "Stay here, okay? It's really hard to track your ass down." He laughed at his own joke.

"Wait. Are they mad?" I asked.

"I know I am." But he didn't look mad.

"I'm sorry."

"You should be. We waited fifteen fucking years for you and Reese to hook up. And then you run off so we can't even congratulate you. Low blow, dude."

I grinned and it felt real that time. "My bad."

"You don't even know. Carson and I stashed a bottle of celebratory champagne when we were seventeen. It's been gathering dust for five years. Now we can't even enjoy it 'cause it's gone to shit." I laughed at him. "All right. I'll be right back."

I'd almost dozed off when my mom and Reese walked in a minute later. They were arm in arm and smiling. But Reese also looked pissed and my mom looked sad.

"You're awake," Mom said.

"Trying to be." For real. Staying awake was hard.

Mom should have laughed at my weak joke. Two years ago, she would have. But the silence that followed couldn't be filled with the easy familiarity of mother and child. I'd grown up. In an entirely different direction from the path she had put me on.

"I told you they were going to kill you," Reese said.

"Yeah, well, they didn't."

"Fuck, I'm glad they didn't." Reese leaned down and kissed me. "You reek like a hospital."

"Better than a morgue."

My mom watched this exchange with slowly growing horror.

"Any chance you guys know what happened?" I was pretty sure I was going to crash any minute, but I needed to know what the hell was going on.

"Excuse me." My mom swallowed hard like she was trying not to cry. Then she bolted.

"So the reunion is going well," I said.

"She's upset." Reese shrugged.

"Can't blame her."

"Nope. Christopher has been trying, but I think she's more mad at him than anyone else."

"Christopher is here?" I felt my eyes close as I asked the question, but I fought and opened them again.

"Breno too. Long story. It'll wait though. Go back to sleep."

"Mmm, 'kay." I closed my eyes. "Wait." I forced them open again.

"What, sweetheart?"

"Stay. Okay?" That was hard to ask. Not because of what I was asking. Not anymore. It was hard because words were hard.

"I will."

"Promise?"

"Always."

I believed her. So I went to sleep.

❖

The next time I woke up, it was to Breno. I was hoping for Ryan. But his father would have to do.

"Why the fuck aren't you in Brazil?" I asked.

Breno turned away from the window he was staring out of.

"You're awake."

Why did people keep asking that? Obviously, I was awake. I'd never been one for talking in my sleep. Well, except for that dream where I would yell. But I hadn't had that in a year.

"Sort of."

Breno sat next to me and smiled in that sad way everyone seemed to have suddenly mastered. "Ryan ducked away from his handlers to e-mail us. He made it clear that we needed to come back and give the Feds everything we had on the DiGiovannis."

"Why? They'll probably arrest your asses."

"He was hoping that we would have enough information for a few arrests. That way the Feds would pull you. If Christopher and I need to do time, then it is well worth your life."

I laughed. "How'd that work out?"

"Not very well."

"No shit."

"No, I mean that we didn't land in the States until after you had been shot." Tentatively, he put his hand over mine. It was awkward, but I didn't care because it was also nice. And I was too sleepy to give a fuck.

"Did you at least give them something good?"

"I suppose." He shook his head. "I'm so sorry, Cooper."

"Don't be. Just tell me that they got 'em."

"I'm not privy to everything that is going on, but yes, arrests have been made. Only time will tell if they stick."

"Got it." I yawned.

"I'm sorry. Go back to sleep."

"Where's Reese?" I was more curious than anything. She had promised. So I knew she was nearby.

"Your father dragged her off to get some sleep."

"Go Dad."

Breno kept talking, but I didn't follow what he was saying. I just let the smooth lilt of his voice carry me to sleep.

❖

After a few days, I was transferred to a different room. Some dude, I think he was my doctor, explained some shit about my being shot. I didn't follow most of it. He said I'd lost a shitload of blood. That was from the one in my stomach. I was growing a whole new collection of scars from that baby.

The one in my thigh wasn't bad. It had just thrown my leg into shock. That was why I hadn't been able to run. The doctor said I'd be walking again soon. That was a plus.

He hadn't been able to tell me why the fuck I was still alive. I asked about the bullet wound in my head. That made him question my sanity because there was no bullet in my head. I'd only been shot twice. He didn't know what had happened to get me there. He only knew that I came in bleeding and they made the bleeding stop.

I appreciated that.

On the first day in my new, fancy room, Ogilvy came to visit me. Probably because I was finally able to stay awake for longer than five minutes at a time. Made conversation a bit easier.

"Cooper. Glad to see you awake." Her business-like tone couldn't hide the blend of kindness and fear lurking beneath the surface.

"Same here. Did you get the fuckers?"

She laughed. Out loud. Point to me.

"We got the fuckers."

"What about the don?" I asked. It was a long shot, but I figured I'd ask anyway.

"After your initial exchange we got the warrant signed for his arrest. We have had a team following him for two days waiting for the signal to arrest him. He is currently in custody."

"Wait, what? What did you get him on?"

Ogilvy looked at me like I was stupid. No surprise. "Really?"

"What did I miss?"

"No wonder you were so casual."

"Huh?"

"You got him to admit that he was paying you ten thousand for killing Ryan. That was enough for an arrest. A nice solid case, easy conviction. Lawrence DiGiovanni isn't going anywhere."

"Shut the fuck up."

Ogilvy laughed again.

"What about Vito and friends? How the fuck am I alive?"

"Mr. Serra is still in ICU. He was shot in the chest. He is under arrest, but he may not wake up to face the charges."

"Vito got shot?"

"Yes, we moved in when you started to panic in the garage, but we missed you."

"Huh?"

"I'm so sorry." She grimaced and shook her head. "We thought we had all of the exits covered, but there was an exit we were unaware of. You owe your life to a lovely young couple who were on their first date," she said.

"I'm so confused." Either she was speaking riddles or I was on some awesome drugs. Or both.

"When you started screaming from the top floor, a couple walking below heard you. I'm told that the young lady insisted that her date call the police. He was on the phone with dispatch when Mr. Serra left the garage. The woman heard screaming from the trunk of a car. They hailed a cab and followed it."

"Seriously?" Who was this crazy bitch? I totally owed her a drink. Or some of these painkillers. Or my life.

"I know." Ogilvy shook her head. "I've spoken to the young lady. She's...strong willed." Diplomatic. "The CPD officers who were helping us monitor your wire were contacted by dispatch. We got lucky. Florence picked up the tail based on the directions from the couple who were following you."

"So you guys were there the whole time?"

"At a distance, yes. Florence was waiting for backup when they began shooting at you. He made the decision to move in solo. And he was the one who shot Vito Serra. Two of the men, Robert Harper and George Divine, then opened fire on Agent Florence."

"Is he okay?"

"Yes. Thankfully, he only sustained a minor injury. Mr. Divine was killed at the scene. My team arrived in time to arrest the remaining participants. Robert Harper, Timothy Lagorio, Salvatore Mancini, Dominic Cross, and Lorenzo DiGiovanni are all currently in our custody."

"Wait, T is Timothy Lagorio?"

"Yes. He is your friend Christopher's brother."

"What the fuck?"

"I believe they are estranged."

"No shit."

"We have recovered—"

"Wait. What about Alexis? You didn't say she was in custody." That one was important. At least it was to me.

"Alexis DiGiovanni? We believe that she left after the parking garage. She wasn't at the scene."

"Yes, she fucking was."

"Are you certain?" Ogilvy was already reaching for her phone.

"I elbowed her in the face when I took off. Broke her nose. There's probably blood."

"We haven't processed the evidence from the scene yet." Ogilvy shook her head. "I'm sorry, I need to go. Thank you."

After that, they had a uniform posted at my door. Why didn't they have one before?

CHAPTER TWENTY-ONE

My mom stepped into the hallway to answer a call. Probably from my dad.

"Can she hear us?" I asked.

"No," Reese said.

"Go check."

Reese rolled her eyes, then got up to look up and down the hallway. She came back and sat next to my bed again. "She's all the way at the other end of the hall."

"Good." I didn't want either of my parents to hear this conversation. It would kill them. And I'd been killing them every day for the last two years. I couldn't add another blow to that.

"Why? What's up?" Reese asked.

"We can't stay here."

"What do you mean? Is it weird to be with the fam again?"

"Yes, but no. I mean, it isn't safe." Reese got a weirdly contemplative look on her face. "The longer we stick around, the more my parents are at risk. Same with Austin and Carson and Derek. And Ade, if she ever shows up."

Ade had conveniently stayed in the hotel the entire time they'd been in Chicago. My parents hadn't let her go more than a mile from them since her fuck-up in Spain. I was pretty sure they were livid with her. And she had to be terrified of me. Especially since I'd gotten both arrested and shot. Exactly like we said I would.

But I wasn't going to rub that in. Really. I figured she had enough going on without me telling her I told you so.

"We can't take off again," Reese said.

"I don't want to. I just don't want to put them in danger."

"Alexis isn't going to get anywhere near them."

"You don't know that," I said.

"Actually, I do. Every time I leave this room there are about twenty cops following me. And we are all staying on the same floor of the hotel. I'm pretty sure that every room without one of your family members has an FBI agent in it. Trust me, okay?"

"I do. It's just that Alexis is fucking insane and—"

My mom walked back into the room. "Everyone is on their way up."

"Cool," I said. I was so into pretending that I hadn't been suggesting that we run away again that I didn't bother asking why they were all coming up.

Two minutes later, my dad walked in.

"Hey, guys." He gave us a cursory nod. It could have been because he was carrying a massive stack of pizza boxes, but it wasn't. He hadn't been able to look me in the eye yet. He'd hugged me and told me he loved me. He'd taken notes on my care when the doctor explained the hell that my body was going through. He'd even made runs to the store for Zebra Cakes and Mountain Dew and Cheetos. But he hadn't looked me in the eye. How do you face your child when they turn into something monstrous?

"The boys will be in soon." He nodded at the door.

Everyone seemed used to the ID checks at the door to my room. Reese said she'd seen about four different cops so far. All of them were quite vigilant with monitoring my visitors. Ryan had said he was going to get a fake ID made with Derek's name just to see if they would catch it. But then he got distracted by something shiny so we never really got a verdict on that one.

"Coop!" Carson.

"Cooper." Derek.

"Dude." Ryan.

"Miss Vivian." Austin.

"Blow me."

Ryan and Carson were each carrying a case of beer. Derek had three bottles of wine. And Austin was somehow balancing four cases of soda. I was pretty sure they had overdone it on the beverages.

"Are we having a party?" Reese asked.

"We were going to, back in EDH, but since Coop got all bleedy again, we decided to party here," Derek said.

It wasn't my fault with the bleeding. Okay, I might have been making out with Reese and then we realized I was bleeding.

"Yeah, man. Two more days in the hospital. Was it worth it?" Carson asked.

"Uhh, have you seen my fiancé?" I asked the room in general.

"Hello, father present in the room." My dad waved.

"Mother too."

"Yeah, brother too." Ryan mimicked Dad's wave.

"Anyway, we decided to bring the party to you," Austin said.

"As opposed to all the other days where you guys wouldn't leave my room."

They'd stuck with me constantly since they'd gotten to Chicago. Which was nice in a suffocating sort of way. I think they wanted to protect me, but they didn't really know what to protect me from. I hoped they never knew what I needed protection from.

"But those other days didn't have pizza," Dad said.

"Hey, kids." Christopher walked into the room.

"Hello, everyone." Breno too.

"Well, now it's a party," I said.

The guys laughed. My parents awkwardly studied their shoes. I was pretty sure they wanted to get a restraining order or something against Christopher and Breno. But my mom had figured out that they made me feel safe. So she let them stay out of a sense of duty. But my dad pretty much looked like he constantly wanted to throw down. And Breno looked like a puppy who wasn't quite housetrained yet. Christopher just stared at the walls a lot.

Carson and Derek realized that there weren't enough chairs for everyone so they went in search of more. Ryan distributed paper plates. Austin started handing out drinks. Nothing says classy like wine from a plastic cup. I wanted a beer, but my dad was taking the whole don't mix pain meds and booze thing way too seriously. So I got Mountain Dew.

I was pretty sure someone was going to come in and break up our party. Weren't there rules about visitors in hospital rooms? No one did though. Maybe it had something to do with the police presence. About five minutes into the most awkward so-called party of my life, I started praying that someone would come kick them all out. But it so wasn't happening.

Everyone sat around my bed, which was annoying. I didn't want to be the centerpiece of the table. I wasn't wearing pants. You can't be the center of attention when you don't have pants.

Austin made a valiant effort at conversation. He would start to tell some story, then realize that it was inappropriate in some way and halt. It was excruciating. But Ryan had never been polite, and thankfully, he decided to stay that way.

"Hey, remember that time that guy shot me?"

Everyone turned to stare at Ryan. Like a bad sitcom. Every head just turned toward him. I started laughing.

"Hey, remember that time I put superglue in your bullet wound instead of stitches?" I said.

"Hey, remember that time Vito decided to kill me so he could kidnap Reese?"

"Which time?" I asked.

"Hey, remember that time you got arrested in Mexico?" Reese asked Ryan.

Carson laughed.

"Hey, remember that time Vito kicked the shit out Coop and that drag queen had to save her?" Ryan giggled.

Austin arched his brow at me.

"Hey, remember that time you guys dressed in drag to hide?" Reese said.

"Which time?" Ryan asked.

Derek, Carson, and Austin laughed.

"Hey, remember that time I killed a guy?" I asked. The room went still. Utterly fucking still. "What? He was evil incarnate and I don't feel bad about it. I do feel bad about not feeling bad about it, though. But Reese made me go to therapy for half a year, and now I can sleep through the night without creepy dreams."

"Vivian," my mom whispered.

"No. It's true. I killed a guy. He was really fucking bad."

Reese was awesome. She could have let me hang myself, but she didn't. "He really was bad. He was going to rape me with a knife. So Coop killed him." Everyone stared at Reese. "Don't worry. I went to therapy too." That didn't seem to make them feel any better.

"What? We've always been able to talk. So let's talk. I killed a guy. It's okay. I have immunity. Anyone have questions?" I asked.

I looked around the room. Ryan was smiling at his half-eaten pizza. Austin's mouth was hanging open. Carson had found something really interesting on my dad's face. My dad had found something really interesting on the wall. Derek had gone deaf. He was eating like nothing was happening. Breno and Christopher seemed to think that was a brilliant move, so they dug into the pizza they hadn't yet touched. My mom was staring at me. Through me. I wasn't sure.

"Hey, remember that time—" I started, but my mom cut me off.

"Be quiet. All of you. Just stop it." She set down her plate. "This isn't a joke. I can't listen to you pretend that it is. I can't."

"Hey, remember that time—" I tried again.

"Vivian, stop."

I stared at my mother, praying for something, anything that would take the cold fury out of her eyes. But there was nothing I could say that would take the last two years away. The pain was there. It always would be.

A voice from the doorway cut through the silence.

"Hey, remember that time you told me I was a naïve eighteen-year-old and I was going to get V killed?" Ade said.

Everyone turned to look at her.

"Yes," Reese said.

Ryan started laughing. "That's funny," he said when we all stared at him. "You know, 'cause that's pretty much what happened."

"Fuck you," Ade said.

Ryan kept laughing. "No, it's good. If you hadn't been all idealistic, then we would still be in Spain and you guys would still be here. I don't know about the rest of you, but there's nowhere I'd rather be."

And my dad started laughing. Just like that.

"Yes, Ryan. This is the most pleasant dinner I've attended in quite some time," Dad said.

Which made Austin and Derek laugh.

"It isn't at all awkward," I said.

Carson and Breno joined in. My mom even smiled a little. Which made Christopher smile.

"Come on, Ade, we're having a great time." Ryan stood and motioned for Breno and Derek to scoot. He pulled over an extra chair. "Sit. I'll get you a plate."

Ade sat. She looked like she was in shock, but at least she was here. Ryan tossed a couple pieces of pizza onto a plate and gave it to Ade.

"Thanks," Ade said.

"I know she's baby-sized, but I think this kid needs some wine." Ryan didn't wait for a response. He just grabbed one of the bottles and poured her a very small glass of wine.

"Ade, I don't think you've been introduced to our father," Reese said. "Breno, this is Adriana, Coop's little sister. She got Cooper shot, but we've decided to forgive her because my asshole grandpa is behind bars and so is the rest of our fucked up family."

"Language," my mom said.

"It is lovely to meet you, Adriana," Breno said.

"You're Reese and Ryan's dad?" Ade asked.

"Yes."

"Where the fuck have you been? You know Christopher was a total dick, right?" Ade asked.

That launched the retelling of a very long story.

❖

That evening after nearly everyone had gone back to the hotel, Reese climbed onto my bed. It was too narrow, but we made it work.

"Careful, don't want to tear another stitch," I said.

"I am not sure that I believe that I was responsible for your last torn stitch." She'd had a lot of wine so her speech was extra perfect. And it made no sense whatsoever. Which I found sexy for some reason. Also annoying.

"You're awesome," I said.

"I know."

"I'm sleepy," I said.

"Me too," Reese said.

"Me too," Ryan said.

Ryan?

"I thought you went back to the hotel. What the fuck are you doing here?" I asked.

"Snuggling. I can't sleep alone." He crawled onto the other side of the bed and stole half my pillow. As if the bed wasn't small enough already.

"Be careful of her side," Reese said.

"You know this is why people say we are weird and codependent, right?" I said.

"Shh, sleepy time." Ryan closed his eyes.

I was going to kick him out. But I kind of liked him being there. So I fell asleep instead.

❖

"Kids, wake up." It was my mom's voice. I didn't need to open my eyes to know that.

"Uhh-uh," I muttered.

"Come on, guys. You can't all sleep in here."

I opened my eyes. That was all I could move because I was sandwiched between the twins on a narrow hospital bed.

"But it's sleepy time," Ryan said.

"I know, honey. But you need sleepy time in your own bed." We may as well have been eight years old again. Her tone hadn't changed at all in the intervening decade and a half. "And Vivian needs good sleep. She won't get that with you two in here."

"We have to stay and protect her," Reese said.

My mom laughed. "You guys can stay if you want, but not in bed with V. One of you will get hurt."

"Nuh-uh," Ryan mumbled.

"Yes huh. I'm afraid you guys are going to roll right off the bed."

"Can't leave. Got to watch Coop," Reese said.

"Come on, honey. You need your rest too and you won't get it here. Go back to the hotel. I'll stay here. That way you two can come back in the morning." Mom rubbed Reese's shoulder.

"Fine." Ryan slowly rolled off the bed.

"Good boy."

Reese climbed out too. "You have to stay here and watch her, okay?" She rubbed her eyes in an adorably sleepy way.

"I have my book." My mom held up a paperback. "I'm not going anywhere."

"Promise," Reese said.

"Yeah, promise."

"I promise, guys. Now go get some sleep. I'll see you tomorrow morning."

Reese and Ryan headed for the door. They were leaning heavily against each other.

"Hey," I said.

"What?" Reese looked back.

"Don't I get a kiss?"

Ryan rolled his eyes. "Fine." He started walking back to the bed, but Reese grabbed him and pushed him aside. He started giggling.

"Tool," she said.

"Whatever." Ryan giggled some more.

Reese kissed me and pulled up my blankets. "Listen to your mommy, okay?"

"Blow me," I said.

Reese rolled her eyes. "Good night."

"Night." I was tired as hell, but I fought to stay awake until they left the room. "Hey, Mom?"

"Yes, honey?" She pushed the hair off my forehead.

"Are you mad?"

"About the twins sleeping in here? No, of course not. It's weird, but I'm not mad about it."

"No, not that." I yawned. "Everything else. Me leaving. That stuff."

"Oh, that." She took a long, deep breath. "I'm...I'm really happy that you are safe. I'm relieved that you're all right. That this"—she nodded in the general direction of my body—"will heal."

"Yeah, but you're pissed, right?"

"You have no idea how pissed I am." She pushed the hair off my forehead again. I was pretty sure at this point that it didn't need to be pushed off my forehead. She just wanted to play with my hair. I liked it.

"So you are pissed?"

"Of course I am. How could I not be?"

"Good point," I said.

"But the anger is the last thing on my mind. I'm just happy you're okay. Or that you will be okay. I'm so relieved that you and Reese and Ryan are safe and that we have you back again."

"Cool."

"But you're grounded for the rest of your life."

I laughed. My mom was making jokes. That had to be a good thing. "I'm twenty-three. You can't ground me."

"Watch me." She almost sounded serious.

"Okay. Whatever you say." My eyes closed. It wasn't my fault. I made them open again.

"It's all right. Go back to sleep."

"Wait. What about the Feds in Europe?"

"What about them?"

"If you wanted us home, why didn't you help them?"

She got a weird look on her face and shook her head. "I don't like the things you did. Not at all. I don't understand it. I'm not even sure I want to understand it. But that doesn't mean I was going to help someone put my babies in prison."

"Serious?"

"I love you, honey." She played with my hair some more.

"So you don't care that I killed people?"

"I do care. I find it very upsetting. But it doesn't make me love you any less. Nothing could change that."

"Thanks, Mommy."

She kissed my head and said good night. I was already asleep by the time she picked up her book.

❖

My mom stayed the entire night. I woke up sometime around two and she was curled up in one of those institutional type chairs in the corner of my room. Her knees were propped against one of the heavy wooden arms of the chair. And her head was turned at an odd angle against her shoulder.

I should have woken her up, made her go back to the hotel. But I liked her being there. I liked that she still wanted to watch me sleep. Reese had stayed the last two nights. Before that, Ryan and my dad had each done a shift. But my mommy still called dibs on keeping me safe, keeping me sane. It was nice. So I let her sleep. And a few minutes later, I drifted off too.

It was just after dawn the next time I woke up. I heard voices in the hallway, gentle murmurs outside my room. I didn't open my eyes, just slowly processed the sound of my guard's voice and another. It was oddly familiar, but off somehow. During daylight hours, there were so many people in and out of my room, I couldn't hear shit.

"Reese DiGiovanni. Yeah, I have your name right here," the guard said.

"Thanks."

Reese was really early. Weird.

My eyes were blurry when I opened them. Mom was still sleeping in the corner. There was a figure in the doorway. She was wearing a hoodie and jeans. Something wasn't right. The door closed softly. She walked over to me and pulled her hood off.

"Oh fuck," I said. But that was all I got out before Alexis had a knife at my throat.

"Quiet, Cooper," she whispered. "If you make a sound it will wake up your mother. Then I'll have to kill her too." I didn't say a word. "You really fucked me over, you know that?"

It didn't sound rhetorical. "You deserved it."

"Fuck you."

"I'm digging the black eyes. Good look for you." I grinned.

"Shut the fuck up." She dug the knife in a bit more. I felt a trickle of blood down my neck. "Do you understand what you've done? I'm going to have to flee the country. I really don't like being on the run. I had it all fucking planned out and you had to go fuck it up. My uncle has been arrested. The whole family is going under."

I shrugged a little. Not too much. The bitch had a knife at my throat. It didn't allow for much movement. Also, she was fucking insane. And murderous.

"Don't you want to apologize? You screwed me. You and your little girlfriend and that bastard." Her eyes had gone dark, the bright blue pushed and shoved until there was only a hint of light. That was when I realized she was going to kill me. I'd known when she walked in, but there was some vague sense of hope. But I knew right then that if the guard walked in or my mom woke up or Batman crawled through the window, that she would just kill me faster.

"Oh, am I allowed to talk now?" I whispered. I really wanted to scream, but I didn't want to make her even more pissed.

"No. Shut up." Alexis tilted the knife a little. It hurt.

I was scared. Hell, I was fucking terrified. After all I'd been through, the irony of getting my throat slashed in a hospital while under a police guard was just insulting. The fact that my mom would wake up to my corpse didn't help either.

"Come on, Alexis. Don't do this. You might be able to get out of it. They don't have shit on you." I tried to scoot up the bed, take a little pressure off my neck. The muscles in my stomach screamed sharp and hard. My lungs constricted at the pain. Alexis just lifted the knife higher.

"Don't lie. They're going to bury me. I'm never getting out of it. So I can't let them catch me."

"So go. Go now before you add another murder to the list of charges."

"No. This will buy me—"

We both went completely still at the sound of the guard's voice. I didn't know if I should call out. Sacrifice someone else when I knew they couldn't save me. Or sacrifice myself and hope that Alexis just let them live. Whoever they were.

Reese. It was Reese for real this time.

"No," the guard said. "Reese DiGiovanni is already in there."

Reese must have shoved him or kicked him, I didn't know. He grunted and it was only a half a second before the door started to open.

Alexis grabbed a fistful of my hair and pulled my head back. "Whatever fucking god you believe in. Start praying." She started to slice my throat. I tucked my chin, grabbed her hand, and shoved. Every nerve in my body burst into heat and light as the pain spread, but I kept pushing her away. I couldn't hear or see. I couldn't fucking breathe. I just knew I had to hold her off.

Suddenly, Alexis's head snapped forward and slammed into my torso. And I reached awesome new levels of hurt. Choking, gasping, crying hurt.

The knife fell. I grabbed my throat and held tight. I didn't know what damage she'd done, but judging by the warm, sticky flow, it couldn't be good. I blinked hard until the haze cleared enough to see.

Reese was dragging Alexis back by her hair. Alexis threw a wild elbow that cracked Reese on her jaw. Hard enough to let go. Alexis spun to face her. The guard finally came into the room. He was limping and breathing hard. Reese must have gone for his junk. He looked pissed. Reese swung at Alexis, but the guard caught her arm and pulled her back.

"Hey, what the hell is going on here?" He tossed Reese against the wall. "Stay there. Who are you?"

His voice must have woken my mom because she straightened and rubbed her face. "Reese, honey, what are you doing here? What's going on?"

Reese was breathing hard. My vision had cleared enough to see her hands tremble.

"That's Alexis DiGiovanni," I told the guard. My voice was rough and hard. "You might want to arrest her."

"Oh my God, Vivian, you're bleeding." My mom jumped up and ran to my side. She pulled the sheet up high to press against my throat.

The cop hadn't moved. He was looking back and forth between Reese and Alexis like he didn't know who to arrest.

"Would you handcuff that woman?" my mom yelled at the guard. "And get a nurse. My daughter is bleeding."

He snapped to attention and took a step toward Alexis. She was still facing Reese so all I could see was her back. As the guard got closer, she reached back and pulled another knife from her waistband.

"Knife," I screamed. But it was too late. Alexis buried it in the guard's stomach, yanked it back out, and pushed him to the ground.

"Stupid cunt," Reese said.

Alexis just kept walking toward Reese, blood dripping from the knife. I felt around in my twisted, blood-soaked sheets until I found the knife Alexis had dropped. I tossed it to Reese. It skidded and hit the wall. She picked it up as Alexis lunged at her. Reese rolled away and got to her knees.

I tried to get out of bed, but the combination of pain and my mother pushing me back made it hard.

"Mom, go get help."

Her eyes got big and she shook her head. "I can't leave you two."

Alexis jumped at Reese again. Reese spun back to her feet, the knife held in front of her. I couldn't tell if it was a warning or a challenge.

"Please, go now," I begged. This wasn't my mom's fight. But I was thinking that wouldn't convince her. "We need help." Maybe that would get to her to leave the room.

Alexis came at Reese again, but this time Reese was between the wall and the foot of my bed. Nowhere to go. Alexis swung at

Reese, but before she could make contact, Mom grabbed the hood of Alexis's jacket and pulled her back. Alexis spun and slashed at my mom. She caught her in the left side. It couldn't have been deep because Mom just stood there and stared at her. Completely shocked that this very real violence had suddenly penetrated her world.

Reese jumped forward and stabbed Alexis in the side. Alexis went rigid. She spun slowly as the knife fell from her hand. Reese twisted her knife and jerked it back out. Alexis dropped to her knees, her eyes wide in shock.

"You bitch," Alexis gasped.

I pushed myself up in bed. I didn't care right then that every muscle in my body hated that idea. Reese pushed Alexis to the floor. Alexis grabbed at Reese's throat, her bloody hands slipping and trying to get a grip. Reese slammed her knee into Alexis's side. Alexis screamed and her hands dropped. Reese kept shoving her knee in Alexis's side, pinning her in place. She reached into the collar of Alexis's shirt and pulled out my necklace, her mom's necklace. I was amazed that her hands didn't shake as she unclasped it. She was perfectly calm. Alexis was pushing against Reese's knee, trying to relieve the pressure. Tears poured down her face.

I felt no sympathy for her.

When Alexis passed out, Reese just pushed down harder. Alexis twitched. Fuck, how was she still alive? Alexis's breathing became stilted and wet. Reese held tight against the protestations of a dying body. I said nothing. Sixty seconds went by. Ninety.

"Die, damn it," Reese whispered.

As if she were granting a final wish, Alexis's body stiffened, then went slack. Reese dropped to the floor, her back resting against the frame of my bed.

"Make sure she's dead," I said. There was an impressive pool of blood on the floor. But that wasn't good enough for me.

Reese shook her head. "She's dead."

"Make sure."

"And if she isn't?" Reese looked up at me. A bruise was forming on her jaw. There were spatters of blood on her arms and chest. Bloody handprints circled her neck.

"Then I'll stab the bitch again," I said.

"Vivian!"

I realized that my mother was still in the room. There was blood on her shirt, but not enough for me to worry. Well, except for the whole flood of trauma I was sure would follow.

"You should sit down, Mrs. C." Reese got back on her knees and leaned over her cousin's body. She put her fingers on Alexis's throat. "She's dead."

"Oh my God." Mom looked about two seconds on the wrong side of freaking out.

"Mom." She ignored me. "Mom, look at me." She turned. "We need you to go get help now. That cop needs a doctor. So do I." She shook her head.

"Use the call button, Coop," Reese said.

Well, that seemed smart. I reached over and hit the call button.

"Mom, sit down," I said. "The nurse will be here soon."

"Seriously," Reese said. "Sit down."

My mom nodded. She turned back to her chair, saw the cop's body, and sobbed. She stepped over him and sat down.

Right then, a flood of people in scrubs ran through the open doorway.

Most of them started working on my guard. One woman broke away and checked Alexis's pulse. With a shake of her head, she stood and checked me. She muttered something about stitches and then I got to add a very sexy gauze pad to my collection of bandages.

The next thirty minutes was like that, a lot of frantic people running into the room. Ogilvy showed up about two minutes before Ryan did. Ogilvy was demanding a statement from Reese when Ryan went macho for the first time in his life and insisted that Reese needed space. Ogilvy backed off. A little.

After that, I was moved to a different room. They threw a couple stitches in my neck. It was super fun. Ryan held Reese's hand and Reese held mine. I really, really didn't like stitches. But when the doctor pointed out how close the wound was to my jugular, I stopped bitching.

"How's my mom?" I asked after the doctor left.

"Your mom?" Ryan asked.

"Alexis cut her," Reese said.

"That fucking whore!"

"Can you just find her and make sure she's okay?" I asked.

"Yeah, yeah totally." Ryan nodded enthusiastically. "You need anything else?"

"No, just that."

He left the room. Reese crawled into bed next to me. The blood on her knee was still wet enough to stain the sheets. I pulled her close until her head was buried in my armpit.

"You saved me."

"Yeah, well. You look super hot when you're naked," she mumbled.

"Dude, you look super hot when you're naked."

"Obviously."

Reese started laughing, which made me start laughing.

"Oh, shit." Reese sat up. "I got this for you." She pulled the necklace out of her pocket. It was stained with blood. She fed it around my neck.

"Ouch. Neck wound." Seriously. Ouch.

"Suck it up. I killed a bitch to get this."

I started laughing again. Which didn't make the pain lessen. At all. "That's not funny."

"Nope." Reese smiled. "I'm probably gonna be totally fucked up now."

"Yeah, but I still like you."

"Okay." She snuggled into me again.

We must have fallen asleep because the door opening woke us up. It was Ogilvy.

"I know neither of you is ready to make a statement yet, but I do need your clothes." Ogilvy held up a bundle of clothes and an evidence bag for Reese.

"Whatever." Reese sighed and got out of bed. She started stripping. Ogilvy kept her eyes trained on the wall. I watched Reese get naked. How could I not? Reese pulled on the sweatpants and T-shirt that Ogilvy had brought for her.

"Thank you." Ogilvy sealed the bag. Blood smeared the inside of it.

"Is she really dead?" I asked.

"Yes." Ogilvy nodded once. "Thank you," she said again and nodded at the bag of clothes. But she made it sound like she was thanking us for more than just that. "Your mother is fine, by the way. Ryan and your father are with her. The wound was shallow. She shouldn't have any problems."

That made me feel better. "Thanks."

"Yes, thank you." Reese sat back down on my bed.

"All right. I'll leave you two alone now." Ogilvy turned and left.

Reese stretched out next to me. I pulled her close and smelled her hair. Mine.

I realized, as I heard Ogilvy's steps echoing down the hallway, that she wasn't coming back. She didn't need to.

We were finally free.

About the Author

Ashley Bartlett was born and raised in California. Her life consists of reading and writing. Most of the time, Ashley engages in these pursuits while sitting in front of a coffee shop with her girlfriend and smoking cigarettes.

It's a glamorous life.

She is an obnoxious, sarcastic, punk-ass, but her friends don't hold that against her. She currently lives in Sacramento, but you can find her at ashbartlett.com.

Books Available from Bold Strokes Books

Trusting Tomorrow by PJ Trebelhorn. Funeral director Logan Swift thinks she's perfectly happy with her solitary life devoted to helping others cope with loss until Brooke Collier moves in next door to care for her elderly grandparents. (978-1-60282-891-9)

Forsaking All Others by Kathleen Knowles. What if what you think you want is the opposite of what makes you happy? (978-1-60282-892-6)

Exit Wounds by VK Powell. When Officer Loane Landry falls in love with ATF informant Abigail Mancuso, she realizes that nothing is as it seems—not the case, not her lover, not even the dead. (978-1-60282-893-3)

Dirty Power by Ashley Bartlett. Cooper's been through hell and back, and she's still broke and on the run. But at least she found the twins. They'll keep her alive. Right? (978-1-60282-896-4)

The Rarest Rose by I. Beacham. After a decade of living in her beloved house, Ele disturbs its past and finds her life being haunted by the presence of a ghost who will show her that true love never dies. (978-1-60282-884-1)

Code of Honor by Radclyffe. The face of terror is hard to recognize—especially when it's homegrown. The next book in the Honor series. (978-1-60282-885-8)

Does She Love You by Rachel Spangler. When Annabelle and Davis find out they are both in a relationship with the same woman, it leaves them facing life-altering questions about trust, redemption, and the possibility of finding love in the wake of betrayal. (978-1-60282-886-5)

The Road to Her by KE Payne. Sparks fly when actress Holly Croft, star of UK soap Portobello Road, meets her new on-screen love interest, the enigmatic and sexy Elise Manford. (978-1-60282-887-2)

Shadows of Something Real by Sophia Kell Hagin. Trying to escape flashbacks and nightmares, ex-POW Jamie Gwynmorgan stumbles into the heart of former Red Cross worker Adele Sabellius and uncovers a deadly conspiracy against everything and everyone she loves. (978-1-60282-889-6)

Date with Destiny by Mason Dixon. When sophisticated bank executive Rashida Ivey meets unemployed blue collar worker Destiny Jackson, will her life ever be the same? (978-1-60282-878-0)

The Devil's Orchard by Ali Vali. Cain and Emma plan a wedding before the birth of their third child while Juan Luis is still lurking, and as Cain plans for his death, an unexpected visitor arrives and challenges her belief in her father, Dalton Casey. (978-1-60282-879-7)

Secrets and Shadows by L.T. Marie. A bodyguard and the woman she protects run from a madman and into each other's arms. (978-1-60282-880-3)

Change Horizon: Three Novellas by Gun Brooke. Three stories of courageous women who dare to love as they fight to claim a future in a hostile universe. (978-1-60282-881-0)

Scarlet Thirst by Crin Claxton. When hot, feisty Rani meets cool, vampire Rob, one lifetime isn't enough, and the road from human to vampire is shorter than you think... (978-1-60282-856-8)

Battle Axe by Carsen Taite. How close is too close? Bounty hunter Luca Bennett will soon find out. (978-1-60282-871-1)

Improvisation by Karis Walsh. High school geometry teacher Jan Carroll thinks she's figured out the shape of her life and her future, until graphic artist and fiddle player Tina Nelson comes along and teaches her to improvise. (978-1-60282-872-8)

For Want of a Fiend by Barbara Ann Wright. Without her Fiendish power, can Princess Katya and her consort Starbride stop a magic-wielding madman from sparking an uprising in the kingdom of Farraday? (978-1-60282-873-5)

Broken in Soft Places by Fiona Zedde. The instant Sara Chambers meets the seductive and sinful Merille Thompson, she falls hard, but knowing the difference between love and a dangerous, all-consuming desire is just one of the lessons Sara must learn before it's too late. (978-1-60282-876-6)

Healing Hearts by Donna K. Ford. Running from tragedy, the women of Willow Springs find that with friendship, there is hope, and with love, there is everything. (978-1-60282-877-3)

Desolation Point by Cari Hunter. When a storm strands Sarah Kent in the North Cascades, Alex Pascal is determined to find her. Neither imagines the dangers they will face when a ruthless criminal begins to hunt them down. (978-1-60282-865-0)

I Remember by Julie Cannon. What happens when you can never forget the first kiss, the first touch, the first taste of lips on skin? What happens when you know you will remember every single detail of a mysterious woman? (978-1-60282-866-7)

The Gemini Deception by Kim Baldwin and Xenia Alexiou. The truth, the whole truth, and nothing but lies. Book six in the Elite Operatives series. (978-1-60282-867-4)

Scarlet Revenge by Sheri Lewis Wohl. When faith alone isn't enough, will the love of one woman be strong enough to save a vampire from damnation? (978-1-60282-868-1)

Ghost Trio by Lillian Q. Irwin. When Lee Howe hears the voice of her dead lover singing to her, is it a hallucination, a ghost, or something more sinister? (978-1-60282-869-8)

The Princess Affair by Nell Stark. Rhodes Scholar Kerry Donovan arrives at Oxford ready to focus on her studies, but her life and her priorities are thrown into chaos when she catches the eye of Her Royal Highness Princess Sasha. (978-1-60282-858-2)

The Chase by Jesse J. Thoma. When Isabelle Rochat's life is threatened, she receives the unwelcome protection and attention of bounty hunter Holt Lasher who vows to keep Isabelle safe at all costs. (978-1-60282-859-9)

The Lone Hunt by L.L. Raand. In a world where humans and praeterns conspire for the ultimate power, violence is a way of life… and death. A Midnight Hunters novel. (978-1-60282-860-5)

The Supernatural Detective by Crin Claxton. Tony Carson sees dead people. With a drag queen for a spirit guide and a devastatingly attractive herbalist for a client, she's about to discover the spirit world can be a very dangerous world indeed. (978-1-60282-861-2)

Beloved Gomorrah by Justine Saracen. Undersea artists creating their own City on the Plain uncover the truth about Sodom and Gomorrah, whose "one righteous man" is a murderer, rapist, and conspirator in genocide. (978-1-60282-862-9)

Cut to the Chase by Lisa Girolami. Careful and methodical author Paige Cornish falls for brash and wild Hollywood actress Avalon Randolph, but can these opposites find a happy middle ground in a town that never lives in the middle? (978-1-60282-783-7)

More Than Friends by Erin Dutton. Evelyn Fisher thinks she has the perfect role model for a long-term relationship, until her best friends, Kendall and Melanie, split up and all three women must reevaluate their lives and their relationships. (978-1-60282-784-4)

Every Second Counts by D. Jackson Leigh. Every second counts in Bridgette LeRoy's desperate mission to protect her heart and stop Marc Ryder's suicidal return to riding rodeo bulls. (978-1-60282-785-1)

Dirty Money by Ashley Bartlett. Vivian Cooper and Reese DiGiovanni just found out that falling in love is hard. It's even harder when you're running for your life. (978-1-60282-786-8)

Sea Glass Inn by Karis Walsh. When Melinda Andrews commissions a series of mosaics by Pamela Whitford for her new inn, she doesn't expect to be more captivated by the artist than by the paintings. (978-1-60282-771-4)